Naked in Naknek

Lolu Sinclair

© 2025 LOST LUST / FOUND Recordings LLC

All rights reserved. No part of this publication can be reproduced, stored in a retrieval system, or transmitted in any form by any means without the prior written permission of the publisher.

This book is a work of fiction. Unless otherwise indicated, all the names, characters, businesses, places, events, timelines, and incidents in this book are either the product of the author's imagination or used in a fictitious manner. Any resemblance to actual persons, living or dead, or actual events is purely coincidental. The use of any real company, product, and/or artist names is for literary effect only. All trademarks and copyrights are the property of their respective owners.

ISBN: 978-1-965155-02-8 (TPB)
ISBN: 978-1-965155-03-5 (KIN)

lostlust.com

Music Playlist

We made an awesome playlist to accompany our story!
We know you will love it.

Scan the QR code to listen for free.

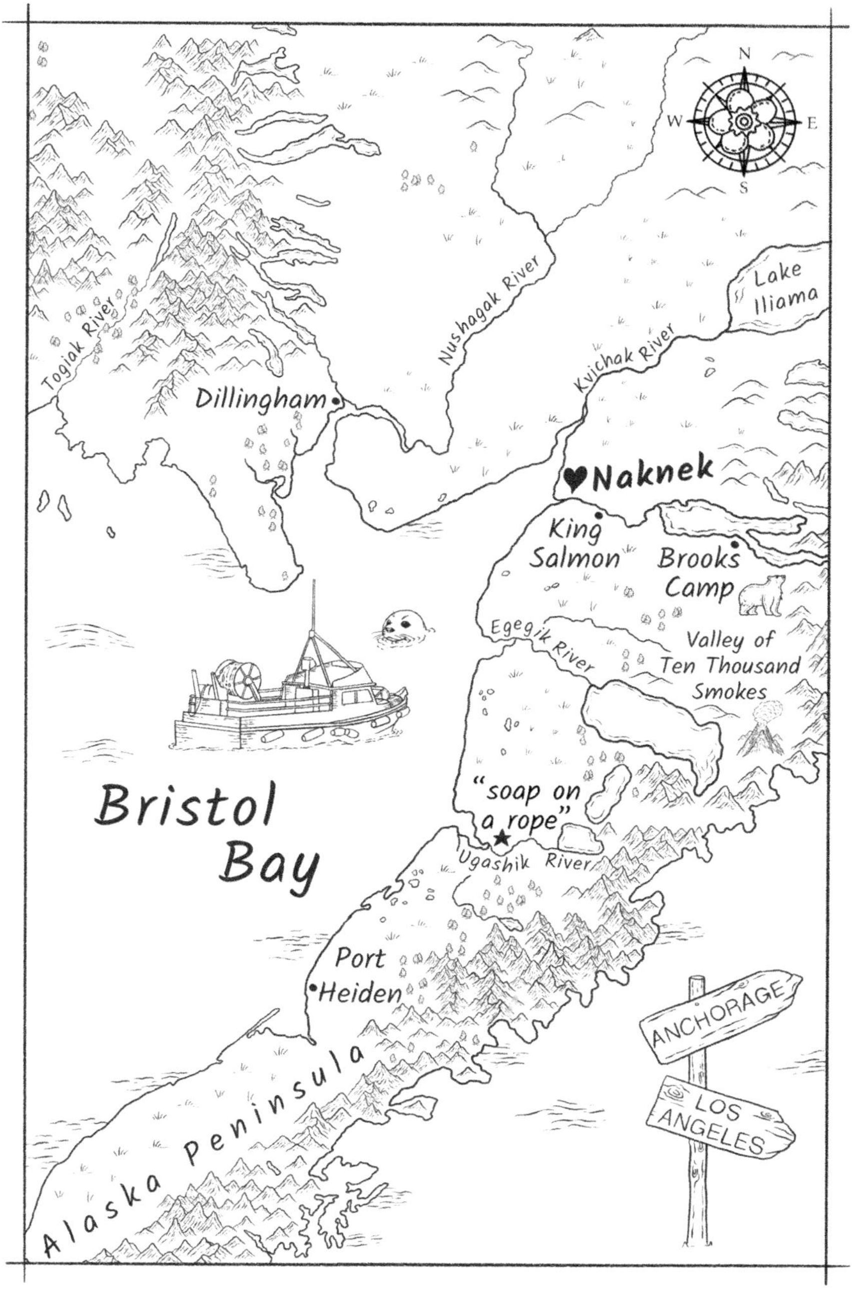
N
W
E
S
Lake Iliama
Nushagak River
Togiak River
Kvichak River
Dillingham
Naknek
King Salmon
Brooks Camp
Egegik River
Valley of Ten Thousand Smokes
"soap on a rope"
Ugashik River
Bristol Bay
Port Heiden
Alaska Peninsula
ANCHORAGE
LOS ANGELES

Contents

1. It's Not Just Straws — 1
2. Nose to Nose With a Chevy Silverado — 12
3. She's Trouble — 27
4. Even if He is a Sexy Fisherman — 36
5. No Turning Back Now — 48
6. Saved by the Kelp — 58
7. Those Little Planes Are Dangerous — 64
8. This Isn't a Pleasure Cruise — 75
9. Whales Are Very Much My Thing — 89
10. If That Helps You Sleep at Night — 106
11. Smart Women Piss You Off — 113
12. Get the Sample and Get Out — 121
13. You Forget the Big Picture — 124
14. Don't Get Too Close — 134
15. I Like Your Fun Facts — 140
16. I Need You to Climb Up — 150
17. I Don't Really Buy into That Stuff — 165
18. I'm Going to Get Naked — 171
19. You Don't Have to Apologize — 187
20. Two Can Play at This Game — 198
21. I Think You Look Perfect — 208
22. This is a Good Start — 221
23. Flying Always Takes It Out of Me — 228
24. Forget Me Not — 242
25. Just Callin' It Like I See It — 250
26. New Kink Unlocked — 260
27. Fuck Off to California — 273
28. This Has Gone Too Far — 280
29. Whose Side Are You On? — 286

30. You're Gonna Have to Get Over Her — 297
31. Culture Shock — 309
32. Humans Are Weird — 315
33. I've Got a Woman to Go After — 321
34. Is That the Opposite of Over It? — 333
35. Buy a Friend a Drink — 343
36. You Haven't Gone Pro, Have You? — 354
37. I'm Not Getting Naked — 367

Also by Lolu Sinclair — 375

Chapter 1

It's Not Just Straws

LILLIAN

A barnacled back breaks the surface as a spray of water announces the pod of gray whales. There are three adults and two calves, which is great news for their waning population.

"Hello, beautiful." I smile.

With my elbows resting on the railing of the research vessel, I look through my binoculars. The Pacific rolls under me, steady and strong. Hope can be difficult to come by these days. Especially if you're an environmental scientist. But two brand-new baby grays remind me of what's possible.

"Okay, I have your chai. Now spill."

I look up to see Trudy standing beside me with a

steaming mug of chai tea. We might be on a research trip on the ocean, but the Pacific Marine Institute is one of the most well-funded research facilities in the country. Because of this, we travel on a state-of-the-art vessel, the *Rorqual*, with all the amenities a person could want, including satellite internet. And chai.

I pride myself on looking nice for work, even at sea. But Trudy looks amazing, even in a boring gray pullover, thanks to her immaculate, gravity-defying box braids and a layer of red lipstick.

"Extra hot chai tea latte with steamed oat milk?" I ask.

"Obviously. Although, I don't know how you can do *extra* hot in the middle of July," she says. "In the middle of the *ocean*."

I chuckle. "The heart wants what it wants." I take a sip of my chai. *Yes ... perfection.*

"Perfect segue," Trudy says, raising an eyebrow.

"For?"

My friend rolls her eyes. "Girl, we've been on this boat for three days, and you haven't said a single thing about the breakup."

I frown for a moment and then realize. "*Ohhhhh.* Oh yeah. The breakup."

Trudy scoffs. "Wow, you're brutal. Don't tell me you've already forgotten."

"Didn't forget." Kind of forgot. Or pushed it out of my mind. "I've been focused on the whales."

"Uh-huh."

I sigh. When I'm at work, I'm *at work*. I forget about

everything when I'm here. Including breakups. "What do you want to know?"

Trudy quirks an eyebrow and purses her lips. "You texted me Saturday night, 'Ended it with Calvin.' And when I pressed you for details, you said you'd tell me everything on Monday. Today is *Wednesday*. I brought you your gymnast-floor-routine-level-of-complicated drink. I want the details."

I shrug. "There's really not much to tell. We only dated three months anyway, so—"

"He was cute, Lillian. Really cute."

"Cuteness doesn't make up for a crappy personality," I say, taking another sip of chai.

"He was nice!"

"Nice doesn't make up for being irresponsible!" I exclaim in response.

Trudy rolls her eyes. "Don't tell me this is about the straws."

"It's not just the straws!" I say through a nervous laugh. It started with the straws. I ignored it at first until I realized every time we went out to get coffee, he'd throw away the lid and get a straw. "He also has a Prime account. And he will order a single tube of toothpaste and nothing else!"

"Plenty of people who work here have a Prime account, girl."

I huff. "It's not just straws and the Prime account!"

"Okay, then tell me what it is! Inquiring minds want to know."

"It's everything. He needed a new car, right? It's his first year out of residency, and he wants to trade in his 2007

Hyundai Sonata. Fine. He deserves it. He's looking at little sporty cars—"

"God, and he's a surgeon. You could have been rich." Trudy moans.

I ignore her. "I say, 'Hey, it'd be great if you got an electric car. They're better for the environment, and they'll save money on gas. And if you buy the right one, they perform better.' Calvin was all into that. In fact, he invited me to come test drive some electric cars with him. We went to like four different dealers. I thought he was going to get a BMW i4."

"As if I know what that looks like," she says dryly.

"Sporty little sedan. That's all you need to know." I pinch my brows together, and my jaw gets tight. "Imagine my surprise when he comes to pick me up on Saturday night. He's not in a little electric sedan. He's in a souped-up Chevy Silverado."

Trudy's eyes widen. Now she's getting it. "A *truck?*"

"A gas-guzzling giant." I collapse back in my seat.

"Oof. Yeah. That's rough."

I hold my hands up. "You get it now? It's two-fold. He doesn't get why it matters so much, *and* he wasted all my time looking for a stupid EV, when clearly he was just humoring me."

Trudy purses her lips. "It does feel like a bait and switch."

"Exactly. That's exactly what it feels like. And if we're only three months in and he's already asking for my opinion just to humor me, I know it won't get better the longer we're together."

Trudy's expression isn't judgmental, but I can tell she's worried about me.

"Don't give me that look."

"What look?"

"The worried, 'Oh no, Lillian might be too picky to find someone' look."

She snorts. "You *know* I don't think that. You just deserve someone great."

"Sure, maybe. But I'm happy on my own. And I'd rather be alone than with a man who has a carbon footprint the size of Yosemite."

∼

Back in my office, I hear a sound and look up from my computer.

"A word in my office?"

My boss stands in my doorway the following day. His dark eyes stare me down. Dr. Harrison is the head of the animal population wing of PMI. He has been for over a decade, as evidenced by his silver head of hair and the deep wrinkle in the middle of his forehead.

"Of course," I reply nervously.

He gives me a curt nod and disappears into the hallway.

I head out of my office and down the hall to Harrison's. His office is quadruple the size of mine with floor-to-ceiling windows looking out at the ocean. I find him standing there, back to the door, observing *his domain*. The

Pacific. He gives me the creeps with his supervillain stature. I'll enter low and hope for the best.

"Sit, Dr. Harvey," he commands.

If it were any other man, I'd be itching to fight. But he's my boss and if I want to get closer to his level of authority here at PMI, I need to play the game. I sit down in the chair in front of his metal desk and wait. He takes his time, turning back around and joining me at the desk, sinking into his chair.

He produces a manila folder from the top drawer and slides it over to me. "I have an assignment for you."

He says nothing more. See? Supervillain behavior.

I open the folder and scan the first few details. "You want me to go up to Alaska?"

"Bristol Bay's coho salmon population has been on the decline for several years now. Sockeye is doing great, but coho is not, which is worrying."

I furrow my brow. That *is* an interesting issue. "Are they being overfished?"

He shrugs. "That is a distinct possibility. However, since coho is the most affected, I have to wonder if there's more going on."

It definitely is a mystery, and my heart races with excitement.

Dr. Harrison opens his hands up. "You've been at the top of my list for a while now. I was just waiting for the right assignment. The work you've done on monitoring the gray whale populations has been extremely solid." Moving on from a project usually means the project isn't needed anymore. We've seen great strides with the whales. I did that.

I smile. "But salmon isn't—"

"Your area of expertise, but I think you'd be a formidable arm of the operation."

That's a compliment. I know it is. Not every scientist is valued for their versatility and adaptability.

Dr. Harrison goes on. "Plus, if you publish, we could start discussing what it might look like for you to graduate to a senior research position."

"Senior research? Really?"

"It's the logical next step should everything go to plan."

I swallow. Things hardly ever do when it comes to research.

"You'd be on your own, but we will make sure you have all the equipment and supplies you need."

"Of course."

"And Naknek is a lot smaller and quite a bit different than Los Angeles."

I smile and nod. "I can imagine."

"Can you?" Dr. Harrison asks with a raised eyebrow. "It will be a couple of months. Not just a weekend vacation."

My shoulders tighten. "I'll adapt. I'm not worried."

Dr. Harrison smiles, a rare sight from him. "You leave in two weeks."

I try to suppress my shock. "That's quick."

"That won't be a problem, will it?"

"No. Not at all." It's not like I have anyone waiting for me at home. No boyfriend to attend to. Not even a pet. I just need someone to water my plants.

"Good. I knew I could count on you."
"Of course. Always."

~

"WHAT DO you *mean* you're going to *Naked*, Alaska?" my sister blurts out the moment she walks into my apartment.

I'm already pouring glasses of wine for us. "Naked? Where'd you get naked from?"

"Um, from your text, obviously."

Sarah holds her phone out for me to see. I texted her immediately when I got the news about my latest assignment. Sure enough. There it is in gray and white: *I'm going on assignment to Naked, Alaska!*

"Is it like a nudist colony or something?" Sarah asks, annoyed with my lack of response.

"Fucking autocorrect." I laugh. "*Naknek*, Alaska. Not *Naked*."

Without another word, I head into my room, and Sarah follows, picking up her wine on the way. "So, no hot naked fishermen?" she whines.

"If the fishermen are naked, we might have bigger problems than fish populations."

Sarah snickers, mischievous little sister mode activated. "I'd say they're going very well if—"

"Sarah!"

"I'm kidding, I'm kidding!" Sarah plops down on my bed next to my suitcase. "Now, tell me all about your research assignment, Dr. Lillian."

We get back on track, and I explain the trip to Alaska to

Sarah while she navigates to the Airbnb page. Sarah's a good listener, and even though she likes to interrupt with her cheeky comments, she never lets me go unheard.

"Oh, my gosh. This cottage is so cute. It's like *Little House on the Tundra,*" my sister says, scrolling.

I laugh as I fold up another shirt. I called her when I got home to help me pack. Of course, Sarah's version of helping me pack is lying on my bed while I do all the folding. No matter, I like her company.

"Thankfully, it has a bathroom. Not an outhouse," I say.

She gasps. "Do you actually have to worry about that?"

I roll my eyes. Sarah is a *real* city girl, working as a corporate lawyer in Century City. "I mean, it's not unheard of up there, but—"

"You can't go. You absolutely can't. No sister of mine is going to be getting out of bed in the middle of the night to go to an *outhouse*. What if you run into a polar bear?"

I return to my closet to pick out a few more things. "I'm not going *that* far north."

"Okay, but you never know. A feral polar bear could—"

"Polar bears can't be feral. They've never been domesticated," I say, sorting through the hangers until I come upon my wetsuit. I pull at the neoprene and consider packing it until I remember the waters in Alaska are much colder than down here in California. I'll need something thicker.

Sarah grunts, throwing her phone down and sitting up. "Why aren't you scared?"

"I'm more worried about sleeping through the

midnight sun than anything." More items for the shopping list—eye mask and melatonin. "And subletting the apartment. That's going to be hell." I already put an ad online. Now, I'm waiting for someone to take the bait.

"Lil, I will pay your rent if you can't—"

"You will do no such thing! My little sister can't pay my rent. That's so *wrong*."

Sarah tosses her hair over her shoulder as if it's no big deal. She's been dying it blonde since she moved to LA. "It's what sisters do. I don't want you to worry."

I sigh and smile. "I'll find a subletter."

Sarah grabs her phone and lays back down. "Whatever you say."

After a few more moments of packing, Sarah hums at her phone screen. "At least it looks beautiful up there this time of year."

"Yeah. Really beautiful." I've never been to Alaska. I've always been in warmer climates for research, even though I specialize in cephalopods. It will be a much-needed change of pace. I need something different from the grind of being overworked and underpaid, which is the life of a researcher at PMI.

"How long is the flight?"

"Five hours to Anchorage," I say as I toss a few pairs of socks into a packing cube. "Then, another hour to Naknek."

"You're really going to be out there, huh? The sticks?" she says with a far-off look in her hazel eyes, the same ones I inherited from our mother.

"The boonies," I add with a spooky flair. "Ooooo . . ."

Sarah winces. "Better you than me."

I laugh. "I'm excited. Nervous, but excited. It's an adventure."

Sarah turns onto her stomach, perching her elbows on the edge of my suitcase. "You're going to be great."

I smile gratefully. "You think so?"

"Duh. You're the smartest woman I know." Her eyes lock on mine. "Now, can we eat? I'm starving. How do you feel about sushi tonight?"

Chapter 2

Nose to Nose With a Chevy Silverado

LILLIAN

Getting to Naknek is a two-day affair. I arrive in Anchorage just past noon, and while Naknek is only another hour away, there isn't a flight until tomorrow. After sending my new subletter instructions on where to find the apartment key, I check how long it would take to drive to Naknek. I was promptly slapped in the face by the statistic that 86 percent of Alaska's towns can't be accessed by roads from the outside.

Flying is a necessity.

From the second I arrive in Anchorage, I'm awed by Alaska's beauty. Six different mountain ranges are visible just from the airport. California can be magnificent, but these mountains with their snowcaps and crags up against the majestic blue sky are unlike anything I've ever seen. They are simultaneously like protectors and overlords. Beautiful and terrifying at once. Tall plants with fuchsia flower clusters line the sides of the parkway. I make a mental note to look up what kind of flowers they are.

A part of me is disappointed I can't stick around a bit longer and explore the nature Anchorage has to offer. Denali is a four-and-a-half-hour drive away, and I've heard the Alaska railroad has some of the most beautiful views in the country.

The next morning, I'm up bright and early to hit the airport and get to Naknek.

I knew the plane would be small, but not this small. It has propellers. *Propellers.* Couldn't those things just break off and fly into the wind? And even if we survive a crash, we'd be doomed.

Climbing the few stairs into the cabin, I can literally *see* the cockpit. I feel sick.

There are only a few other passengers, which means I get a double seat to myself, and we take off on time. I don't enjoy flying to begin with. And I like it even less when my stomach lurches with every bump and dip as we ascend to cruising altitude, which does not seem high enough in my opinion.

It's loud too, so my noise-canceling headphones don't quite do the trick. I decide to pass the short flight by looking at a book I picked up from the airport gift shop called *Alaska's Wild Plants*. I know all about marine life, but plants have always eluded me. So, time to get smart.

That keeps me pretty distracted until I look up from

the book and out my window, realizing we're flanked by mountains on both sides. I'm filled with dread for a split second, calculating how the hell we would survive the Alaskan wilderness if we crashed. But that thought is quickly replaced with marvel.

The sharp, pointed tops of the surrounding ridge are breathtaking. How can you not be amazed at the earth and what a gift it is?

Unfortunately, the landing is no better than takeoff in terms of my anxiety. The landing strip is *literally* gravel. Isn't gravel bad for traction?

The plane bounces twice as the tires hit the ground, but no one seems worried except for me. I'm more than grateful to be alive once the plane slows to a stop. When I unfold myself out of my seat and make it out of the tiny aircraft (alive, in one piece), I step onto the lone dirt runway that seems too short for a plane to take off.

With my luggage in hand, I set out across, greeted by a rickety plywood shed proudly labeled "South Naknek International Airport" above an empty window frame. There's a "Lounge" sign above the open doorway. Inside, there's a single wooden bench and an old landline phone hanging on the wall. The air is filled with a faint smell of damp wood and stale air.

A guy from my flight, decked out in red flannel, blue jeans, and work boots, catches the look of utter confusion on my face. "Looking for the car rental office?" he asks.

"Yeah," I say with a sigh of relief. "How far is it?"

"About a ten-minute walk. But I'm heading that way now if you'd like a ride."

"No, thanks," I reply, forcing a polite smile.

"Suit yourself." He shrugs, climbs into his pickup parked behind the shed, and drives off.

It would have been much easier to drive with my rolling suitcase, backpack, and overstuffed purse. There aren't any sidewalks and the roads are dusty, not to mention having to cross what is technically a two-lane highway to get to the rental place. But I've seen too many hitchhiking stories gone wrong to get into a stranger's truck.

And the second I step onto the property, the man from my flight steps out of the main building to greet me. The same one who offered me a ride. Red flannel and everything. That's not embarrassing at all.

"Told you I'd give you a ride," he says with a chuckle, a clipboard tucked under his arm.

"Better safe than sorry," I say. "I didn't talk with you on the phone this morning, did I?"

He looks down at his clipboard. "You're Lillian Harvey?"

"Yes?"

"Follow me."

He didn't answer my question, but I'm not going to press.

The man leads me to my rental, and I immediately go slack-jawed when I come nose-to-nose with a Chevy Silverado.

"Just sign here and—"

"I asked for a sedan," I say, pointing limply at the truck.

"Upgrade," he says.

I glance around the lot, which is full of cars in various states of . . . I can't say disrepair. Maybe *mid*-repair. "There isn't anything smaller?"

"You came at the tail end of tourist season. I'm running on fumes here."

"But, I mean, I can't drive that!"

He claps me on the shoulder. "Course you can, Lillian! Believe in yourself. The only difference from a little sedan is it runs on diesel."

The blood drains from my face. "*Diesel?*"

"Yup. And it's your lucky day; diesel just dropped in price 'round here." The man pushes his clipboard into my line of vision again. "You gonna sign?"

I take the pen in an absolute daze. Maybe there's another rental place where I can find a better car. I'll pay out-of-pocket if I have to. I can't be driving *this* thing around my entire time here. For one, it's humongous. For another, it is absolutely outside of my moral compass to drive a *diesel* engine. I'm not making a scene, though. I will not be the temperamental city girl.

The man, Ed, hauls my bag into the bed of the truck and helps me up into the cab. This thing is massive, like riding three horses at once. But I grin and bear it, fumbling to three-point turn it out of the parking lot.

Ed flags me down in the rearview before I can pull out onto the Alaska Peninsula Highway. I roll down my window and peek over the monstrosity of a vehicle.

"Just want to let you know, Lillian, people hitch around here. Don't make a big deal of it, alright?"

"Hitch?"

"Hitch*hike*?" he clarifies, pushing his chin forward.

I renegotiate my hands on the steering wheel.

"Don't know where you're from, but around here, it's not some dangerous thing, alright?"

Yeah, he should tell that to that serial killer who used to hunt women down in the Alaskan wilderness with his plane.

"Good . . . um, *karma*," he says with a snap of his fingers.

I force myself to smile. "Thanks for the tip."

He slaps the side of my truck. "Alright. Take care."

I just need to get to the cottage and drop off my things. Then . . . *chai*. I can already taste it.

∽

NAKNEK IS as scenic as it is decrepit. The buildings all look rundown and weathered. All the blemishes are even clearer under the summer sun. I'm sure these buildings have done their duty all these years, bearing the Alaskan winters.

And yet, while the town is a bit rundown, the surrounding nature brings it to life. The Naknek River is wide and still, with boats coming in and out of Bristol Bay. Salmon season is ending, so I wonder what accounts for all the busyness. I'm interested to hear from the local fishermen how their yield has been this summer.

Across the river, I catch glimpses of South Naknek, where many of the docks and some canneries are. I still haven't figured out how people get across. Apparently in the winter, the ice is solid enough to drive on, and they literally use a plane to get kids to school on the south bank.

My worst nightmare.

The drive is short, as I expect is true of everywhere in the Naknek area. My rental cottage is one of a small neighborhood of cottages that has long-term and vacation rentals alike. They're all carbon copies of one another—blue metal roofs with light wooden walls.

After struggling to get my bag down from the truck bed, I head into my cabin, my home sweet home right on the Naknek river.

Inside is smaller than I anticipated. I was particularly impressed that the pictures had shown a kitchen separate from the living space, but they must have used a wide-angled lens on the camera because the galley kitchen is nowhere near as big as the picture made it look.

I'm also shocked when I flop down on the bed and realize it's two twins pushed together instead of a full.

A bed is a bed. This is all for science, anyway. Function over form, hm? That's the Alaskan way.

My phone buzzes in my pocket, which surprises me considering the limited cell service out here. It's a text from my sister.

So? Are they naked?

I laugh, rolling my eyes. Her horny brain cells really work overtime. I respond in kind.

Sadly, not :(

I force myself up from the bed to check out the rest of the cabin. There's a door out the back of the house that

Naked in Naknek

leads down a grassy hillside to a stony beach. At least the views are expansive, even if the insides aren't.

I know I'm going to be spending a lot of time in here going over my data and writing reports, so I might as well see what Naknek has to offer.

Which means it's chai time.

∽

THERE ISN'T REALLY a downtown in Naknek. Buildings are just peppered wherever they landed. I make a beeline to the only place that appears to carry what I desire.

The Half-Hitch coffee shop is a long, brown structure right off the main road that looks like the freight car of a train. All the signage is homemade and hand-painted, and there's a hand-carved bear out front. There are a few foldable tables and chairs, all occupied by people enjoying the "nice" weather.

I pull my truck into a semblance of a spot. This thing is so embarrassing and gauche, but it's not the only truck here. I'm sure all *those* drivers, though, know how to get out of this sort of thing. I kinda just slide down and hope my feet hit something.

Inside, the Half-Hitch is as homegrown as it is on the outside. None of the chairs match, and the wooden floor looks like it could use a new finish. But dang, if it isn't cute. It's bustling midday and, though I don't drink coffee, the smell always makes me salivate.

I take a big inhale. Beans, sugary pastries, and . . . is

that fish? Do I smell *fish*? And not like someone cooked fish, but like someone used raw fish as cologne.

I guess this *is* a fishing town.

Over the barista is a menu, but there's also a peculiar board with a list of names, titled "Buy Your Friend a Coffee." I stare for a few seconds, trying to understand. Before I do, I'm distracted by a boom of loud laughter from a table in the corner. There are four guys piled around it, dwarfing the table to an impossible degree, like it's dollhouse furniture.

The first man who catches my eye is young and scruffy. His hair is cropped short like he's in the military. There's something attractive about him, despite his rough and tumble appearance.

Next to him is the oldest fisherman at the table, as evidenced by his dusty chestnut beard reaching the center of his wide chest. He leans back in his chair, glum as he grumbles about something.

There's one with his back to me. I get flashes of his face. His skin is of a deeper complexion than the others. I bet he has some native Alaskan heritage.

Finally, I turn my attention to the fourth man at the table, who sits opposite me. I didn't notice him at first because of his dark cap. However, when he takes it off and runs his hand through his thick, dark hair, he has my full attention. His full beard looks well taken care of by the shape and length. I hate when a man's mouth gets lost in a beard that's too bushy and feral. This one is just right. It highlights a pair of strong cheekbones and frames his bright smile.

The man tilts his head from side to side, stretching out his neck muscles. Then he pauses and smiles at me.

My stomach drops as our eyes meet. His are luscious brown. My heart launches into a gallop.

Fuck, he's hot.

There's something in those eyes that's both handsome and haunting. I've seen it in sailors before. There's a certain sparkle from those who love the sea more than anything on land. Men who know the sea hold stories in their eyes, and I'm always curious to know more.

I look away. I can't handle the strength of his stare, that tug inside me wanting to know more. I didn't come here to meet a hot guy in a coffee shop I came here to work, keep my head down, and do what I need to do.

"You ready?"

I flip around to face the barista. He's tall, lanky, and can't be over sixteen. "Hey, sorry about that."

"What can I get for you?" he asks.

"Could I get a chai tea latte with oat milk?" I drop the "extra hot," keeping it simple this time.

The kid purses his lips before looking over his shoulder at . . . well, there's no one there, just coffee equipment. "Uh, we don't have oat milk."

"Oh! Oh, duh." Why did I say duh? That was rude. "Do you have any dairy alternatives?"

He looks again. "Almond, I think."

"Okay! Well, that's fine. We'll do almond." I ignore all the water it takes to grow almonds and how the toxic fertilizers are hazardous to bees. When I think of the bees, my heart hurts. "Chai tea latte with—"

"We don't have chai," he says blandly.

What am I even doing here if they don't have chai? "Ohhhkay. Do you have ... tea? Any kind of tea?"

The little asshole smirks at me. I know he's just a kid, but he doesn't need to smirk at me. "I think we have English breakfast."

He *thinks?* "That's fine. I'll do that."

"Cool."

I find a table and sit down with my laptop, hoping I can forget any of that happened. A couple minutes later, a woman comes up beside the table, cup in hand.

"Did you get the tea?" she asks in a sweet-as-honey voice.

"Oh, yeah, that's mine. I could have gotten myself you didn't have to—"

"Do you want milk or sugar?" she plows ahead, batting her big eyelashes at me.

"No, this is great."

The woman places the tea on the table, and to my surprise, she doesn't walk away. Oh no, she sits down across from me. "I'm sorry about Josh. He does his best, but he's just a kid. You know how it is."

"That's okay. I should have looked at the menu before I ordered," I say sheepishly.

She holds out her hand toward me. "I'm Gwen. I own this place."

I take her hand and shake. Sizing up her features, I realize she's not very old. In fact, I don't think she's much older than me. But there's a bit more texture to her skin and

Naked in Naknek

a few silver strands in her swoop of bangs. "I'm Lillian." I'm going to keep the "doctor" thing to a minimum. No reason to rub it in people's faces. "Your place is very cute."

"Oh, thanks. A work in progress. Although, it's been that for the past decade." Gwen sighs. "You're here for Fishtival?"

I think I've misheard. "I'm sorry?"

"Fishtival!" Gwen exclaims again. "It's a celebration we have around here at the end of the fishing season. You know, kind of a celebration for all the fishermen, welcoming them back to town since they've been in and out on the rivers for so many months. It's been going on for, gosh, I don't know. Well, at least since before I was born. That's why town is so active today. Everyone just came from the parade."

"There was a *parade*?"

"It lasts all of five minutes, but hey! It's something!" she says with a bright smile.

Gwen tells me about all the details of Fishtival. There's a flea market and a pool tournament, activities for the kids, and even an art gallery right here at the Half-Hitch. I hadn't even noticed all the art on the walls. There's everything from fiber arts to watercolor. Some of them are absolutely beautiful.

Gwen gestures toward the counter where the barista has his nose buried in a book. "Josh might not be great at the coffee thing, but he has a knack for macrame." Her eyes widen. "So if you're not here for Fishtival, and you're definitely not a local, what *are* you doing here?"

"I'm here on a research assignment from the Pacific Marine Institute."

Gwen laughs. "Well, you've come to the right place. We've got marine everywhere." She jerks her thumb over at the men in the corner. "My brothers are fishermen. All the men in my family have been fishermen, actually."

I glance back at the table. A different man with cropped dark hair stares at me. When our eyes meet, he looks away and says something to his friend, not missing a beat of the conversation. Can he tell I'm an outsider? Already? I have to change the subject. "Um, can I ask you about the board? The buy a coffee—"

"It's just a silly thing we do. You can buy someone a coffee ahead of time, and we'll write it up on the board, so the next time they come in they'll be surprised. Cute, huh?"

I smile. "Very." You couldn't get away with that in a big city. No way, no how.

∽

THE NEXT MORNING, I head down to the dock to find the boat PMI hired. My bag is stuffed to the gills with everything I need for my research and then some. I'm off. It's the lack of sleep, I think. Despite my best efforts, the near continuous sunlight is strange. I had my curtains open for too long and didn't realize how late it had gotten.

Thank heavens for melatonin.

The docks aren't particularly welcoming. There are fishermen lumbering every which way. I thought Fishtival was to celebrate their return from the salmon fishing season, but apparently, that was only symbolic. Plenty of them look like they're ready to go out in their tall rubber boots and waterproof overalls.

I look down at the email from Dr. Harrison to check the information once more. I'm looking for Captain Tim Sinclair, and if I don't spot him, I should find his boat, *Net Profits*. I chuckle at that. I love a punny boat name.

I can't tell if these fishermen just can't see me, or they're choosing not to because one by one, they blow by me like I'm not even there.

"Excuse me?" I peep, hoping someone will hear me.

No dice.

I try to find an approachable subject when a pair of eyes meet mine. It's one of the guys from the Half-Hitch. The one with the short hair. He's sitting on a crate repairing a net, I think.

He looks away to busy himself with the net he's repairing, but it is too late. He's made his bed, and now he has to sleep in it.

I go over to him, paying no mind that he's trying to ignore me. "Excuse me?"

"Hmph."

I'm not sure if that was a statement or a question. "Do you know Captain Sinclair? Net Profits?"

He eyes me hard and sticks his tongue into his cheek. Damn, who pissed in his cornflakes? He leans back and yells out to a man nearby, "Kirk!"

The man looks up. He's the quintessential image of an old fisherman with haggard hair and deep wrinkles.

"Net Profits?"

Kirk shakes his head. "Left Naknek a couple days ago."

"What?" I almost shriek.

"I said, 'Left Naknek—'"

"I heard what you said!" I snap and cringe, realizing I was rude. "Thank you."

The man fixing the net asks, "What do you need with Sinclair?"

"He was supposed to take me out on his boat. I'm a researcher from the Pacific Marine Institute."

The man stares at me for a moment. I can't tell if he's impressed or . . . unsettled.

"Captain Sinclair was supposed to take me out on the rivers to collect samples of—"

He laughs. "Sinclair expects everything up front. He probably swindled your boss."

I clench my fists at my sides, my shoulder straining with the weight of my bag. "Well, what am I supposed to do?"

"Dunno."

"Don't *know*?"

The man rises to his full height, and *again*, these guys are huge. "Call your boss, sweetheart."

I seethe as he walks away. *Sweetheart*. "Jerk," I say under my breath. I've had quite enough mortification for the day. I need to figure out how to get a boat. Fast.

Naknek might be charming, but I'm not sure it likes me.

Chapter 3

She's Trouble

MATTHEW

If it weren't for coffee, I'm not sure I could get out of bed every morning. Coffee is my wife and my mistress, and that's all I'll say on the subject.

Today, I get a late start. I usually like to be out on the water first thing in the morning, but it's been a long and anemic season for salmon. I'm not too . . . let's say, inspired to get out on the water and troll.

My guys meet me at my sister Gwen's coffee shop most mornings. The Half-Hitch is the hub for the fishermen. It's the closest one to the harbor, and the patrons are the least likely to give you the side-eye if you smell like bait. We like to give her our business, get the bean water, and make a plan for the day.

I'm the last one in this morning. Jesse and Tuma are already at our usual table, coffee steaming.

"There's the lazy ass," Jesse says, with a wicked grin over his shoulder.

Tuma's too busy to look up, trying to get the right ratio of sugar to cream in his coffee by alternating between the two.

I wave my hand at Jesse, a "get out of here" motion, as I approach the counter. Winnie, my six-year-old niece, stands behind the register, eyes level with the counter as she adjusts a small plastic T. rex and a brontosaurus across from each other.

"Battle of the century, huh?" I ask as I lean over the counter.

Her grey eyes flick up at me, and she smiles. Her grin is missing two teeth right at the front. They grow up so fast. "Of the Jurathic period," she says excitedly. "Although, the thee-rex is a Cerathosaurus because they're from the Crethaceous period, but—"

"What did I say about dinosaurs on the counter?" Gwen calls out from the kitchen.

Winnie scoops up the two dinos and plunges them into the front pocket of her overalls as her eyes flick to me nervously.

"Dinosaurs? What dinosaurs?" I ask loudly, giving Winnie a very dramatic wink.

Her little face scrunches up into a smile. When she does that, it's like going back in time to when Gwen was little. Cut and paste.

Speaking of, Gwen wafts in, throwing a rag over her

shoulder and narrowing her eyes at me. "Don't teach her to lie, Matthew."

I shrug. "I know dinosaurs when I see them, and there are no dino—"

"Not today, okay?" My sister sighs.

I know when to back off Gwen, and that's as good a sign as any. It's a look I've come to know well over the past eight years.

Gwen taps Winnie on the back, and the little girl scrambles out from behind the counter to go play dinosaurs somewhere more appropriate.

"You good?" I ask.

"I'm fine," she says. "Coffee?"

I reach into my pocket for my wallet. I really need a new one. This one I've duct taped to hell and back, but hey, it gets the job done.

"Put that away," she says with a wave of her hand.

"Come on, Gwen. I'm gonna pay for my coffee."

She turns around and puts a few pumps of coffee into a paper cup with the Half-Hitch logo. "It's just drip. No skin off my back."

I ignore her and take a few bills out of my wallet. "Every penny counts." It's not easy to keep a business afloat in Naknek. After peak season drifts away, it can be a ghost town around here.

My sister shakes her head, sliding the cup of coffee across the counter toward me. "You're the one who's been complaining about the market price for sockeye this season. It's like the more you catch, the less you make."

Gwen holds my dollars out to me, but I ignore her,

sticking my wallet back in my pocket. "I'm going out for coho later. I'll be fine."

She finally gives in, stuffing the dollars into her register. "What's the point of Fishtival, if you all have to go back out?"

"We're fishermen. We fish."

"You know that's not how it used to be."

I sip my coffee and ignore the lump forming in my throat. No. It's not. Sockeye season alone used to be ridiculously profitable—an abundance of riches. We got time off to be with our families and actually enjoy the fruits of our labor. Now, with the sockeye market tanking, we're lucky if coho season yields enough to make ends meet. The coho aren't as plentiful as they once were, and every year it feels like there's less to go around. The door to Half-Hitch opens, letting in a nice Pacific breeze. Ian Brown lumbers in. When people talk about *lumbering,* he's the definition.

I give him a nod. "Hey, Ian."

"Hey, mate."

Ian's been in Naknek twenty-some years, but hasn't shed his English accent or slang to match.

Gwen plates up a scone for Ian. "Scone, rhymes with *yawn,*" he said the first time he brought up the idea to her. He had to explain he didn't want any of those American triangles with berries and crystallized sugar on the top. What he really wanted was a *biscuit* with fresh cream.

But Gwen always does her best to satisfy the customer, and that's what she did. They're a crowd favorite now. I step to the side and let Ian belly up to the counter.

"No sign of Stevie today?" he asks.

"I'm afraid not," Gwen says.

I glance up at the Buy a Coffee board and smirk. I'm not sure how many years ago Ian bought a coffee for Stevie Nicks, but the man is holding out hope and I have nothing but respect.

"Damn. Well, you'll never get away from the sound of the woman who loves you," he says in consolation.

I snort, patting him on the shoulder. "You're a real romantic, Brown." I turn to join Jesse and Tuma at our table.

A few fishermen give me a nod or a wave as I go. There are familiar faces I grew up with, but others I've become acquainted with over the past few months too. We get a lot of seasonal workers at the canneries and on the boats during salmon season. A lot of them will get their promised ticket back to Anchorage pretty soon.

A conversation has broken out between my usual table and two others with fishermen all talking about something that's got most of their faces looking sour.

Drama.

"What's happening?" I ask as I take a seat next to Tuma.

"The scientist," an older guy, Kirk, says. Somehow his wrinkles even have wrinkles. That's how worked up he is about whatever subject they're discussing. "Brown said he was renting his cabin to some science center down in California and—"

"She's *trouble*." Another old timer, Lefty (thanks to being born with his left leg shorter than the other), snorts. "Gotta be trouble."

"Who's gotta be trouble?" I try to butt into the conversation again.

"You haven't heard?" Lefty says.

I shake my head. "Obviously not. That's why I'm asking."

"Your own brother ran into her on the docks yesterday morning," Lefty continues, jamming his finger toward Jesse.

I glance at my brother. He's got a layer of stubble that would be easily taken care of with a shave, but he doesn't give a rat's ass about looking clean-cut. Other than keeping his hair out of his eyes, so it's easier to make eye contact with women. His words, not mine. "Is this a new pastime, or—"

My brother has a habit of giving young female tourists a . . . different perspective of Naknek, let's say. However, he doesn't take my joke well. "Not like that. You think anyone I'd be interested in would be hanging out at the docks?"

"Will someone tell me what's going on?" I ask.

Tuma pipes up from beside me, thank god. He's the only one who makes any sense around here because he hasn't spent his life nipping the bottle like the rest of us. "She's a researcher. Apparently, she hired Sinclair to take her out to get some samples. That's what she told Jesse."

"He probably realized he'd sink his boat if he went out with a woman," Jesse says with a smirk.

I kick him under the table. Not only is it a ridiculous superstition amongst fishermen and sailors, but it's abjectly false. And, we have a highly respected female captain working out of Naknek. "Don't be a dumb-ass."

"Whatever she's doing is bad news," Kirk says. "Mark my words. Bad. *News*."

"What's she studying? I mean, surely, it can't be that bad."

"Bah!" Lefty yelps, crossing his arms over his wide chest. "We don't need someone sticking their nose where it doesn't belong."

"Amen to that," Jesse says.

I glance around the Half-Hitch. Plenty of people here are what we'd call outsiders. They're here to work, sure. But how different is it, really? "What's she studying?" I ask.

Everyone looks at me blankly.

"Really? You're getting all up in arms about some girl who's doing some research, and you don't even know what she's studying?"

"You talking about Lillian?" Gwen shouts from the register.

"Who the hell is *Lillian*?" Kirk responds unhelpfully.

Gwen puts her hand on her hip. "She's here with—who is it?—Pacific Marine Institute, I think. She came in the other day. She wanted chai, but we don't have chai. Poor thing."

I remember her. The woman who came in looking totally out of place with a long auburn ponytail and colorful windbreaker. Not from these parts, I can tell you that. You remember all the women around here, especially when you're my age and single. The pool is small and, for the most part, taken.

I try not to get my hopes up when someone new comes to Naknek. They're here for a time. Not forever.

Something about her, though. *Lillian.* She struck a chord in me that hasn't been struck in a long time. I stole a few glances while she talked with Gwen. Her long legs, sun-kissed skin, and full lips curled in a perpetual smile—a mysterious smile—drew me in.

It's rare that anything surprises me around here anymore.

But she did.

Kirk grunts. "Aren't there some laws around that? Just letting researchers... research? Doesn't seem legal."

"Did she tell you what she's studying?" I ask Gwen.

"She didn't tell me, but I googled her. She's got her picture on their website and a little bio. Apparently, she's a researcher in the animal population department. Could have to do with our fishing problem."

"There's no problem," Lefty says.

I snort. "Yes, there very damn well is."

Lefty shakes his head. "Things come in cycles. Circle of life."

"Whatever it is, we don't need her snooping around," Jesse says, smacking his open palm down harshly on the table. "What's she gonna do with that research? Give it to the government. Then they're going to start coming after us instead of fixing the actual problem."

"You know the actual problem?" I test my brother. "You know how to fix it?"

Jesse rolls his eyes. "I'm saying it doesn't matter. We're going to be the problem because we're the thing they can control. They can tax the shit out of us and make us buy more permits. None of us need that on top of a shit fishing season."

Tuma and I exchange a glance. He smiles and gives me a shrug. This is the way of things. We bitch and complain, but we still do our work.

I'm not interested in today's bitch fest, though. "I'm gonna get something to eat. I'll meet you on the dock," I say to Tuma before getting to my feet and exiting the conversation without so much as a goodbye.

Chapter 4

Even if He is a Sexy Fisherman

LILLIAN

"I'll do what I can. In the meantime, use this as an opportunity to be proactive," Harrison said at the end of our phone call yesterday when I informed him of Captain Sinclair's disappearance. I don't ask if he was taken for a ride by Mr. Sinclair. "If you can save the institute some money, that will reflect highly on you."

I'm not sure what exactly he's suggesting. Negotiate with the local fishermen? Use my feminine wiles to secure a boat? I decide not to think about it too deeply or else I'll get rage-fueled heart palpitations. I'll do my job and if that means putting my nose to the grindstone, so be it.

But if he thinks for a second, I'll try to save the Institute money by *flirting*? The man is sorely mistaken.

Activity in Naknek seems contained to the docks and

Naked in Naknek

the few watering holes in town. I drive to The Half-Hitch but see the fisherman from the dock who called me *sweetheart* lumbering in, so I decide to take my chances elsewhere.

Which is how I end up at The Sea Witch, the local diner. "Like sandwich!" Comic Sans declares at the top of the laminated menu.

Naknek really is charming around every corner.

I take a seat at the counter, which gives me a full view of the diner. It doesn't look quite like the other diners I've been to in the lower forty-eight. It's got a pitched roof with visible wooden beams, a linoleum floor, and long communal tables. Even the counter is more like a bar, as evidenced by the lines of liquor bottles along the wall. I guess any place around here has to serve multiple functions if it wants to get by.

I order oatmeal and fruit and ask, haplessly, if they have chai. They tell me they have Fireball. I pass and settle for a coffee instead. I don't like coffee, but I do need that little hit of caffeine.

Down the bar from me are a couple guys I assume are fishermen because they're talking about, well, fish.

"I'm gonna have to help my brother up in Fairbanks this winter with his ice fishing business," the one man says, looking down into his cup of coffee. "To make ends meet."

"You gonna leave the girls here?" the other man asks. He's younger with patchy facial hair and big sunken eyes that look both tired and more alert than I've been in years.

The first man leans back in his chair and rubs a hand

over his bald head. We'll call him Baldy. "Yeah, but what can I do? Fish don't give a shit."

My eavesdropping is interrupted by the server arriving with my oatmeal. I thank her distractedly, not wanting to miss what they're saying.

"It's been getting worse. This is your first year here, so you haven't seen what I've seen, but the coho don't bite like they used to.".

My already-piqued interest is piquing even harder.

"What do you think it is?" Patches asks.

Baldy shrugs. "I don't know. Doesn't help to know either because knowing doesn't *do* anything."

I take a quick inhale. Baldy's talking about leaving his family for the winter to make ends meet. That's a huge sacrifice.

I could help with that. I need a boat, and I have money from the Institute to pay for it.

What's the harm in asking?

I lean toward the men. "Excuse me."

They both look up at me, their expressions stoic.

"Are you talking about coho salmon?"

Baldy raises an eyebrow. "You listening to our conversation?"

"I—ha! I couldn't help but overhear."

The two men exchange a look. This isn't going well.

"I'm actually studying the coho population in Bristol Bay. I'm from the Pacific Marine Institute," I say, maintaining a smile despite their cool demeanor.

Cool turns to cold. Patches purses his lips. "You're the scientist."

"Yes! That's me."

Baldy grunts and looks at his coffee as if it's primetime television.

"I need a boat to get some samples of the water and the riverbeds, and I'm trying to find someone to help me out."

"Help *you*?" Patches scowls.

Jesus, even if I did use my feminine wiles, they wouldn't make up for how annoyed these guys are with me already. "Yes! Of course, not for free. The Institute would pay you. And I just thought, since I heard you talking about how the season was slow—"

"We don't need your pity money, ma'am," Baldy says without looking up.

"It's not pity, it's—"

Patches rears up on his chair and gives me a hard look. "You heard him. We're not interested."

And with that, they go back to their conversation like I don't even exist. Like we aren't even breathing the same air. I don't mean to stare at them, but I'm flabbergasted. People have been so nice to me since I arrived in Alaska, but suddenly, the tide has turned. Is it because they know I'm a scientist?

"Finton's an asshole. Don't take it personally," someone says next to me.

I turn to look at the source of the voice and find the bearded fishermen I saw laughing at Gwen's the other day. The one that made me stop in my tracks and think, "*Damn*."

I'm thinking *"damn"* again now that we're up close and personal like this. When my eyes meet his, amber and inviting, my mouth grows dry and my thoughts scramble. He's even more attractive this close. Soft lips part the darkness of his beard, the hard ridge of his nose, and brow bone. Usually when you get close to someone, you can see all their imperfections, but he's . . ....

Stop staring and say something.

"Wh-which one is Finton?" I ask.

The man chuckles. "The one who doesn't look like he's finished puberty."

I smile and he smiles back, pink lips amidst that well-groomed beard. Oh *no*.

Before I can reply, the server comes up. "The usual, Matthew?"

"Please," the man—Matthew—replies.

I busy myself by looking interested in my oatmeal, although it's gotten cold and sticks uncomfortably to my spoon. However, distracting myself doesn't really help. Some people just have an aura about them; something that invites you in. And Matthew has that. It's exciting and terrifying at once.

"You're looking for a boat?" Matthew asks as he settles onto the seat beside me, his legs so long he can prop himself up on the edge of the stool and have his feet flat on the ground.

"You heard that, huh?"

He leans on the bar and folds his hands. "I did."

I glance at him and wait for him to say more.

His dark brows pinch in the middle, and he gives me a sympathetic smile. "I'm afraid you're going to be hard-pressed to find someone open to helping you."

My heart falls. "Why's that?"

Matthew sighs. "You've got a reputation around here."

I scoff louder than I mean to. "A reputation? I just got here."

"I know, and you've already made quite an impression on Naknek," Matthew says.

I'm all turned around. On one hand, he's making me flustered because he's handsome as hell. And on the other, I'm angry. "I'm just here to do a job. Like the rest of you."

Matthew smiles and gives the server a nod as she stops by with a glass of orange juice for him. "Listen, uh . . . " He raises his eyebrows so they meet his beanie. "Lillian, right?"

He must have talked to Gwen. He's one of her brothers, I guess. "Yeah."

"Well, *Lillian*," he says my name . . . nicely. His tone is genuinely kind. I guess I can appreciate that, even if he's not saying things I want to hear. "We have our way of doing things around here, and people don't take kindly to outsiders coming and sticking their nose into things."

I shake my head. "I'm not *sticking* my nose into things. I'm trying to help, but no one will even give me an opportunity to explain why I'm here."

Matthew opens his palms up to the sky. "Okay, then go ahead and explain. I'm listening."

I huff. "Are you actually going to listen, or are you going to take what I say back to your crew and try to run me out of town?"

Matthew leans on the bar and rubs his chin, hand

shuffling through his beard. It's such a subtle movement, but it's stupidly hot. "Between you and me, Lillian."

I narrow my eyes at him. I don't give my trust that easily, even if he is a sexy fisherman.

"Promise. We might all be suspicious as hell around here, but we're earnest to a fault. I don't lie," Matthew says.

He even sounds earnest. Even if he's lying, it's not like it'll hurt telling him my plight. He'll just go back to his friends and tell them I'm exactly what they thought. That I'm hiding something or trying to pull the wool over their eyes. "Fine. I work for the Pacific Marine Institute in Southern California. I've been sent out here because coho salmon populations have been on the decline. You know this, of course."

Matthew lifts his chin. "I do."

The simplicity of his response sends chills down my spine. "Right. You all do. So, you know better than anyone why it's important we figure out *why*. Because this is your livelihood. And I want to help with that," I say, pressing a hand to my chest. "I want to figure out what's going on, so my team can make recommendations to help. I'm here because I care, not because I want to get in the way."

The server comes back with a plate made for a man like Matthew. Eggs, bacon, toast, the works. I bet he burns a lot of calories working on the boat. I will not let myself get distracted by thinking about all the muscles he must have, definitely not. "Um, anyway, I understand that I'm an outsider, but surely you all can understand it's important we figure out what's happening so your livelihood isn't on the line, right?"

Matthew makes me wait while he takes a bite of food. At least he has the decency to chew it all up and swallow before he speaks. "Your logic is sound."

"Thank you."

"If you were in California," he says, punctuating the air with his fork.

I blink. "What?"

I have to wait for another bite of food. "It's not the fact you're *doing* the research. It's what comes after. Because, what? You're going to run back to California and show them your data and then?"

"Well, we'll give recommendations to the government and—"

Matthew snaps his fingers and points at me. "Bingo."

"Sorry?"

He pats his mouth with a napkin. "You are going to find out information, which, I grant you, is important information to have. And then you're going to give it to the government, who will, under the guise of helping, put more restrictions on us and interfere with the way we do things. Make sense?"

I know as well as anyone the government is fallible. And that's putting it lightly. Do they actually have our best interests at heart? Debatable. However, the Environmental Protection Agency is one of the better branches of the government. I trust them more often than I don't, which you can't say for the IRS. "Don't you feel you're already being restricted though, based on what's happening with the coho populations?"

"Of course we do. I mean, many of us used to work one

fishing season a year. *One.* Now to make ends meet, we have to go out on the boat for longer and longer. That's hard on us and our families."

I smile, unable to contain my excitement that we're on a similar page. "Exactly! That's not fair to you all. You deserve to be able to make ends meet and more without the expense of your family."

Matthew shifts in his seat, leaning in closer to me. "But if you all come in here with your recommendations, and you tell us we have to stop fishing for coho to get the numbers back up, that doesn't change what we need to live on."

"I—" God, this is way more complicated than I'd like it to be. "I suppose, but—"

"Coho goes for more money. So, while our numbers might be lower overall, it's still a significant portion of our income. How do we make up for that in the meantime?" Matthew gestures to present the answer. "More time on the water. More fishing. More time away."

I'm at a loss for what to say. I have plenty of arguments, sure, but none of them have the pathos his do. At least not pathos he'll hear. The plight of coho salmon surviving and thriving is a formidable one. But how does that stack up to a fisherman trying to explain the livelihood of a community?

He smiles, solemn and sympathetic. "I'm not trying to give you a hard time. I'm just trying to give you the Cliff Notes of how things work around here. We need to do things on our terms." Matthew pinches two fingers together and taps the counter. "And that's important to us. Okay? We don't have a lot, but we work our asses off to take care of what we do."

"I don't doubt it," I reply.

"So, when someone like you comes in here . . ." Matthew gestures to me, his hand swiping through the air like an artist's paintbrush. "No matter how polite and pretty—"

Did he just call me pretty?

"It's our natural and earned inclination to be suspicious, standoffish, and, if I'm honest . . . " Matthew leans in closer to me. We're much too close for strangers. "Try and run you out of town."

I gasp, a mixture of shock and *delight* at his closeness.

Matt backs off much too quickly for my liking. "Not me, of course. But Lillian, no one is going to give you a boat and help you out with your project."

I cross my arms over my chest. "So, you *are* trying to run me out of town."

"I'm not, I swear, but—"

"Then, let me pay you to take me out on the rivers, so I can get my samples."

Matthew freezes and watches me for a moment with those stunning brown eyes. A smile creeps across his lips. "I can't do that."

"Then, you're just like the rest of them," I say. My turn to take a bite of my gloopy oatmeal and make *him* wait.

Matthew looks off, his mouth ajar, like he knows the beginning of what he wants to say, but not the ending.

Finally, he looks down and laughs. "They'd give me hell if I took you out on my boat."

"That's fine," I say. "I'm not leaving until I'm done with the project anyway. I'll figure out a way to get out there." I sound a lot more confident than I actually am. "I don't back away when it comes to my work, Matthew. Because it matters. It *really* matters. Not just to me. But to the whole world, even if they don't know it."

He settles his teeth into his lower lip. It's almost utterly sexual, so I focus on my oatmeal to keep from being distracted. I can tell he is thinking about something, and he is taking his time responding. "Okay, tell you what. I can't help with my boat, but I could take you out in my plane."

"You have a plane?"

"More common than you'd think around here."

"So, how will going up in your plane help me when I need a boat?"

Matthew leans back in his seat, spreading his legs wide. He's so masculine it hurts. "Well, I'm running an errand in Dillingham. You could get a view of the entire bay and the rivers. It could give you an idea of the area, what you're working with, and help you come up with a plan for how you get that boat."

I stick my tongue into my cheek. What I need is a *boat*. Not a plane. But his offer isn't nothing. And besides, if he's offering me time with him one-on-one, maybe I can soften him. *Not* with my feminine wiles, no. But maybe, if I can get him to see I'm a human who really cares, he'll give me a bit more rope to work with. "Okay. When do we leave?"

Matthew's eyebrows jump slightly like he's surprised I agreed. Then, he smiles.

And that's a smile I'd like to bottle up and save forever.

Chapter 5

No Turning Back Now

MATTHEW

I grab the propeller blade and give it a once over, making sure there are no nicks or scratches. It's the final inspection step before taking my Cessna 206 up and out of Naknek.

Since my run-in with Lillian yesterday at The Sea Witch, I've been wondering what the hell I'm doing. I'm not sure if my curiosity has gotten the better of me, or if I'm thinking with my dick, which is *always* a bad idea.

Hearing her talk about her work and the passion in her voice struck something in me. It's clear she cares about figuring out what's happening to the coho. And that's admirable. However, she doesn't understand the implications. What could happen to us if the government knows too much and ends up adding more rules and strictures.

We like the wild. We like to be out of the fray. It's not that we're ungovernable, not by a mile. But we prefer things to be as they are, not as they could be. The enemy you know versus the enemy you don't.

And while I don't see her as an enemy per se, Lillian is truly the unknown enemy in many of my friends' eyes.

Just as I release the propeller, a black truck pulls into the gravel parking lot of the Naknek airport. I watch as the truck comes to a stop and the driver's side door opens. To my surprise, Lillian emerges in a pair of jeans and a chunky sweater, her hair long and free over her shoulders.

Dammit, she looks good. I should have prepared myself better for this.

Lillian jumps down from the cab, looking pissed as hell as she slams the door. She resituates herself and puts on a smile before heading in my direction.

"Morning," I call out.

"It's still morning, huh?" she asks, looking up at the sky.

I laugh. I've grown up with the midnight sun every summer since I was born. I never think twice about it. "You're from sunny California, aren't you?"

"Yeah, not *this* sunny," she says, stopping just in front of me.

I find myself at a loss for words. I kept my cool in the shoddy lights of The Sea Witch yesterday, but she's gorgeous. Her beauty is obviously unchanged, but I didn't have to look directly at it. Now, daylight illuminates her every glorious feature. Her heart-shaped face, apple cheeks, the forest green of her eyes.

Yeah, you might have been thinking with your dick on this one, Benton.

"Am I too early?" Lillian asks.

"No!" I respond too urgently. "I mean, uh . . . no. I just fueled up and checked that everything is in good working order, so after I do a cabin check, we should be ready to go."

"Great."

"After you," I say, gesturing up the steps.

Lillian leans forward and then stops. "I'd prefer to follow you if that's alright."

She's trying to conceal her nervousness. I see right through it, though. I know plenty of guys who avoid going up in the air, even if their life depends on it.

"Sure, no problem." I go up the steps and she follows.

"Is this an old plane?" she asks as she settles into her seat. Well, settles as much as someone can when they're on edge of terror.

I try to laugh it off. "Well, it's not an original production model, I'll tell you that."

Lillian's forehead wrinkles, her mouth pursed in worry.

Of course she's not familiar with airplane history, dingbat. "They made the first 206s from the '60s to the '80s. But this one is from the early 2000s. Cheaper to buy that way, but I promise everything is up to snuff in terms of parts."

Lillian tries to smile, rubbing her hands on the arm rests. "It's bigger than I expected."

"Yeah, I bought it a couple years ago." Gotta move it along. I am rambling. "Sometimes I rent it out for charters and—you know—it's good for the extra income." I hate that she's right. That we're struggling out here. Sockeye used to be *it* for a lot of us. Now it's sockeye here, coho there, investing in a business if you're lucky. Diversifying income. A deadly phrase.

I check the equipment, see we're ready to go, then turn to Lillian. "You have everything you need?"

She opens her bag, produces a camera and a notebook. "Ready as I'll ever be," she says with a sigh.

"Don't be nervous," I tell her as I grab a headset for her.

Lillian takes the set from me. "I'm not nervous."

"Don't lie, either."

Lillian's lips twist to the side in a smile. "Is it obvious that small planes scare me?"

"They scare everyone to an extent. If you're not scared, you're going to mess up. But don't worry, I'm licensed."

She balks. "Oh, great! At least you're licensed."

I turn away with a laugh. The only other woman I've had up in the cockpit with me is Gwen. And that's a different can of worms. She's always backseat driving. If she had her license, she'd for sure be a better pilot than me. "I'm not just licensed. I'm good."

Lillian puts the headset on. "We'll see about that."

I reach over and adjust the mic, so it's in front of her mouth. Her lips are glossy, looking just the right amount of sweet and soft.

I draw away and put my own headset on. "You hear me okay?"

"Loud and clear!" Her voice comes through the headphones loudly.

"You don't have to yell," I say through a chuckle.

She flushes a shade that matches the undertones of her hair. "Sorry."

"Okay, let's hit it."

After getting clearance from ground control and doing all final checks, I get the plane situated for takeoff on the runway. Lillian is braced in her seat beside me, white-knuckling the notebook in her lap.

"You okay?"

"I just realized people always tell you not to get into cars with strange men, not airplanes. And now here I am. In an airplane with a strange man."

Poor thing is running through every worst-case scenario in her head, the top of the list not being that we could crash, but that I'm some creep. Sometimes I hate being a man. No, sometimes I hate *other* men for being shitty men.

"My sister knows I'm here, by the way. And my mom. And my friend Trudy, so if you do anything—"

"I'm not going to do anything other than show you the rivers, take you to Dillingham, and bring you home," I say as genuinely as I can. "Remember, I'm not a liar."

Lillian heaves a sigh.

"You wanna get out?" I offer, although, to be honest, if she said yes, I'd be sorely disappointed.

She lifts her head and rolls her shoulders back. "No. I've come this far. No turning back now."

I grin. I like this girl.

Takeoff is smooth, which puts Lillian at ease. I hear her let out a long, slow breath as if she'd been holding it. I take her south first, explaining each river as we pass over it.

"The Egegik River is where you go for good sockeye runs," I explain. That's where I got some of my best fishing done this season, although the market price is marginal compared to years past. "Been a mass exodus from Egegik. You think Naknek is small..." I say with a chuckle.

Lillian does her best to take photos as we fly over. For someone scared of flying in small planes, she's glued to the window the whole time.

After about another half hour south, we pass over the Ugashik River.

"Look at all those tributaries," Lillian muses. "Pretty diverse fish population down there, I'd imagine?"

I glance at her, a bit surprised. I shouldn't be shocked. She's a scientist. This is her life. But she's stepped into *my* world. And I want to show it to her in all its glory. "It's farther than a lot of us like to go from Naknek, but you can always find something down there." The tradeoff being burning the fuel and the time. "Used to be great for coho," I mumble to play off like I'm unconcerned.

I loop the plane around until we're headed over the bay in the direction of Dillingham. Beneath us is the open expanse of water, which always gets my heart going. I've known a couple people who have lost their lives in accidents thanks to how unpredictable small planes can be. However, I've got a seaplane. Worst comes to worst, I land us right in the bay.

"What do you like more? Being on the water or in the air?" Lillian asks me.

I pause for a moment.

"Sorry, I shouldn't distract you."

"No, no, I'm thinking. They're different. You know?"

Lillian nods. "Yeah, of course."

"Depends on the day, I guess. Sometimes I get sick of being on the water. But other times being in the air is exhausting, so—"

"You're like a duck," Lillian says.

I laugh. "I never thought of it like that."

Out of the corner of my eye, I see Lillian's cheeks flush. Adorable.

Why does she have to be adorable too?

And she proves easy to talk to when she's not steeped in taking notes or trying to frame a photo. She's a good listener too. I end up talking much more than I thought I would. I tell her about the black sand beaches as we pass over them and the Japanese glass floats that are found there sometimes. "They're all handblown glass. And they often used old sake bottles to make them." I hold up my hand, cupping it slightly. "Like a little ball. Although they were made in all different sizes. They were used to keep nets afloat. People still go searching for them. It's a big deal."

"Sad they stopped making them," Lillian remarks.

"I've got a few in my house. Maybe you can see them some time." Did I really just invite her to my house? "Or I'll bring one to show you. To The Half-Hitch."

Dude, shut up you're making it worse.

"That sounds amazing."

I'd offer to take her some time, but I don't want to get ahead of myself. She wants something from me, and

Naked in Naknek

I'm... I'm just being kind. Going out of my way for a relative stranger. No use offering more than necessary.

Except, her excitement, her giddiness is totally infectious.

"You know what's funny?" she says. "I grew up thinking the tundra was always snowy and cold, but it's not, right? I mean in the summer..."

"It can be, but it's also filled with wildflowers in the summer. Fireweed and daisies and all sorts of things."

Lillian leans closer to the window. "Fireweed, those are the magenta flowers, right?"

"Yeah, they're everywhere. They grow like, well, like weeds."

She giggles.

"They even make fireweed jam and syrup."

"Really?"

"Oh yeah. It's good. Different, but good."

She shakes her head. "It's so cool how much you all live off the land around you. I mean, that's what every civilization is based on, and when you live in a big city, you forget that because everything is asphalt and concrete. But then you see wildflowers, and you're like *wow*. The earth just does that."

I don't respond. Her wonder makes me appreciate what I have, even if it can be hell sometimes.

"I sound so stupid. Oh, my god."

"No, not at all. Promise." I gnaw on my lower lip. Aw, fuck it. "You can find wild blueberries down there too. It's peak season for them. There's a—" I swallow. "There's a place close to Naknek people love going, but it can get really picked over this time of year, which is why I prefer to go south when I have to overnight on my boat."

"You go blueberry picking?"

I raise an eyebrow. "Do I not look like I go blueberry picking?"

"No, you don't. Big, burly fisherman type picking berries. It's a funny image."

"I can be gentle," I say.

"I didn't say you couldn't be."

I glance over at Lillian. Our eyes meet for a moment, a moment that sends a shiver down my back and right to my — I clear my throat. "Anyways, um, we're passing over the Togiak now." I explain the aspects of the Togiak River, how untouched it is, and how great the fishing is, but how far out of the way it is. With more boats going out that way this season, the nets end up being a bit lighter.

We land in Dillingham, smoother than a landing in Naknek thanks to the paved runway. I taxi my plane to the apron, where my friend, Derek, is waiting in his truck with the radio. I'm compelled to ask him to drive us into town, so we can grab something to eat. It wouldn't take long to refill and head back to Naknek. Fifteen minutes, or twenty, with a quick little jaunt over Kvichak.

"You want to go into Dillingham and, uh, we could get a bite to eat, and you could see the river up close?" I ask Lillian.

Her face immediately brightens. "I could get a sample!"

"A sample?"

She reaches into her pack and pulls out a couple empty vials. "Well, a water sample. I don't have my diving gear to get soil from the riverbed, but I need both for my research."

I might be wary of her research, but her enthusiasm is charming as hell. "Is that a yes?"

Lillian's mouth spreads into a sweet, girlish smile. She nods. "Yeah. Let's do it."

Something pulls in my chest. It's a feeling I don't know how to describe and know would be dangerous if I let it get out of control.

Best to quash it now. Because there's nothing to gain from losing myself over Lillian when I know once she has what she needs, she'll cut town as soon as possible.

Not to mention the fact that our worlds are more different than she even realizes.

Chapter 6

Saved by the Kelp

LILLIAN

The diner is old with fixtures that look ripped right from *Grease*. And it smells like grease, too. The fryers are cooking up something that smells delicious.

I pour over the menu. Meatloaf, salmon burgers, pickled kelp. Pickled kelp? I'm going to have to try that.

"Get whatever you want. On me."

My eyes shoot up to Matthew. "What? Why?"

He closes his menu and dresses up his cup of coffee with a packet of brown sugar. Cute. "Because I said so."

I point to my chest. "I was going to buy lunch."

He pulls a face, lips bending down at the corners and brow furrowed. "That's ridiculous."

"No, it's not. It's the least I can do for tagging along on your trip."

Matthew leans back. His knee brushes mine for a split second. Shouldn't do anything to me, but it does. It sends electric pulses through me. We've been so close all morning, and all that time my thoughts have been topsy turvy over the dictionary definition of "tall, dark, and handsome" sitting across from me. "If I recall, I invited you to join me. Wouldn't be very polite of me to make you pay for lunch." He sips his coffee, seeming nonplussed.

"You invited me begrudgingly. I know you're doing me a favor."

Matthew shakes his head. "Wasn't begrudgingly."

"Alright, well, whatever you want to call it then," I say, tossing a hand in his direction at the nits he's picking. "I want to pay for lunch as a thank you."

"Nope, I'm a gentleman. I'm paying for lunch," he says with a direct and pointed look.

I cross my arms over my chest. "Where I'm from, the only reason a man would buy you dinner is if you're on a date."

Matthew pauses. I assume he's gathering his wits or about to give me a crash course in the Alaskan way of things, which I will happily listen to. However, he doesn't do either of those things. Instead, he says, "Call it what you want."

My jaw nearly drops. Has this been a date the whole time? No way, right?

Matthew's attention diverts from me to the server, who is also running the cash register and, from time to time, popping in the back to argue with the cook. "Yeah, I'll have a double cheeseburger with fries and add a slide of slaw."

The server doesn't even bother writing it down. "And you, hon?"

I glance down at the menu again, my mind racing to pick out the right thing. At least I know the salmon is probably locally sourced, right? "I'll do the salmon burger. Do you have sweet potato fries?"

The server smiles. "No, ma'am."

At least she didn't laugh in my face. "Okay, then I'll do the garden salad with the dressing on the side."

"Something to drink?"

"Water's fine."

She starts to step away, but then I remember: "Oh, and could I get a side of the pickled kelp?" I ask.

"Gotcha," she says without looking back at me.

Matthew's staring at me. I feel a warmth crawl over my skin. "What?" I ask, busying myself by putting the menu back in the metal holder near the wall of the booth.

"Huh?"

"You're staring."

Matthew is caught off guard for a moment, eyes widening, lips parting. Then, he laughs. An awkward laugh. Maybe he didn't realize he was staring at me. "Oh, sorry, didn't mean to. I was just ... that was fascinating."

A laugh hops out of me. "Fascinating?"

He rubs his hand along the side of his face, his beard scraping his skin. "Yeah, I mean, you both fulfilled the stereotype in my head and then subverted my expectations."

"What stereotype?" I say with a teasing lilt at the back of my voice.

"You know what I mean. California-type of woman," Matthew says, lowering his chin.

I fold my hands on the tabletop, leaning closer. "What's a California-type of woman to you?"

"The type that orders sweet potato fries when they aren't on the menu," he retorts. "And orders dressing on the side."

"Touché. I have to ask, though."

He rolls his eyes. "You don't eat potatoes to watch your figure?"

I open my mouth to deny it, but I can't lie. I definitely backed off the starches after moving to Los Angeles. "Sweet potato fries are like the norm in California."

"I bet they are."

I kick him under the table, not too hard but enough to get my point across. "Don't be rude."

Matthew laughs, that bright smile appearing on his face. The one that drew me to him in the first place.

This really *does* feel like a date.

Saved by the kelp. The server returns with a small white dish of green loops of it. "Enjoy," she says before scurrying off to handle another table.

"And *that*," Matthew says, wagging a finger toward the dish. "Was what surprised me."

"What? That I'd try pickled kelp?"

He shrugs. "You can't blame me for being a *little* surprised."

I stare down at the bowl of kelp rounds. "Have you tried pickled kelp before?"

Matthew appraises the bowl with narrowed eyes. "Can't say I have."

"*Wowww,* and you call yourself an Alaskan."

He ticks his head to the side. "Fair play. I've had raw kelp before."

"Brag, why don't you?"

Matthew is beaming. Glowing even. I thought I'd be more reserved for longer with him, but he makes it easy to come out of my shell. "People have been eating all kinds of kelp around here for a long time. Pretty easy to harvest too but not super profitable."

"Unless you pickle it," I reply.

"Got me there."

"Okay, well, then you'll try it with me," I say, picking up my fork and skewering a piece of kelp. "Ready."

Matthew does the same.

We eat the kelp at the same time. It's much crunchier than I expected compared to a dill pickle. But it tastes the same. The same herbaceous saltiness. However, there's a brine to it you don't get with pickles, something inherent about the kelp itself being steeped in seawater.

"Mm," Matthew says with a nod. "S'good."

"Really good," I reply and pick up another ring.

Matthew is quiet, resting a finger against his lips as he watches me eat.

"You're staring again."

"Yes, I am."

I stare back, less affronted this time. I allow myself to

sink into his amber eyes. If he wanted to keep me at a distance, he's not doing a great job at it.

"And I shouldn't," he says, looking off and sipping his coffee.

"Why's that?"

"Not very gentlemanly, is it?"

Our food arrives before the conversation can continue, and I'm disappointed. I would have enjoyed him looking at me a bit longer, gentlemanly or not.

As we tuck into our meals, Matthew quietly picks up a handful of fries and puts them on my plate.

I resist telling him he doesn't have to do something like that. It's clear it's part of his character. He wants to do it. And I like that.

"Your salad looked sad," he says as a defense.

"It does look a little sad, I guess." Two cherry tomatoes, some too thick cucumber slices, and a gloopy dressing. I pick up one of the fries and dab it into the glob of ketchup on his plate. "Thanks."

"Anytime."

I may not know Matthew very well, but I genuinely believe he means "anytime." I wouldn't be surprised that, for the right person, he'd do anything.

Chapter 7

Those Little Planes Are Dangerous

LILLIAN

When we touchdown in Naknek, wheels sloughing against gravel, I get a swell in my chest of exhilaration combined with terror. I realize I've forgotten all my nerves. I didn't even blink when we got back on the plane in Dillingham. Something about being up in the sky, seeing Bristol Bay from above, and talking with Matthew took me out of my head completely.

Once the plane has slowed down to a cruising pace, Matthew throws me a look. "All in one piece?"

I smile, pulling my notebook closer to my chest. "As far as I know."

He chuckles, a sound that lives low in his chest. It's a

sort of primal sound, something that feels untouched and unjudged that makes my heart flutter.

Which isn't great, all things considered. I'm already at a disadvantage when it comes to respect and power here in Naknek. The last thing I need is to start crossing the streams and flirting with Matthew. Okay, flirting *more*.

Matthew slows the plane to a stop and gets up, opening the cabin door and pulling the stairs down. He lifts his hand toward me when I'm at the top of the stairs. "Watch your step," he says.

I take his hand, roughhewn with calluses and hard work. If I let my hand linger in his, I'd run my fingers over all the divots and ridges and learn the labor of his palms. But I want something more than my hand in his. I want his boat. And that's not a euphemism.

Once I'm standing on the gravel, I pull my hand from his. It's more difficult than I'd like it to be, but I manage it. *No more of that, Lillian.* "Well, that was certainly enlightening. Thank you for offering your time and your plane."

"It's no trouble. Nice to have company," he says, diverting his gaze.

"I'd like to pay you for your time."

"No."

"Or the gas—"

"I already told you, that's not necessary."

I let my shoulders slump. "You went out of your way to show me the bay. You bought me lunch. It's the least I can—"

"Like I said. Nice to have company."

Our eyes catch for one moment, just a moment too

long. Then, we both look away. I try to laugh at myself because I'm getting all flushed when the reality is the awkwardness comes from the fact he knows I want something from him. And I know how this town feels about me.

"Anyway . . ." I check the time on my phone. "I have to get home and call my family."

"Ah, well, don't let me keep you."

"Oh, no. It's fine. They just want to hear about how things are going and if I'm surviving up here in the great wide . . . North." Is that a thing? Is that what they call it?

Matthew snorts and runs his hand over his head, pulling off his beanie and revealing his thick head of hair. It's all tousled and mussed from being covered, like someone's just ran their hands through it. I wish it had been me. "Yeah, I'm sure you have to tell them all the details about what a different world it is up here."

"No, not a different world, that's not—" It is different, but that's not meant to be a judgment. I'm fucking this up royally. "That's not what I meant, Matthew."

"Relax. I didn't take it like you were being rude."

"Good. Because I have nothing but admiration and respect for the way things operate up here. There are a lot of differences, but I think there are more similarities than anything," I say. "Don't you think?"

Matthew purses his lips and rubs them together.

"I mean, we both like pickled kelp," I add. Dammit, I've said too much. He probably thinks we're not similar at all. After all, I'm the do-gooder Californian, and he's trying to keep things the way they've always been up here.

Naked in Naknek

To my surprise, he finally gives a soft nod. "I think you're right."

"Good. *Good.*" *Chill, Lillian. Don't freak him out.* "I mean at the very least—"

"I'm still not sure about the boat," he says.

I stop, my eyes widening. "Okay. That's okay. I didn't expect..."

I didn't, but I hoped. I really hoped spending some time with me might show him I'm not a jerkoff from California who wants to ruin Naknek in the name of environmental virtue.

If I knew him better, I'd say his whale-eyed look was apologetic. Don't want to get my hopes up, though.

"It's not a no. I'm just not sure."

"That's understandable. You've got a lot on your plate. A lot of pressure, probably." If everything he says is true and all my interactions are evidence enough, people around here can't stand me. He'd be taking a huge risk helping me out. Potentially othering himself from his community. And this isn't LA. There aren't millions of people. There are a couple hundred. So, I respect it. Even if it hurts a bit. "I've got to go."

"Lillian—"

I back away toward my truck. My stupid, humongous truck. "Thanks again. This was so enlightening."

"Lillian, wait, I—"

"Thank you for lending your expertise," I say, flashing a final smile, before climbing into the truck.

Thankfully, Matthew doesn't try to call after me or run over and knock on the window to continue the conversation. However, when I give him a final look, he's standing at the tail of the plane, worrying his beanie in his hands and staring after me with concern riddling his brow.

Not concern. Pity. It doesn't matter if he likes me. We've known each other for a day and change. That is nothing in comparison to a life built in Naknek where everyone knows everyone, and everyone understands what this world means to them.

I'm just an outsider.

I drive off before I hurt my own feelings.

~

"THOSE LITTLE PLANES ARE DANGEROUS, LIL," Dad says, looking down his nose at me through the camera of the computer. My parents still live in Michigan at the house Sarah and I grew up in. Their faces are scrunched into one window and Sarah is in her own, the lowlights of her lush West Hollywood apartment glowing in the background.

"Dad, that's how you get anywhere around here," I say through a laugh. "There aren't a lot of official roadways, and, besides, a flight takes twenty minutes, and driving would take like a whole day in some cases. Planes are like everyone's second car."

Mom shakes her head more in awe and disbelief than any sort of judgment. "It really is the Last Frontier up there, isn't it?"

"I guess," I say with a shrug. "I mean, it's like anywhere in small-town America, just a different kind of culture

Naked in Naknek

than a Podunk town in Indiana or something. Although, they don't have chai. Can you believe it?"

"Yes, I can," Sarah says, swirling a glass of wine in the frame.

I roll my eyes and lean back on the rickety bed. "Well, I've been having to drink regular tea, and sometimes even coffee."

"A tragedy," my father says wryly.

"No oat milk either. *That's* a tragedy," I say with a pointed finger.

"Anything else, princess?" Sarah asks.

Mom scolds Sarah softly, but I just roll my eyes. "I mean, could you send me a boat? My connection fell through, and the fishermen around here are . . ." I try to find the right word.

"Are they giving you a hard time, Lilypad?" Dad asks.

"I mean with a town called *Naked*—" Sarah starts.

I smack my hand against my forehead. Not in front of the 'rents, Sarah.

"Naked?" Mom scoffs, taken aback. "What on earth—"

"It's a joke, Mom!" I cry out to intercede.

Mom sniffs, lifting her chin. "Well, where does a joke like that *come from* unless people are being too forward, or . . ."

My attention flicks to Sarah's frame. She's snickering behind her hand. Little sisters are *the worst*. I decide to ignore it. Explaining the whole autocorrect thing will be more trouble than it's worth. "I mean, other than an errant 'sweetheart' here and there—"

Sarah snaps out of her laughing fit, her brow hardening. "Now *that's* unacceptable!"

Ah, my sister. Always righteous and strong-willed. I love her for that. "It's patronizing, sure, but they're not all—"

"I'll come out there and whip them into shape, just say the word," Sarah says, then gulps some more wine.

I shake my head. "It's not all bad. I mean, the guy who took me up in the plane is a fisherman. He's probably the only one even considering taking me out on his boat." Even if that chance is slim to none at this point.

"I don't like the idea of you going out alone on a boat with a man," Mom says, shaking her head.

"Matthew is a gentleman, I promise." A gentleman who has my pheromones on high alert.

Sarah's expressions are strong enough to read through the gritty connection. Her eyebrow rises, and her lip twists into a smirk. "A gentleman?"

I don't like where this is going.

"How old is he?"

"*Sarah!*" I whine, voice pitching up like it did when I was a kid and wanted her to get out of my room.

"I'm just *asking*."

Dad takes off his glasses and rubs the bridge of his nose. "Girls—"

"Like is he a gentleman in a kindly older grandpa type way, or a gentleman in a young and eligible way?"

I cringe. "Sarah, that's not important."

"So, he's young and eligible, got it." Sarah's smile turns wicked.

Naked in Naknek

I throw my hands up. "You were just saying how you were going to come out here and give them hell for calling me sweetheart, so—"

"Look, I'm not an idiot. I know there must be some hunky fishermen out there. I've always liked blue-collar men. The kind who knows how to fix a sink, you know?"

Dad pushes himself up from the kitchen table where my parents have been smushed together in the frame. "I don't want to hear this."

Sarah laughs while I just shake my head. "You're ridiculous," I tell her.

"And *you're* blushing!"

I am totally blushing now that I can't get Matthew off my mind. I get a flash of his knee knocking against mine at lunch today, and my stomach *swoops*. "I'm not!"

"I'm just saying, Lil. You might be there for work, but that doesn't mean you can't be there for pleasure too."

Mom gasps. "Sarah!"

I snap my laptop shut and collapse into my pillows. Well, that was nice until it got out of control.

It's late afternoon here in Alaska. I could stay in and lounge since this day had more than enough excitement with my plane ride, lunch, and all the information I got from Matthew. But I don't want to waste any time in Naknek, especially since I still don't have a boat. Maybe if I get out of the cabin, I might stumble upon something or someone that can help me.

So, I head out in my truck. The hulking mass of metal is a knife to the heart every time I drive the thing. I follow the main road, the "highway," until I see a sign for Red

Salmon Cannery. There's no gate or anything, so I figure it's safe for me to check out. Might be good to get a lay of the land and get an impression and understanding of all the parts of what makes fishing so important to Naknek.

I turn down a side road, looking for someone, anyone who might be able to lend me some information. I spot a man walking past the outbuildings toward me.

I drive to catch up with him and roll down my window to call out, but recoil at not only the smell, but the taste of fish in the air. I'm used to fishy-smelling things, being in marine biology, but this is stronger than strong. "Excuse me?"

The guy jumps, and I realize he can't be more than twenty years old.

"Do you work here?"

"Yes, ma'am." He has a thick Southern accent.

I smile. "You're not from here."

"No, I'm not," he says with a sheepish smile. "Neither are you."

I shrug. "Guilty. You working here for the season, then?"

He leans on the open window. "Yes'm."

"Could I ask you some questions?" I ask. "I'd love to hear about your experience."

The kid looks over his shoulder. "I was just walking into town for some cigarettes. You give me a ride? We can talk?"

My heart thumps with unease, but then I remember what the owner of the rental place said on my first day. That people hitchhike around here, and it's not something

Naked in Naknek

I should be scared of. Still, it goes against everything I've ever been taught. "Sure. No problem."

The guy, Peter, turns out to be as harmless as anyone could be. He almost always ends his sentences with a polite "ma'am" and does his best to take up as little room as possible.

As we drive, he tells me his story. "I'm from Cape Girardeau, Missouri. *Misery*."

I laugh. "Even you guys call it that?"

"Yup. I guess it works for some people, but if you don't fit into what people expect . . . well, that's why I struck out on my own. Follow the work, that's what I do."

I nod. "You're far from home, then."

He laughs. "Yes, ma'am, but I don't mind. I like being able to live in new places and meet new people."

I shift my hands on the wheel as we drive. "You don't ever feel like an outsider around here?"

"Oh, sure, I do. I mean, you knew I was an outsider the second you heard me talk, right? But so many people at the cannery are people like me. You know, just . . . different. From different places."

"That must be nice." I pause. "Why do you work in the cannery instead of on a boat?"

Peter gives me a double take. "Pardon me for saying so, ma'am, but you have to be a bit of a lunatic to do something like that."

"To go out on a fishing boat?"

Peter points to the side of the road toward the Trading Company Store to direct me as he says, "Fishermen are their own breed. And I'll admit, they all seem really fond of each other. Like a family. We all get close at the cannery, but we're not risking our lives like they do out on the water."

I pull the car to a stop. "Do they lose people often?"

"They lost two this year from around here. I overhear things, you know," Peter says, then slides his hands down the front of his jeans. "This is a small town. Everyone knows everyone. But out there, you have to be close because out there you have to fight."

"I never thought of it like that."

Peter smiles kindly at me. "They can be surly and mean lookin', but . . . I think they love harder than they let on. I think they have to."

Chapter 8

This Isn't a Pleasure Cruise

MATTHEW

I stare at the bubbles on the inside of my glass, the white foam creeping down until it joins the beer in the bottom. I'm out with the guys, but my brain is somewhere else entirely.

Since the second Lillian drove away from the airport, I haven't been able to shake her. She cares about what she's doing. I know she does. That much became obvious to me through our time together, and the way she went from buoyant to crestfallen in an instant.

But clearly, she just wants something from me. It's not earnest or genuine. It's business.

It's all just business.

Still, my rationalization can't eclipse the way I feel

about her. Those fluttering feelings in my stomach. I haven't had those in years.

"You're being awfully quiet, Matt."

I look up at my brother across the table. "Long day," I say. "You know how flying takes it out of me."

Tuma leans in with a smile on his lips, his thin eyes growing even thinner. "You got the new radio?"

I nod. "Yeah, I installed it this afternoon."

"Finally," Jesse says, holding his hand up to flag down Fred, the namesake of the bar, Fat Fred's.

I glower at my brother.

"You should have let me know you were going. I would have gone with you," Tuma says.

"Thanks man," I reply with an earnest smile. "But um . . ." Might as well tell them. It's not like they can do anything now that Lillian's been up in the air with me. "I ran into that scientist the other night, and she asked about using the boat and—"

Jesse balks. "Don't tell me you said *yes*."

Now I wish I had just to piss him off. "No, I didn't say yes. But I offered to take her up in the plane and show her the bay."

"That was nice of you, mate," Ian says.

"Ian!" Jesse snaps.

"What? Just because we don't like what she's doing doesn't mean we've got to treat her like a leper, Jesse," Ian shoots back, running his thumb over the corner of his horseshoe mustache then adds with a dry smile, "Besides, I'd think you'd be champing at the bit to get a moment alone with her."

Naked in Naknek

A flame of jealousy alights inside me.

Jesse guffaws. "Sure, she's good-looking, but no. I'm not interested in smart girls."

"You're missing out, you bastard," Ian replies.

"I think what Jesse means is that smart *women* are too smart to fall for his bullshit," I mutter.

Jesse narrows his eyes at me. "Jealous much?"

I finish off my beer. "Not at all."

Fred cuts through the tension with a replacement beer for Jesse. He goes to grab my drink, but I hold up my hand to signal I'm done. It's too easy for one to turn into five if you're not careful. Just to feel something. Especially, when it's still light out at ten o'clock.

Once he's gone, we are quiet as the gears shift. There's no use getting into arguments, but it's hard when you work with family. And, given the way things work around here, everyone becomes family at some point.

"You're too nice, man," Jesse finally says.

I shrug. "I don't know. Everyone's giving her a hard time for being an outsider, and I thought maybe I could get a good read on her instead of all this fearmongering."

"Fair," Tuma says.

Ian sits up, his eyes zeroing in on the door. "Well, what do you know, here comes your girl now."

"She not my—" Wait. She's *here*? I whip around in my seat. My cheeks flush when I see Lillian in the doorway of the bar. Her hair is up out of her face now, making her look a bit taller. Although, that could be the heeled boots she's wearing. She shuffles to the side to let a couple of guys leave. I watch her inhale sharply, her chest puffing like she's putting on her armor. I'll give her credit. She's brave to keep on showing up, even though she knows how people respond to her.

"Please tell me you didn't invite her." Jesse groans.

"I didn't," I say. But I sort of wish I had, so she'd be walking over to me. It was close to impossible to tell her I wasn't sure about the boat, but I had to. After that lunch, I just knew being close to her was going to make me act stupid. And I don't act stupid. Can't afford to.

Lillian heads to the bar as she scans the tight, dingy interior. Despite the brightness outside, Fred still turns on all the neon signs and branded Tiffany-style lamps. It's got ambiance. Not necessarily a nice one, but an ambiance for sure.

"She looks so . . ." Tuma trails off. "I don't know. Alone."

That's because she literally is, as she waits for someone to notice her waiting to order a drink. She's got a book tucked under her arm. She really came out here to read? No wonder she's not Jesse's type.

But she's mine. That's obvious, and there's no use lying to myself about it. I like a woman who is interested. Interested in everything. The world around her; the world she doesn't know yet. Because I'm curious too. I think you have to be when you spend your life out on the water. You're always looking at the horizon, wondering what's just beyond. Forcing fear to take a backseat.

Maybe we're more similar than we are different. Those differences, though, are huge.

"God, she brought a book to a bar. She's one of those." Jesse snorts into his beer.

Naked in Naknek

"Why are you such an asshole?" I ask without pulling any punches.

Jesse's face curdles, ready to give it back to me. However, Tuma intercedes before anything can happen. "You say that like it's a new thing, Matt." Now Jesse turns his attention to Tuma, but no one can stay mad at Tuma. He's like Winnie the Pooh in an Aleut body. Softspoken and kind, even when people don't deserve it. "Alright, give me your hand," Jesse says, waving at Tuma.

Tuma rolls his eyes and holds out one hand. Jesse grabs it, and instead of arm wrestling like you'd expect brawny sailors to, they start thumb wrestling. Like two little worms rolling around, trying to pin the other down.

"I'm too old for shit like this," Ian mumbles.

While Ian refs the thumb wrestling, I watch Lillian leaning over the bar to talk to Fred over the din. Her ass is right there, and even I am easily distracted when it comes to an apple bottom. My god, I can just *picture* my hands fitting around her, pulling her onto my lap. Not the time or the place.

I pull my eyes up to keep my desire from getting out of control. Fred saunters off to get her a drink and, as if sensing I'm watching, Lillian looks over her shoulder at me. Her surprise lasts only a moment before she smiles and gives me a little wave.

Something expands in my chest. I smile back.

"Having fun?" she mouths at me. At least I think that's what she mouths. I get a little lost thinking about how her lips would feel against my neck.

I shrug and then glance at a chair at the empty table next to us. I put my hand on it and nod toward it.

Lillian frowns for a moment. "Are you sure?"

I shrug again, letting my lips dip down.

Lillian considers my offer. She smiles. "Okay."

I shouldn't have invited her over, but I can't deny how good her acceptance feels.

"Dammit! Unfair. Your thumbs are too long!" Jesse exclaims.

Tuma scoffs. "You're the one who challenged *me*!"

"Fair is fair, Jesse," Ian says.

I grab the bottom of the empty chair and yank it between Tuma and me. "Move over."

"What? Why?" Tuma asks but obliges.

"Lillian's coming to sit with us."

My brother's entire body tenses. "You've got to be fucking *kidding*."

"No, you need to learn a little bit about respect. You don't have to get along with her, but you—"

Lillian appears over Jesse's shoulder. "Am I interrupting?"

"Yes," Jesse says as I eagerly say, "No." I give my brother an angry look.

Her eyes widen, cheeks going slack. "I can go," she says, backing a step away.

Thankfully, Ian manages to wrangle up his English politeness. "Nonsense, love. We've got a seat for you and everything."

Lillian takes the seat next to me and gives me a thankful smile.

"Watcha reading?" I ask, placing my hand on the back of her chair and then quickly retracting it for fear I'm crossing a line. Tuma clocks me and snickers behind his hand.

"Oh!" She looks at the book in her hand as if she forgot it was there. "It's a book about Alaskan flowers I got while I had a layover in Anchorage."

"You read that for fun?" Jesse asks.

I sigh. "Lillian, this is my brother Jesse. Sorry, he never stopped being an angsty teenager."

"Yes, we met briefly before, but nice to make it official," Lillian says.

Jesse merely looks at me. I ignore him. "And this is Tuma and Ian."

Tuma and Ian exchange pleasantries with Lillian. At least *they* haven't forgotten their manners.

"Lillian's here for research," I say to give the illusion they didn't already know.

"You study plants?" Tuma asks, playing along, while Jesse grumbles, "I know."

"No, marine life," Lillian says. "But it's good to have a comprehensive knowledge of an environment. Plus, it genuinely interests me."

Tuma's smile brightens. "My wife would like you. She knows all about plants and . . . well, everything," he says.

The way Tuma talks about Katoo makes me jealous. I haven't been lucky enough to meet my match. They've been together since they were kids, shared so much history, and a few children too at this point. Tuma might be my best friend, but his is Katoo.

"She's also the reigning queen of the salmon-filleting contest," Ian adds with flair.

Lillian laughs. "There's a salmon-filleting contest?"

"Don't see what's funny about that," Jesse says.

"Weren't you just leaving, Jess?" I say in a voice verging on a growl.

My brother glares at me. He takes his beer and lopes off into the bar to hopefully find people who appreciate his bad attitude.

"Sorry about him," I murmur to Lillian.

She touches my arm. "It's okay." And though she releases me, I still feel her touch, nerves remembering the exact position of her fingers on me. "I don't mean to sound judgmental. If anything, I'm the pleb here. I just love how no matter where you go, there are special customs and cultures and—"

"Well, Tuma is Aleut," I say, gesturing at my friend. "His family are Native Alaskans."

Lillian pauses. "That must be an honor and quite the undertaking to preserve your culture."

Tuma's eyebrows rise. "It is. Both those things."

Ian and I exchange a look. Non-native Alaskans often don't know how to broach the topic of what it means to be a Native Alaskan. It's both surprising and impressive Lillian isn't afraid to get right to the heart of the matter when so many around here are willing to ignore it.

"You know, there are a lot of dying practices our elders have passed down. A lot of people have left or opted for a more, eh, conventional way of living," Tuma says. "And you know, when you have children, you don't want to hold them back from the lives they want. But I hope mine have some desire to preserve our culture."

Lillian listens with rapt attention as Tuma speaks. She is not distracted by anything else in the bar, shining all the light in her eyes on him. Tuma's usually quite shy around strangers, but Lillian has a knack for making people feel comfortable.

A lump grows in my throat. Maybe the way she speaks to me isn't that special after all.

"Where are you from?" Tuma asks. "Before California."

I cough. What happened to pretending?

Lillian laughs and looks askance at me. "So, you've heard of me?"

Tuma grabs his root beer and hides his face behind it as he drinks.

"Hard not to hear about a newcomer, love," Ian says, leaning back in his seat. "I should know."

"Oh, really? You?" Lillian says, her eyes widening in clearly melodramatic shock.

A laugh bubbles out of Ian. "I know, it's hard to believe."

I laugh a little too. She's sharp, I'll give her that.

"Originally," Lillian picks up Tuma's question. "Michigan." She holds up her hand and points at the knuckle of her pinky. "About here. Right on the lake, actually. Similar to Naknek, but different."

"Very different, I'm sure," I say.

"Far cry from the ocean, isn't it? Lake Michigan?" Ian says.

Lillian tilts her head from side to side. "In some ways,

yes. I mean, sure, you've got the obvious that it's salt water versus fresh. And we have different marine life because of that, but both water systems are incredibly biodiverse."

Oh, we're getting into the lingo now. Good thing I love to listen to her talk science.

"And like Naknek, where I grew up has an economic dependence on water. Ours isn't dependent much on fishing. But tourism and the crops. Commercial shipping." Lillian stops to sip her beer.

None of us speak. Something about the way she talks, both commanding and casual, has us hanging on her every word.

"And, of course, we're experiencing impacts from climate change in both places." Lillian tips her shoulder up. "Erosion, spreading of invasive species, warming waters." She licks her lower lip and keeps her eyes down on her drink. "Population decline."

"That's why you're here, right?" I ask.

"Yes, you're correct," she says, something enveloping her voice that sounds more . . . flirty than professional.

Which I can't say I mind.

"The declining coho salmon population has become a high-priority issue. It's time someone does something about it. And if we have the data, we can accomplish a lot. You may have heard I was supposed to go out on—"

"Lillian," Ian interrupts. "Look, I know we all appreciate what you're doing in theory, but in practice . . . I don't know one guy around here that would loan you a boat."

Lillian sits up a bit straighter, glancing at me and then

Naked in Naknek

back to Ian. "But you said it yourself, outsider sees outsider. Wouldn't you—"

"Oh no, no, no. I worked hard for the title of insider." Ian grabs his beer and gets to his feet. "Listen, love, best cut your losses. Quit while you're ahead. You're bright. Just use it elsewhere."

I look hard at Ian, trying to get him to look at me, but he ignores my gaze. He gives the table an open-handed wave before joining a couple of guys at the pool table.

Tuma gets up too. "I better get home to Kat. Been out late too much, and now the season is over." He gives Lillian a sympathetic smile. "Perhaps, I can introduce you to her sometime."

"I'd like that," she says, forcing her lips up the way she did when she left me at the airport.

Fucking heartbreaking.

Tuma leaves his empty glass and hustles out of the bar like his life depends on it, leaving Lillian and me alone in a sea of people.

"You don't have to sit with me," she says, gripping the base of her glass.

"I'm not gonna just leave you sitting here," I reply. "Unless you want me to go."

"I just know what it could do to your reputation. Clearly."

I want to tell her I don't care about that shit. But if that were true, would I have been trying to close myself off to her? Withhold my boat? I care about it a little. "I don't care about that enough to leave you here on your own." And that's the truth.

Lillian doesn't say anything for a long time. Then, she lifts her head and sets her jaw tight. "I know what the hell I'm doing." Her voice is low and dark, and in other circumstances... might be an incredible sound.

Not now, though. "I know you do."

Her voice says sharply, "No, you don't. You're all scared I'm going to screw things up for you. But newsflash, things are already screwed up."

My muscles tighten. "That's not our fault."

"I didn't say that," Lillian says, rubbing her hands over her eyes.

"But that's how the government will treat it. That's how activists *treat* it, as if—"

"Matthew, I'm not an activist. I'm a *scientist*. I'm not working off my feelings. I'm working to make the world better through facts and figures. For us. For *you* and all your friends and this damn town. And you all hate my guts," she exclaims.

Lillian drinks her beer. A lot of it. Gulping it down to make it hit faster. Can't blame her for that.

She slams the glass down and lets out a heavy sigh. "Do you know how disheartening that is?"

I glance around the bar. Ian is now shooting pool, and Jesse is chatting with his woman du jour, a tiny woman with a black pixie cut and an arm full of tattoos. I know the name of almost every person in this town. It can be exhausting, but I've never felt like I didn't belong.

And Lillian is sitting here against all odds, trying to have people *see* her. And they keep turning away.

Not me. Not anymore.

"I'll take you out on my boat," I say, making sure no one overhears me.

I watch the news wash over her. Confusion. Recognition. Her jaw drops. "What?"

"I said I'd—"

"Really?"

"Shhhh! Lower your voice!"

"I could kiss you. Oh, my god! I could just—"

"Please don't make a scene." I'd accept a kiss, but not when we're out in public like this. Not when someone might think I'm a traitor for giving her too much rope. Not when it would be impossible for me to stick to only *one* kiss.

Lillian beams from ear to ear. "Are you sure? I know, it's not—"

"Don't give me an opportunity to change my mind. You got me hooked. Don't let the reel go."

She giggles. "Okay."

I shift in my seat to get a little closer to her. "Tomorrow morning."

"Yes."

"Early, alright? This isn't a pleasure cruise." Isn't it? In a way?

Lillian nods. "Got it. I promise I'll be early."

I bite down on my lower lip. "Naw, I'll pick you up. Don't want people to see your truck there." Overkill much? "And goes without saying, but don't *tell* anyone."

She twists an imaginary key in her mouth.

Lolu Sinclair

Keeping secrets in a town as small as Naknek is like putting toothpaste back in the tube. But I'll try. Or else I'll never hear the end of it.

Chapter 9

Whales Are Very Much My Thing

LILLIAN

When Matt comes to pick me up, he's flabbergasted at the size of my backpack. "You staying overnight or something?"

I heft the thing into the cab. "Just have all my equipment. Sample kits. Hip waders."

"You came prepared."

"Of course. It's my job. What did you expect?"

Matt taps his fingers on the steering wheel of his truck and tilts his head to the side. "Fair."

Once I'm settled in my seat, Matt nods to the cupholder in the center console. "I, uh, got you a coffee from the Half-Hitch."

"Oh . . ." I don't have it in me to burst his bubble by telling him that coffee is a once-in-a-blue-moon sort of thing for me. But the desire to not drink it is overridden by the thoughtful gesture. "Thank you so much."

"Brought some creamers and sugar packets because I wasn't sure—" He reaches into his jacket pocket.

"Black is just fine," I say, even though sugar and cream would make the taste ten times more tenable. Matt makes me feel a bit . . . out of sorts, I suppose. Like only half of my brain cells know how to function, because the other half is solely focused on him, his dark beard, and the huge muscles I know are hiding under his jacket.

I'm pleasantly surprised when we get to Matt's boat and it's a little itty-bitty thing, especially compared to the *Rorqual*. However, even other boats in the bay seem bigger than Matt's. Many of them, what I've learned are called seiners, are piled high with nets and equipment, emblematic of lawns back in Michigan stuffed full of lawn ornaments.

But Matt's isn't very long, thirty-two feet, he tells me, with a silvery metal bottom. At the bow, written on the hull is the name of the boat: *The Bristol Belle*.

I've never liked how boats are treated as if they're inherently female. But when I see a boat so well cared for, I have to imagine the men who ride it take it as a great honor that she keeps them safe on the seas.

"It's a gillnetter," Matt explains when I ask about it. "The nets we use catch the fish by the gills."

I inwardly wince at the thought. Those poor fish. It's important I place the values of Naknek and its people above anything now, especially if I want access to Matt's boat in the future.

Naked in Naknek

Matt helps me onto the stern with an outstretched hand. I get to feel his palms again, the calluses and the warmth. "Watch your step," he mumbles.

It's early on the Naknek River, but not too early. Since the salmon season is reeling to a close, some of the boats are sitting at the dock, while others have already headed out for their final catches of the season. This means I haven't been seen getting onto Matt's boat. At least as far as I know. I push the thought aside.

Because it's a foggy, damp day, Matt decides we should stay in the cabin as he drives us up to the Kvichak River. It's like being back in the cockpit of his plane yesterday, the two of us side by side in our chairs, him helming the ... helm.

"So, uh ... how does this all work? Your samples and things, I mean," Matt says as he settles into his captain's chair.

I push aside thoughts of how sexy he is, taking control of his boat. Nothing better than a capable man. "Yeah, so, there are a few pieces of it. It boils down to samples from the river and then the fish themselves. First, I'll gather water from different spots to check for things like oxygen levels, temperature, and pH. These give clues about the overall health of their environment. I'll also take some sediment from the riverbed to see if there are any metals or chemicals settled there that could be affecting the salmon."

"And samples from the fish?" Matt asks with a raised brow.

I try to laugh, uneasy about telling a pro fisherman that

I, a complete and utter novice, need to figure out how to catch a coho. "Yeah, you're going to need to give me some tips on how to fish," I say.

"I thought you were trying to protect the salmon, not fish them." There's a distinct, subtle smile on his face, like he's got me cornered.

"No, I am, I just . . . you know, getting to see them up close and take stock of their health is important to my study. And I can take some non-invasive samples. Fin clippings, scale scraping."

Matt goes quiet as he does a couple of things on the control panel before taking hold of the wheel and directing his boat away from the dock. "I can do that for you. Get you a look at the fish, I mean."

"Oh, you don't have to—"

"Be easier than making you into a quality fisher." His thoughtful eyes flick to me, then back to the river. "And we can release 'em back or eat them. They won't go to waste."

It would certainly save me a lot of pain over the situation. "I could add some money onto the fee, so you wouldn't be losing out on a catch. I just can't in good conscience—"

"Don't worry about it. Good practice. I haven't done much slow fishing in a while anyway. One at a time with a rod, you know?" Matt replies with a genuine smile. The thought actually excites him.

It excites me too. The image of him on the rocky shore casting into the water and waiting for a bite. Probably so adept and talented at the job that it's second nature. Makes my heartbeat quicken just a bit.

"Be about an hour out to Kvichak," he explains as he maneuvers the boat to the mouth of the Naknek River and into Bristol Bay.

Gillnetters don't move very fast. I don't know what I expected. Still, though, it's fast enough to make the town of Naknek roll by. It might be a gray and damp day, but there's something so beautiful about it. In LA, you so rarely get anything but sun. Sun, sun, sun. It's a different kind of exhausting. I miss the seasons sometimes. And while Alaska has its own forms of repetition, being here is cleansing. Other than the drama of getting my work done and the side-eyes I get from most of Naknek, I feel welcomed by the landscape. By the environment.

That's got to count for something, right?

Once we're out on the bay, we join a peppering of other boats on the placid water. It's so *quiet* out here, partly because Matt and I don't seem to know what to say to one another. We sip our coffee, he points out something on the shore, and I make a note of it.

This is work. For both of us. I'm doing my research. He's my boat for hire. The situation doesn't call for niceties.

And yet, I'd like to share them.

"Uh." Matt captures my attention, but as soon as my eyes are on him, he clams up.

Is he . . . nervous? "Yes?"

"We sometimes see whales around here, if that's your thing," he replies, words catching in the back of his throat.

"Whales are very much my thing," I say. "I just finished up a project tracking pods of grays."

Matt nods and his voice opens up with excitement to share more with me. "Yeah, you can see those from time to time this time of year."

I beam. "Guess I should keep my eyes peeled."

Turns out Matt has lots of facts about the wildlife here, which shouldn't surprise me. It's his willingness to share that warms my heart. He points out an eagle he spots overhead. "Angry fuckers if you run into them during a catch." Later he points toward an untouched, undeveloped shore where something lumbers. "Bears, too."

I squint to make out the bearish shape. From such a distance, it almost feels like I'm at the zoo rather than in the wild. It takes a few moments for me to realize just how stupendous it is to see a bear that is truly free and wild. "Grizzly?"

Matt shakes his head. "Brown bears. Grizzlies *are* a type of brown bear, but you don't see them by the water. Grizzlies live inland."

"I didn't know that."

"Where there's salmon, there's bears. But there's enough to go around." Matt smiles but seems to stop short of adding something.

I can fill in the blank though. *For now.*

"This is the river that connects with Iliamna Lake, right?" I ask as we enter the Kvichak's wide, expansive mouth.

"You got it."

"And Lake Clark from there?"

"Are you trying to impress me?" Matt asks with a glint in his eyes and a lopsided smile.

"I—n-no, I was just—"

Matt chuckles.

"I was just reading up on the Pebble Mine proposal and . . . you must be happy about the veto." The proposal to mine a significant mineral deposit nearby caused consternation for years until the Environmental Protection Agency effectively banned any mining activities in the area. Even the Supreme Court overruled the state's request to be relieved of the EPA's embargo.

"It's been a relief, but we never get too comfortable. You know, that's why so many of the fishermen are wary of you."

I nearly lurch out of my seat. "I have nothing to do with—"

"What I mean is, we see threats from development all the time. We fight it. The fishermen, well, most are local, and they take offense when they're pinned as the problem."

I sigh. "I didn't pin them as a problem."

"I know you didn't. Yet."

Matt stops the boat long enough at the mouth of the river for me to get a sample of water. I make a mental note of how great it would be to get a riverbed sample from the mouth too, but that would require my diving suit, and I didn't bring it. I was afraid I might be asking for too much.

We go farther down the Kvichak, until Matt points out a beach of gray stones and pebbles that looks suitable for my work. We get in the skiff and putter over to the shore, my whole bag in tow, which is almost like a third passenger.

I step out of the skiff, water coming up to my calves in my rubbery hip waders. "Might take me a bit since I have to test for a few things in real-time here. But once I have the sample and it's packed in my cooler, I'll be ready."

Matthew pulls the skiff up to the shore. "No rush. I'm actually going to go check on a spawning site while you work."

A man who can speak science to me is my favorite type of man. This isn't just academic science either, this is lived experience science, which is a whole other energy. "Alright, I'll be here," I say as I sling my bag to the ground.

"You got bear spray in that pack?"

"Oh, no. Forgot to pick that up."

Matt reaches into his jacket pocket and produces a large, cylindrical canister which he lobs at me. "Take this."

My reflexes surprise me, and I manage to wrangle the can out of thin air. I glance at it, then at Matt. "Um. Thanks," I say.

Matt nods, pushes his lips together, and then jerks his thumb over his shoulder. "Well, I'll be out that way. If you holler, I'll hear you."

"Sounds good."

Matt heads off down the rocky beach and into some tall timber. He knows where he's going and what he's doing, walking with confidence and no hesitation. For a big man, though, his steps aren't demanding and hard. Every step conveys a respect to the ground beneath him, as if they are synchronous rather than separate. If only more people understood that separating ourselves from the earth has only made things worse.

Once I force myself to look away from him and *focus*, I place the spray beside my pack and sort through my equipment. It's not hard to lose myself in the work. I want to move quickly, but carefully, especially with the field testing I have to do—pH, turbidity, and color. All things I have to observe immediately. After the tests are done, I grab my sediment corer and push it down into a shallow point in the riverbed, filling the tube with dirt, sand, and silt. The water is fucking *cold,* which I guess I should have expected. But I'm still surprised at just how biting it is against my skin.

I stow the sample and mark it before wading back into the water, venturing further from the shore to collect additional samples for testing back at the cabin. One by one, I stick them into the cooler I have hung on my elbow. Science is precise work, but it isn't elegant. The squatting and avoiding water getting into my waders, the bent elbows, the nearly losing the cap of a vial but saving it at the last second... all far from glamorous.

I turn to slog out of the water but stop short when I see movement through the trees. It's the same bulky movement I saw from the boat. At least, I think it is. I'm a marine biologist, not a mammalian biologist.

I tiptoe to land, if that's possible through water. Just as I make it to shore, a bear emerges from the trees. Not as big as a bear could be, but that doesn't really matter. Because a bear is a bear no matter how small.

What do they tell you to do around bears? Be big and wave your arms? Or arm in this case, since I can't disturb my samples.

Hopefully, it hasn't seen me.

I feel like I leave my body as I watch the bear. Whether it's wonder or adrenaline, I don't know. He swings his head through the air, sniffing or just enjoying the scenery. I read somewhere that bears understand the concept of beauty which is quite sweet.

The bear lumbers a few steps forward, big paws padding seamlessly across the ground. Just like Matt, really. Except it has claws. It's going toward my pack. I don't have any food in there, I don't think. It's probably just curious.

I start waving my free arm to make myself bigger. I'm supposed to yell too, right? "Hey! Bear!"

The bear is unfazed, getting closer to my pack. Fuck, fuck, fuck. Why did I leave the spray right there on the ground? This is some fucked up dramatic irony.

With a burst of unearned confidence, I bound over to the bag and grab the strap, yanking it back toward me. This throws me off balance, sending me falling into the rocks on my ass. I scream as my cooler of tubes flies through the air. Pain ricochets through my backside and tailbone as I hear the metallic clang of the can tumble amidst the rocks.

The bear skitters back in surprise, which would be settling if it wasn't for another bear emerging from the trees. This one is bigger and runs quickly into the clearing with deep huffs.

Did I mess with a cub? Oh *no*.

The bigger bear spots me and moves toward me with

urgency. I try to push myself to my feet, but between the weight of the pack and the sliding rocks, I'm floundering.

Time slows down. Not enough for me to make sensible choices, but plenty of time to think and wonder.

Do I run? Do I leap into the skiff and try to get back to the boat? What about Matthew? Where'd that stupid can of spray roll off to?

The mother bear hip-checks her cub out of the way and continues to huff and barrel toward me. I cower, making myself small, hoping if I play dead and docile she'll forget I scared her.

When I think all is lost, I hear someone shouting words I can't identify in the swell of my terror. However, when I hear the sharp sneeze of an aerosol can, I force myself to look up. It's Matthew, standing in front of me, not more than a couple yards from the bear. He has the yellow can of spray, and is spraying it toward the mama bear.

She roars, a combination of a donkey's bray and an elephant's trumpet, before recoiling.

Matthew steps back, a hand reaching down. For me? Before he can make another move, the mother bear cajoles her cub back into the woods, away from the cloud of bear spray.

I don't think I'll ever move again. That's how tense I am.

Suddenly, Matthew crouches in front of me. His hands fly to my shoulders. "Are you alright?"

My eyes land on his. I open my mouth to speak, but I can't. I think I'm in shock.

"It's alright. They're gone, you're—" He runs his hands

up my arms, unspooling my wound-up muscles. "Are you hurt?"

"I'm sorry," I manage to squeak.

"What? No. No, let's—"

"I grabbed my bag from it. I shouldn't have grabbed my bag."

"Lillian, it's over. You're okay. And I'm okay. There's no use beating yourself up about what could have happened, alright?"

I blink at him, unable to express my gratitude that he's not chastising me even though I deserve it. I'm gripped by fear again when I remember. "My samples!"

I try to jerk to my feet, but Matt tugs on me. "Easy, easy. Let me." He gets up and goes to the cooler, swiping it off the ground.

The second he leaves me, I'm terrified that the mother bear will see me through the trees.

"I think they might have gotten a little shaken up," Matt warns.

I don't even want to look at the damage. "I'll have to take them again. I'm sorry, I'm—"

"Lillian, it's *okay*. Okay?"

His voice is so calm and delicate I think I might burst into tears.

Matt looks back down into the cooler, then toward the woods. "Why don't we head back to the boat, okay?"

He approaches me, hand outstretched to help me up. I let myself take it and hold on all the way to the skiff.

Once we're back on the boat, Matt sits me down on the deck and disappears into the cabin. I rub my tender tailbone, expecting him to drive us down the river a bit farther, but he emerges again with a rectangular black bag. He sits across from me to unpack it. I realize quickly it's a collapsible fishing rod.

I watch him carefully, allowing the stress to abate. His handling of the rod is deft and unquestioning.

Once it's all reeled and ready, he stands and holds the rod out, handle toward me.

Confused, I follow the length of the rod up to his eyes.

"Come on," he says, tipping his head toward the port side of the boat.

"You want me to . . ." I hold my hand out and hesitantly grab the rod.

"Let me bait the hook for you," he says before reaching into his pocket and producing a slippery minnow.

"Where'd you get that?"

A humored grunt rumbles from the back of his throat as he pierces the small fish with the hook. "From the river, obviously."

"Just now?"

"Yeah, while you were working, so I could catch you a salmon." With the rod baited, Matt moves behind my left shoulder. "But now, you're going to do it."

His hands rest tenderly on my elbows. "I thought there wasn't time to make me a fisher."

Matt moves his hands to my forearms. "Move it back over your right shoulder."

With his help, I bring the rod back, the hook twinkling in the light.

Pointing out at a rocky outcrop where the water swirls

and bubbles white, he says, "You're aiming for that back eddy right there, where the current is reversing."

Except I'm not doing much at all. Matt's grip tightens, and he controls the cast. The hook flies through the air, the reel hissing for several seconds until it hits the water, exactly where he wanted it.

"Now, we wait," Matt says, moving to lean on the railing beside me, so he can keep an eye on the line. "No promises. Just have to be patient."

I've all but forgotten about my close encounter with the bear. "You're trying to distract me," I say with a knowing smile.

Matt's head tips back with laughter, bearing his throat to me. I'd like to kiss his Adam's apple. "That depends. Is it working?"

I bite my lip. "Yes."

"Good."

I like him, which is not safe. Liking people too much is a good way to get disappointed. "I'm surprised you're not angry with me."

"For what?"

"For being stupid and nearly getting trounced by a bear," I say. "Talk about a city girl, right?"

Matt shakes his head. "Happens to us all at one point or another."

"You're being nice."

"Yeah, so? You'd rather me be mean to you?"

I hesitate. "No."

"That's good. I like being nice to you."

I whip my head toward him, my cheeks heating up.

Naked in Naknek

However, Matt isn't looking back at me. His entire body tenses, eyes focusing on the water.

The line tightens.

"This is it," he says. "Get a hold on the reel and..."

I don't have to do much. In an instant he's behind me again, helping me keep a grip on the rod and reel the catch in. Matt makes it seem effortless, though, the rod bends as the fish fights hard to free itself.

"That's it," he says, voice ragged in my ear.

I suddenly want to know exactly how he sounds in the bedroom. The biceps pressing up against me don't help either. I hold my breath until the moment the fish becomes visible over the railing. A silvery back, pinkish bottom, and a mouth like two hooks press together.

"There she is," Matt says. "That's your fish, Lillian."

I let out a stunned, excited gasp. "Really? That easy?"

"Not usually." Matt chuckles. "But today's your lucky day."

We pull the struggling salmon onboard. Matt holds her effortlessly as I get my samples as quickly as possible. Then, he tosses her back in. I can't ignore that it probably was like throwing money away for him. "You didn't have to do that," I say. "Any of this, but especially that."

Matt shakes his head. "Man of my word."

Then, he comes up to me, toe to toe, towering over me. His eyes search my face. "Are you feeling better?"

"I'm fine."

"Be honest. I'm actually asking."

That's nice. "I'm ... better now." For a multitude of reasons.

All having to do with Matt.

∼

BY THE TIME Matt drops me off at the cabin, I've forgotten the horror of my run-in with the bear and let it turn to complete and utter mortification.

"Well, this is me," I say stupidly once Matt puts the truck in park.

He grabs the strap of my backpack from the floor.

I ignore the fluttering in my chest as I get out of the truck and go to the cabin door. Matt follows, backpack slung over his shoulder like it's a bag of feathers. I type in the code and pop the door open. "Um, thank you for everything today."

"Of course."

"For the thing with the bear, especially. That was so embarrassing."

"Happens to the best of us," he says.

I roll my eyes. "Yeah, no, it doesn't. And you know it."

Matt smiles softly and shrugs.

"Just don't tell anybody, for my pride."

"Secret's safe with me, Lillian."

I swallow. I don't even want to think about how much work is left to do and how I'm going to figure out another way on the water. The likelihood of someone being as kind as Matt is low. "Anyway, thanks again."

"You've got to get samples from the other rivers, right?"

I let out a tired laugh. "Yeah. Don't remind me."

Matt watches me for a moment from under his dark

brown brows. "I'm going out on the boat with Jesse and Tuma tomorrow to do a bit of fishing on the Egegik. You should come if you're up for it."

I blink in disbelief. "Um . . . what?"

"Yeah, you could get your samples, and you said you wanted a look at some of the fish, right?"

"I thought this was a one-time secret thing."

Matt nods. "It was."

Was. Past tense.

"I think it might be good for them to see you in your element. That you're not the big, bad wolf."

I laugh louder than I intend. "They definitely wouldn't think that if they saw me with those bears."

Matt laughs but lets it peter out before he speaks. "What do you think? Tomorrow?"

There are so many reasons that make me want to say no. All the doubts and insecurities that have been aching in me for the past few days. But it's not possible for me to reject an invitation from Matthew when I feel all mushy and warm around him. Saying no would be a betrayal to my heart.

"Okay. Tomorrow."

Chapter 10

If That Helps You Sleep at Night

LILLIAN

The next morning, I wake up to my travel playlist, a combination of powerhouse female musicians like Fiona Apple, Aimee Mann, and Patti Smith. I'm supposed to meet Matt at the docks which means no more hiding. None at all.

I decide to get an English Breakfast tea from the Half-Hitch before heading to the docks. It's not chai, but it's better than nothing. Once I leave the cabin, I notice it's sunnier today, which reflects in my mood as I head to the Half-Hitch jauntily with a smile on my face.

When I arrive, I see a man leaning against the building, smoking a cigarette. He looks like a true mountain man: deep and craggy wrinkles, dark hair overrun with salt, and a wild beard to match. He stares at me as I approach, and determinately tosses his cigarette down and snuffs it with a stomp.

As if he's been waiting for me, he slides his hands in his pockets and steps forward, blocking the door. "You're the girl."

He doesn't say it like he's a fan. "Sorry?"

If I hadn't had an interaction with a bear just yesterday, this would be way more intimidating than it is. "Listen, my son's a bit soft around the edges and sometimes doesn't know what's good for him, but he's one of us. You got that?"

His breath is sour and smoky which is altogether unpleasant.

I try to add up all the things he's saying to understand, but his words are coming fast, and my brain is working slow. "Your son? Are you Matt's dad?"

He ignores my question. "I don't know what you've said to him or what you've *done* to get on his boat, but I'm warning you not to get too comfortable." He says it in a lascivious, dripping way.

"What I've *done*?" Like I've . . . "How dare you insinuate something like that."

He stares at me. Through me. His beady eyes are like spiders crawling over my skin.

"I'm here to do a job. That's it."

"If that helps you sleep at night," he says, voice like scraping gravel.

My stomach dips, and for a split second, I feel like

crying. To have my intentions misunderstood repeatedly is one thing. To be made out as some sort of villain, someone who is *trying* to hurt, is another.

The door to The Half-Hitch swings open, and I'm prepared to step out of the way until Gwen appears, hand on her hip. "Dad, what are you doing?"

"Just talking," the man mumbles.

"Sure, you are," Gwen snaps, then waves her hand away from the door. "You're driving away customers."

Her father turns but takes a second to glower at me. "I'm leaving. I'm leaving."

Gwen and I watch him lumber over to a rusted red truck. He really does resemble Matt. The frame of him.

Gwen touches my shoulder, and I nearly jump out of my skin. "Are you alright?" she asks.

I rub my chest, trying to calm my nervous system. "That was..."

"He can be scary if you don't know what to do with him. But he's all bark, I promise." Gwen gives me a sweet smile that almost erases the unpleasantness of that encounter. Almost. "Come inside."

The Half-Hitch is nearly full of locals gathered at their tables. I'm starting to recognize a lot of the faces around here. My eyes meet the gazes of a few, and I try to maintain an easy smile, but their curiosity and judgment are unsettling.

"Tea?" Gwen asks when we get to the counter.

"Please."

When I pull my wallet out, Gwen shakes her head. "No, no. On the house."

Naked in Naknek

"Gwen—"

"Not after my father accosted you out there," Gwen says.

I put my wallet back in my bag, trying to decide what to say. "I really wasn't prepared for how people would respond to me here."

Gwen's eyes, the same as Matt's, have a sympathetic glean in them. "I really am sorry about him. He hasn't been the same since my mom passed."

"I'm sorry for your loss," I say. They're hollow words I try to make as emphatic as I can.

Gwen sighs as she pours hot water into a cup. "It's okay. It was long enough ago now that his bad behavior really doesn't have an excuse."

Behind the counter, I notice a little girl sitting on a stool with her head buried in a book with a dolphin on the front, which makes me smile.

Gwen notices me looking. "That's Winnie, my daughter."

"Hi, Winnie," I say.

"Hi," Winnie says back without lifting her eyes from the page.

Gwen tsks. "Winnie, you have to look at people when you talk to them."

"It's okay," I say. "I was the same way."

Gwen smiles, then places my tea on the counter in front of me. "Winnie, this is Lillian. The scientist."

Winnie's eyes shoot up, big and round. "Oh."

I laugh. "Well, that got your attention."

"Uncle Matt told her all about what you two did yesterday on the Kvichak, right, Win?"

My heart swells at the idea that he told stories of our time together to his family. That feels nice in a way I'm not terribly familiar with.

Winnie nods. "Yeah, it thounds cool." Then she smiles, showing off empty spots where her teeth should be.

"Then maybe I can tell you about the studies I did on dolphins when I was in grad school. If dolphins are your thing," I say.

Winnie's mouth opens, and she grips her book harder. "*Yes.* Yes, *please.*"

Gwen laughs. "Okay, another time, though. You go in the back. I want to talk with Lillian about some things."

Winnie's face falls. "Okayyyy." She hops off her stool and trudges to the door in the back.

"Nice to meet you, Winnie," I say after her.

She gives me a shy smile over her shoulder before disappearing.

"She's so cute," I say.

"Thank you," Gwen replies with a humorous roll of her eyes. "Anyway, I know people are talking, Lillian. About you."

"So, I've heard." I sigh.

"I was honestly surprised when Matt told us he took you out on his boat. Matt's a nice guy, but he's still a Bristol Bay fisherman. You know, it's like a secret club that even I don't know how to get into."

I lift my tea to my mouth. It's too hot, steam singeing my nose hairs. "Well, your dad seems to think I did some, let's say, unsavory things to convince your brother to help me."

"Dad thinks everyone is doing unsavory things to get anything. It's his own personal conspiracy theory."

I blow on my tea, then take a drink. It burns the tip of my tongue. "I appreciate you being nice to me. It's more exhausting than I realized having people giving me looks all the time."

"Well, you've got a friend in Winnie and me. And Matt too, of course."

I didn't know it was "of course," but I certainly don't mind that.

"Matt's a good guy," Gwen says. "And people respect him around here, which is why they're a little uneasy he's decided to help you out. Doesn't surprise me in the least, but . . . the way they see it, they're a team. And if you're not with them, you're against them."

My shoulders collapse. "But I *am* with them."

"Not to them you're not," Gwen says with an apologetic smile. "You have full-time Bristol Bay families trying to get by, and then you have the seasonal fishermen who have to spend their time away from their families in Anchorage. And that doesn't even factor in the dynamics between white people and the Aleut. It's personal."

"I get it. I really do. Or . . . I'm trying to."

Gwen nods. "I can tell you are."

I'm still on edge and don't want to be here under all the prying eyes of the locals. "I've gotta go meet Matt down at the—"

Gwen starts buffing the counter and throws me a kind look. "Okay. Take care, hon."

Once I'm safe in the cab of my truck—I can't believe I'm taking ownership since I hate this thing—I let out a big sigh. What a day it's been. And it hasn't even started.

And now I have to get on a boat with more foes than friends.

Joy.

Chapter 11

Smart Women Piss You Off

MATTHEW

"Your girl's here," Jesse says as I finish repairing a small patch of net.

I don't look up. "She's not my girl."

"Sure, that's why you're risking our lives by inviting her on board."

I drop the net and push myself to stand, rising to meet my brother. We are about the same build, though he has a couple of inches on me. I'm older though, and that's not easily forgotten. "You're going to be a perfect fucking gentleman for the first time in your life, alright?" I say.

"She's a—"

"I *know* what she is, and I *know* smart women piss you off."

"I didn't say they piss me off, I said—"

Tuma doesn't look up from sharpening his knives. "They intimidate you."

My brother scrunches his nose, and before he can say anything else, I grab his shoulder. "Just be cool. It's one day. Maybe you'll warm up to her. Besides . . ." I lock my eyes into my brother's. "If you're not on good behavior, you don't get paid."

Jesse opens and closes his mouth like a fish and then groans. "Fiiiine."

I laugh. That was the deal we made last night after he said "no" about a dozen times to coming out on the boat with me. I'll give him a cut of Lillian's fee *and* pay him for a day on the boat the way I would during the season. As long as he's on his best behavior, which remains to be seen.

"Hi."

I turn toward the dock where Lillian is standing tall and radiant in the morning sun, her auburn hair tied back, and her head held high. "Hey! Long time, no see."

She smiles, but there's something meek about it. She's not still embarrassed about the bears, is she? I admittedly played it cool given the situation, but there was no use scaring her more. That was a close call, closer than I've experienced in a long time.

I take Lillian's bag, which is somehow heavier than yesterday, and then her hand to help her onto the deck. "You remember Tuma?"

"Yes, nice to see you again," she says.

"You, too."

I glance at Jesse, who is by the wheelhouse door. "And hopefully you remember my brother a little less."

Jesse rubs one arm shyly. "Um, hi, Lillian."

"See? Did that kill you? Anyway . . ." I turn back to Lillian. "You ready to take a run with authentic Bristol Bay fishermen?" I ask, spreading my hands and jabbing them out like I'm a carnival barker.

Lillian does not seem enthused. "Sure. Ready as ever."

I put my arms back at my sides, ignoring Jesse's snickering. "Everything okay?"

"I, um—" Lillian glances at me then looks away nervously. "I ran into your dad at The Half-Hitch on my way over here."

My jaw falls. "Oh, god."

"Yeah, he hates my guts," she says with a soft laugh.

"That's Wayne Benton for you," Tuma mumbles.

"Sorry about him," Jesse offers. Jesse might not like Lillian, but even he knows that running into Dad is like meeting a feral animal in the dark. It either ignores you or wants to tear you apart limb from limb. "He can be a real bastard."

"That's why Jesse is the way he—" I add, stopping short when something bonks off the back of my head. A yellow buoy topples to the ground, and I glare back at my brother. "The hell?"

I'm ready to go toe to toe with Jesse for embarrassing me in front of Lillian. It's not that my pride is bruised. Okay, maybe a little, but I run a professional outfit. I worked a long time to get where I'm at, to be taken seriously. I don't need my kid brother making a mockery of it.

However, Lillian laughs, which catches me off guard.

She hides her pink lips behind her hand and blinks up at me. "Sorry."

There she is. "No, no. It's funny."

Now, Tuma laughs with a 'Bro, you're so obvious' type of laugh. I'm trying *not* to be obvious, but it's hard around Lillian.

Her whole demeanor has brightened, and now, her expression matches the sun. "Gwen took care of me. No apologies necessary."

"That's good. That's good. Um. Weather's good today if you want to sit with me up on the flybridge."

"That'd be great."

"We'll head south, get to the mouth of the Egegik, and do what we did yesterday. Go down the river where you can get your samples, and—"

"Actually, I was planning on diving to get a sediment sample today."

I stare at her. "What?"

"It's going to be a more effective sample, information-wise," Lillian explains. "Contaminants settle in the deeper parts of the riverbed, which will give me a better sense of—"

"We're contaminating the riverbed now, are we?" Jesse pipes up.

I get ready to shut him up, but Lillian's in her element. She holds her own. "Contrary to your belief, Jesse, I've never accused the fishermen of being the cause of the coho salmon population decline. You've decided that all on your own." She lifts her chin. "I'm here to determine *potential* causes of the problem and diagnose issues that could be hurting the salmon. I have no preconceived notions other than the obvious effects of climate change. So, if you let me do my job, you might learn something."

Jesse is red in the face. He's at a loss for words.

"This is why he doesn't like smart women," Tuma says to me. "He can't keep up."

"I can keep up!" Jesse huffs.

Tuma laughs while I address the problem at hand. "I understand you might need to dive for your research, but the water out here is much colder than in LA."

"I bought a heavier wetsuit for the occasion," she says. "I've also got a mini tank and a pump to refill it if I have to.

Dammit. I don't want her going down there. All my instincts tell me it's a bad idea. "Well, besides that, the currents are strong."

"I'm a strong swimmer."

"I'm sure you are, but you haven't swum in a Bristol Bay current."

Lillian narrows her eyes. "I need my sample."

"And you're on my boat, and I need to keep you alive," I tell her.

She crosses her arms. "That wasn't part of the deal."

I almost laugh. "I didn't realize I had to negotiate for your survival now." The conversation might be serious, but I love bickering with her. I wipe the budding smile away. "No, I'm sorry. I can't let you."

Lillian's shoulders sag.

"All we have to do is tie a rope around her, don't you think?" Tuma offers. "I mean, we've got plenty of rope."

I perch my hands on my hips and glare at my friend.

Whose side is he on? "I'd be happy to go down myself at a different time to get your sample, but today—"

Lillian interjects, "Oh, come on! You loop some rope around me, and if something goes wrong, you yank me out! You're fishermen, isn't that what you do?"

"We fish fish, not women," I say.

"Well, we know *you* don't," Jesse jabs.

I pinch my fingers, leaving a small gap. "You're this close."

"I think you're underestimating her, Matt," Tuma says, holding up his pristinely sharpened knife. "And you know Katoo would castrate you if she found out you'd done that." He slides the knife into its sheath and smiles.

"So, what's it going to be, Matt?" Lillian asks, crossing her arms defiantly. "My sample or your balls?"

～

THERE IS nothing sexy about scuba gear, except maybe the skintight suit.

But Lillian somehow manages to make all the bulky gear and silly flippers look *really* sexy. Of course, her confidence adds to it quite a bit. She wears it well and clearly has done stuff like this plenty of times. I should have known her confidence wasn't foolish. But I remain resolute. Lillian might know diving, but she doesn't know diving in Bristol Bay.

Lillian tucks her shiny hair into the diving hood, pulls it up over her head, then grabs her goggles and crowns herself with them. "Okay, tie me up, Captain."

My hands holding the rope go limp as she raises her arms up. I was ready to take it all seriously until she made my brain turn to mush again. I've never been one for tying people up, but if that's what Lillian wants, I'd happily do it for her.

"What are you waiting for? You said the current's good for now."

"Nothing. Nothing, I . . ." I bite my tongue and step up to Lillian, feeding the rope around her waist. "No one's ever asked me to tie them up before." I can't help myself. She walked into it.

Lillian's hazel eyes go wide. At first, I think I might have offended her, but just as that thought starts to settle, she says, "First time for everything."

She's flirting back with me. I don't know if I can survive this. "Jeez, Lillian," I mutter, making another loop.

"What?"

"You're . . . making me lose focus," I reply.

Lillian's eyes flutter, and she smiles. "Oh. Sorry."

After I've done enough loops, I tie a bowline knot around Lillian.

"Make sure it's a good knot. Don't want you to lose me."

"Don't worry, I'm very . . . knotty." I want to facepalm. Nothing's sexy about dad jokes.

Lillian, however, bursts out laughing. "That was good, Captain."

The captain thing shouldn't be quite as satisfying as it is, but it goes straight to my dick. Thankfully, I'm done with her and can step away before anything gets out of hand. "Okay. All set."

Tuma and I help Lillian onto the deck railing. "I'm pulling you up the second I think something's wrong, clear?" I ask.

Tuma and Jesse take the rope while I stand by to keep an eye on her in the water.

"Aye aye, Captain," Lillian says before pulling her goggles down and back-rolling into the water.

I hold my breath as she disappears. Given the harsh currents here, Lillian has had to use a technique called negative entry which forces her to go under immediately instead of getting acclimated at the surface.

The initial pull of the rope has Jesse and Tuma bracing with wide stances on the deck, but quickly, the rope relaxes. They exchange looks of surprise. "Strong swimmer," Tuma exclaims.

I can still see Lillian's form under the water. Thankfully, we bartered on a depth of only fifteen feet. Still, I have to remain vigilant. I don't want to lose her on my watch. I can't.

And not just because I'm the captain.

Chapter 12

Get the Sample and Get Out

LILLIAN

The second I plunge into the water, I realize Matt wasn't exaggerating. The water is mind-numbingly cold, so much so it takes me a second to get my bearings. It doesn't help that the current cuts through my middle from time to time, setting me off balance.

You've done this a million times, Lillian.

Except I've never been quite as uneasy as I am right now. I faced aggressive seals off the California coast, nearly been lost in the clouded, sunless waters of the Amazon estuary while studying pink dolphins, and, as a younger, inexperienced diver, suffered from decompression sickness.

But Bristol Bay is a triple threat. Cold, cloudy, and dangerously full of strong currents.

The water is a murky haze of fine particles and floating debris. My vision is limited to a few feet.

I breathe slowly, taking in the moment. I need to remain calm, so as not to lose my composure. That way, I can get my sample and be done with it, before I go numb.

I touch the rope around my waist, and my heartbeat settles the tiniest bit. Matt's up above, intent on keeping me safe. And Tuma. And I guess Jesse too. He wouldn't go so far as to try and get rid of me like this, would he?

Focus, Lillian. Get the sample and get out.

With new resolve, I swim like a frog until I reach the seafloor, my head tightening with the change in pressure. The cold bites through my gloves, numbing my fingers as I adjust my grip on the sediment corer, careful not to stir the silt too much as I sink it into the seafloor.

I firmly push it down to achieve maximum depth.

The current shifts, pulling so hard I nearly lose my grip on the corer. I steel every muscle in my body until the current weakens enough for me to pull the corer up.

I take a deep breath, allowing the oxygen from my mouthpiece to flood my lungs. I've been taking such shallow breaths I forgot how good it feels to *actually* breathe.

The current returns and tugs my oxygen apparatus free, sending a rush of salt water into my mouth. Panic courses through me as I reach for the mask, but the cloudy water and shock make it impossible to find. My initial panic at losing the mask escalates to full-blown terror as I struggle to breathe, and though I could probably hold my breath for a minute or two, my chest feels ready to explode.

I need to get to the surface now.

I need to breathe.

Chapter 13

You Forget the Big Picture

MATTHEW

It's a tense few minutes here on the boat. I'm white-knuckling the railing and holding my breath whenever I notice the tiniest shift in the current or movement of the rope.

Suddenly, the surface of the water bursts open. Lillian gasps for air, and then she coughs, water sputtering from her mouth. The skin of her face is pale, her lips blue.

"Pull her in! Come on!" I instruct the guys while getting up on the edge of the railing, straddling one leg over the side so the second I get my hands on her, I'll alleviate the strain of the rope. I don't fucking care about the cold water. When you've lived in a place like this your whole life, cold is all there is. There are various levels of cold, and the bitterness of the water is only one version. I'm used to it.

Lillian reaches for my hand, and I take it.

"I got you. Come on." As I pull, I realize she's got no strength left. I hang a bit farther off the side and slide my arm under hers to get a better grip. "That's it. I got you."

Between the three of us, we get her up onto the deck again. I sit her down quickly, pull her hood down from over her ears, and take the piece of equipment from her hand.

"Careful," she chokes out, reaching after the metal tube before coughing again.

She's fighting for her life, and she's worried about the sample? The priorities of this girl. I place the tube down carefully on the bench beside me.

We need to get her warm as fast as possible, especially if shock is setting in.

She continues to cough. I pat her back hard to dislodge any water in her lungs.

"That's it. Get it out," I tell her.

While I attend to Lillian, Tuma and Jesse rush off to get blankets and towels, then put on some hot water for tea. There's an order of operations to something like this, one we're all familiar with. We've all nearly fallen victim to hypothermia at some time in our fishing careers. It's just a part of the job.

Except watching Lillian struggling strikes fear in my chest. I am awash with guilt that I didn't protect her. I should have insisted I go down instead. I shouldn't have let her.

"You w-w-weren't kidding. It's f-uhhh-cking cold," she says, trying to smile through her chattering teeth.

Despite my concern, I laugh and touch her cheek. I'm surprised by the action myself, but Lillian leans into my touch and grabs onto my wrist. "You got what you came for?"

She nods, trying to form more words.

"It's okay. Don't talk." I start working on the knot. "We have to get you into dry clothes."

Lillian's chest heaves as I work. "I g-got you all wet."

"Don't worry about it," I tell her and add with a smile, "Hazard of the job."

She traps me there with a smile of her own. "Thank you, Matt."

I could make her blue lips turn pink again if I do what I want to. But it's not the time, and it's definitely not the place.

But if it was, I'd kiss her. I'd kiss the hell out of her.

∼

AFTER LILLIAN IS BACK to a stable temperature in the cab, we head to a good location to put out a gillnet. She insists sooner than I'd like that she's warm because she wants to watch us work. "I promise I won't get in the way."

And she doesn't. She watches, quiet and unmoving, almost like she isn't here.

Almost.

Because from time to time, I am drawn to look back at her. Sometimes she's taking in the scenery, and other times she's watching the work with a pinched expression. And on a couple of occasions, she's looking at me.

Naked in Naknek

We get a few fish in the net and pull 'em in. Some sockeye, which are almost out of season, but a couple of arctic char and coho, too. Not as many as we'd like. That's for sure. I take one and hold it out for Lillian to inspect and take notes on. She talks to it sweetly as she takes some photos and admires its silver coloring.

"Alright. Done trying to make a pet of it?" Jesse growls from his corner. He's been on pretty good behavior since Lillian's dive, but now that she's not close to freezing to death anymore, he's got his sour attitude again.

Lillian watches as I hand over the fish to Tuma to be cleaned and scaled.

"Um, we usually eat a couple," I explain to Lillian. "Boat food, you know. I don't know if you're a vegetarian or something, but—"

"I'm not. I've tried, but . . ." She smiles sheepishly. "It's just too restricting for me. I try to eat food that's been sustainably sourced and—"

"So, you'll have some?" I ask.

She shyly lifts one shoulder. "What could be more sustainable than eating a fish I just watched you catch?"

I'm hit with a confusing wave of pride. Like I've done something right in her eyes.

I give a quick nod. "Have it ready in a jiff."

Boat food is simple. Rice and fish. Filling, stick to your ribs food. And yet, as I work in the galley to whip it together, I wish I had something to make it a bit *more*. Because Lillian seems like a woman who expects more. And why wouldn't she? She's from Los Angeles, one of those cities where "excess" should be in the name. Why wouldn't she want more if she can have more?

Still, though, I've got two hungry sailors to attend to, and given their mostly good behavior, I don't want to get them on my case. Salmon and rice it is.

I'm shy as I hand Lillian her bowl of white rice and salmon chunks. "It's not much, but—"

"Smells amazing," she says, taking the bowl.

"That's what's amazing about fresh fish," Tuma muses as I hand him a bowl. "It's not fishy at all. It has a sweet smell."

"Mm, yes. It does."

I settle on a crate across the deck from Lillian, and though my stomach is screaming for sustenance, I wait for her to take her first bite. When she does, her face turns from curious to something akin to relief. "Oh, my gosh. That's so good." She takes another bite. "So fresh. I've never had fish this fresh."

"Not even in California?" Jesse asks, judgment flaring in the final word.

"I mean, maybe you can get it on a fishing boat in California but . . ." Lillian shakes her head. "I've never had anything like this."

I'm way more smug than I probably deserve to be for a bowl of white rice and salmon. I'll take it though. Anything I can do to please her.

God, I'm a mess.

"Thank you," she says, her eyes pinned to mine. "For everything, but you know, for catching and cooking it. This is truly such a special experience for me."

Meals with us guys are quiet. We tuck in, we eat a lot, and we eat it fast. But Lillian's voice adds to the usual soundtrack of water lapping at the boat and soft breezes.

"I think Alaska is probably one of the only places that most people understand what the earth offers them. That's why I was so excited to take an assignment up here. In the city, you're focused so much on yourself and what you're doing that you don't think about what the world around you is offering . . . or what you might be taking away from it."

"You grew up in Michigan though," I point out. "That must have been different from Los Angeles."

Lillian throws a hand up. "It's different, sure. But it's not like everyone knows a farmer or engages daily with nature the way you all do. Everyone here knows a fisherman, right?"

"Couldn't swing a cat and not hit one," Tuma says.

"Exactly. You're all engaged with the process in some way or another, whether by practice or association. You all get it." Lillian stops and takes a few bites. "I want to feel that way more often. Sometimes it's easy to get caught up in all the details, that you forget . . ." Her eyes connect with mine. "You forget the big picture."

∽

By the time we get back to the harbor, the day has been long, and yet, I don't want it to end. I'm not ready for Lillian to walk off my boat. I want to get lost in her thoughts for hours. All day and all night. When was the last time I stayed up all night doing something as frivolous as talking with a woman?

Over a decade, that's for sure. I've dated here and there, sure. But a fisherman's life doesn't leave a lot of time to give to someone else. Someone who wants to be with me has to make sacrifices, and I haven't found that person. The one who will make the sacrifices because I'm worth it. It's a two-way street, of course, but the one thing I can't sacrifice is my work.

It's too much for people. Everyone needs me to meet them halfway, and the best I can do is a quarter.

Even less now that the coho counts are down.

When we pull back up to the dock, I send the guys off to do their closing tasks and make sure the boat is in shape for the next trip. They both say their goodbyes to Lillian, leaving the two of us alone. "Let me walk you to your car."

"You don't have to."

I point at her backpack which is the size of an adolescent ape. "You're going to carry this thing all the way back to your car?"

"I'm a strong woman!" she shoots back, a smile plain on her face.

I back away from the bag. "So, you *want* to carry it?"

Lillian eyes it, then shakes her head, pieces of her auburn hair framing her face.

I pull the heavy thing over my shoulder. "That's what I thought."

After helping her onto the dock, we plod toward the parking lot. I'm slow partly out of exhaustion and partly trying to squeeze every moment I can out of today.

Lillian lets out a weary sigh. "I think I could sleep for days."

"After the way you swam today, I understand why."

"You really weren't kidding. That was a hard swim."

"Glad I had you tied up, huh?"

Lillian's eyes widen.

"I, uh, didn't mean—"

She laughs. "You're so funny when you get flustered."

I scratch the back of my neck. I didn't know I was the flustered type, but when it comes to her...

"I'm glad you had me tied up, Matt."

Dammit.

"I mean, I clearly needed it," she adds, bringing me back to the reality that I had her wrapped up in a rope to keep her alive, not for... not for any other reason.

"This is me," she says, gesturing toward the hulking Chevy.

I unload the bag into the truck bed and let out a sigh. "Well, give me a call if you need me to unload that for you later."

Lillian smiles. "I just might."

It isn't really a joke. If she calls, I'll come running.

"It was cool to see you in your element. With the guys."

I slide my hands into my pockets to keep from doing something awkward with them. "Well, thanks. I'm sorry Jesse can't get his head out of his own ass."

"I thought he was just fine. And hopefully now he's a bit softer on me too."

"I'm sure he is," I say, although maybe I'm getting that confused with the way *I'm* feeling.

Lillian touches the door handle before pausing. "I'll make sure PMI sends off payment to you ASAP."

"Oh, thanks."

"Of course. That was the deal."

"When do you want to go out again?" I ask.

Lillian's tiredness evaporates and turns into warm hope. "You want to do it again?"

I want to do lots *again* with Lillian, and some other stuff for the *first* time too. "You're not done with your research, are you?"

"No, but I didn't want to assume. I know how you're sticking your neck out for me."

I step a bit closer and lower my voice. You never know who might be around. Who they'll talk to; what they'll say. "Don't let my dad get in your head. He's a hardass, and he's . . . he's not me." I swallow. "I want to help."

Her cheeks dimple with her smile. "Cool. Then, I'd like that."

"Cool."

"Give me a couple of days with the data. And to recover."

I chuckle. "Sure, sure. Top of next week, maybe?"

We work out the details, anticipation and excitement bubbling under our words. When all is said and done, Lillian climbs into her truck, gives me a wave, and drives off.

I stand in the gravel parking lot for a while, tracing the sole of my foot over the rocks, trying to gather myself before I go back to the boat. No matter how much time passes, though, my chest still tickles and my cheeks are flushed.

I think about how badly I want to kiss her for the rest of the day. I dream about it too.

If I haven't hit the point of no return with Lillian, I'm pretty damn close.

Chapter 14

Don't Get Too Close

LILLIAN

I zip my sweater up to my chin as another chill whips through the air. It's so peaceful out here on the rocky shore, watching boats go by, birds flying through the air without any fear, and the sun going in and out of the clouds.

Though my fingers are slow from the cold, I am too at peace to consider going back inside. And what's the rush? I have time. Not to mention, by being out in nature, I'm studying the environment and observing other elements that could be affecting the coho salmon population.

Even if the people of Naknek don't feel like I belong here, I can't deny I feel like I do. At least a little bit.

A good deal of that feeling is thanks to Matt. He's been checking in with me over text from time to time. Every time his name appears on my screen, I can't deny my giddiness. I feel like a teenager again talking to a boy I like. I thought that was a feeling of the past. That attraction naturally became less fluttery and more pragmatic.

Not the case when it comes to Matthew Benton. Not at all.

A bird flies diagonally across the river toward me, the telltale mottled brown plumage of the willow ptarmigan, the Alaska state bird. They're everywhere, reminiscent of pigeons in their multitude and their puffy shape.

Several more ptarmigans fly past. Some of them cry out to one another. I look in their direction to see what's scared them.

"Holy shit," I whisper.

Down the opposite bank about twenty feet, obscured by bramble and shrubbery, is a humungous moose. The last of the Ice Age megafauna as it were. And boy is this moose *mega*. Bigger than a horse with stalagmites of antlers climbing to the sky.

He's magnificent.

The moose moves slowly toward the riverbank, bending down to get a drink. I've heard moose can be combative and aren't to be trifled with. I would assume that from his size alone.

But this is a once-in-a-lifetime moment. I need a picture, at the very least.

I stand up from my chair, cringing at the way the pebble beach shifts under my shoes. As carefully as I can, I tiptoe down the bank, pulling my phone out of my pocket. I start recording, centering the moose in the frame.

"This is crazy," I whisper as if my sister is here, because I already know she's not going to believe me without photographic evidence.

The moose laps at the water, the waddle on its neck dangling back and forth. What a beautiful creature. How is it that something so big gives me such cuteness vibes? I just want to squeeze it.

"Don't get too close," a woman's voice comes from nowhere.

I gasp as I whip around and realize she's down the bank from me holding a fishing rod, watching me. "I-I wasn't going to!" Great, now I'm shouting. I turn back to look at the moose.

The moose is unfazed by my yelling, simply standing at his full height and enjoying the scenery.

I guess they aren't scared of humans.

I look back at the woman. She's snickering, tossing her dusty blonde cropped hair out of her eyes. "Didn't mean to scare you," she says. "They're harmless, but you gotta stay out of their way. You won't outrun a moose, honey. Won't be worth a post on Instagram."

I shove my phone back in my pocket. "Yeah, sorry. I didn't see you there."

She doesn't respond, focusing on the fishing rod again.

Guess she doesn't want to make conversation. I smile awkwardly and start to walk away.

"It's bad luck to have women on boats."

I turn around. "Sorry?"

She spares me another look. A small smile, narrow eyes. I'm not sure how old she is. She could be my age with weathered skin from the elements or from smoking. Or maybe, she's just older.

"That's what they'll tell you."

"Who will?"

"The other fishermen." Her line tugs, and she reaches for her reel, but stops. "That's what they told me anyway."

The line slackens again. There's an elegance about her movements, and the awareness of the water that tells me she doesn't just know what she's doing, she's an expert. "They kept you from fishing?"

The woman snorts. "Hell no. I have my own boat. My own crew."

"Why aren't you out then?"

The woman's face hardens a bit. "It's an expensive business, fishing. Can't go out as much as I'd like. As much as I need."

A crack forms in my heart. Isn't that the ouroboros of it all? To make money, they need to go out on the water, but to go out on the water, they need money. And the cycle that used to work so well is starting to falter.

"I'm just letting you know why people are giving you a hard time for going out on Benton's boat."

It's rare you're confronted with the knowledge people are talking about you right to your face. "So, you've heard about me."

"We all have, honey."

I purse my lips.

"Name's Marina," she says.

"Lillian. Although, you probably knew that."

Marina nods. "Yeah, Gwen told me." Her line tightens

again, and this time, she reels it in. The fish fights, but Marina doesn't. She is even-keeled the whole time. When the fish emerges, it's a silvery coho. She doesn't seem surprised at all. She just *knew* what it was. "Bingo."

Marina removes the fish from the hook, then reaches for a sharp object. I avert my gaze, stifling the painful flip of my stomach knowing she's quickly putting the fish out of its misery.

"I'll be the first to get pushed out if we start having to deal with licensing and strictures down here," Marina says, calling my attention back with the clicking lid of her cooler. "I'll have to stay in Anchorage all year or find some other summer fishing season."

When I look back at her, she wipes her hands on her pants, staring me down. And while her stare is amber and intense like a flash of lightning, it doesn't seem like she's trying to strike me down. I see worry there. The only reason I haven't seen it before is that the other fishermen all posture and puff their chests at me, trying to scare me off with their hardheadedness. When the truth is, everything boils down to fear. "Why don't you stay here all year round?"

"Natives don't take to the non-natives around here in the off-season, and frankly, I can't blame them. Not after all the years of white people destroying their culture." Marina looks out at the river, not returning to her rod immediately. "Still though, Naknek is home, and I'd hate to leave here."

"I'd hate that, too."

She lifts her chin, sizing me up. "We're used to empty promises around here."

Naked in Naknek

"I understand," I say. "I really admire the work you do. Seriously, I know it can't be easy."

Marina smiles. "I appreciate that."

She seems genuine. For that, I'm grateful.

Marina grabs her rod and her cooler. Done for the day. "They're going to do their best to make you feel unwelcomed here, Lillian. But we women stick together, right?"

My lips grow into a grin. "Yes. I think so."

"Good. That's good." She starts up the beach and turns back to look at me. "I'm rooting for you."

I watch her go, unsure what to say. The relief flooding through me is so powerful tears drop from my eyes. I wipe them away quickly and look back across the river.

The moose still stands there, tall and watchful over his domain. He turns his big head in my direction. And while I'm in awe, I'm not terrified of him.

I think maybe he just sees me and accepts me. Like I belong here too.

Chapter 15

I Like Your Fun Facts

MATTHEW

"Got it," Lillian says. She screws the top on her latest vial, hazel eyes zeroed in on the water.

"That's it?" I ask.

She places her sample into her small cooler that sits between us at her feet. "That's it!" When she looks up at me, she smiles, bright and pretty. "I'm ready to head back when you are."

I glance back at the boat anchored on the bay. We're at the mouth of the Ugashik, early afternoon. The Ugashik is the farthest river on Lillian's itinerary, so we started out early from Naknek. Thanks to the pristine conditions on the water and the lightness of my boat, we made good time. Of course, that was still seven hours and change on the water, just the two of us.

Naked in Naknek

We won't get back to Naknek until late. I had half a mind to tell her we should just anchor overnight, but I didn't want to make her uncomfortable. Especially when the conditions below are so cramped. Though Lillian and I have become familiar as of late, I doubt we're at the sleepover phase of our relationship.

I wouldn't mind a sleepover whatsoever, though. Under different circumstances.

"There's a patch of wild blueberries on the tundra, a short ride up the river. Want to stop and pick some for the ride back?"

Lillian's eyes widen. "Oh!"

"I mean, we won't get back until late anyway. I wouldn't blame you if you wanted to get on the road or—uh—the water, but—"

"No, I'd like that!" she exclaims. "I want to see a big burly man blueberry picking."

I chuckle and rev up the skiff. "When you say it like that, you make me sound like a nursery rhyme."

Lillian grabs her seat as I pull farther down the river, water spraying upward and onto our skin. "Does that threaten your masculinity?"

"Yes. Don't let the guys hear," I say wryly.

She laughs and looks at me. I keep my eyes on the river, not willing to break my concentration to have her make me weak with a look. Nevertheless, my skin is warm under her attention. "Gosh, this town is even smaller than Naknek."

I glance at the buildings peppering the rolling greens

as we pass them. "Pilot Point? Yeah. Population is in decline too."

Lillian frowns, watching the buildings roll by. "That's sad."

"That's Bristol Bay," I say with a sigh. "Towns are already small enough. Now, everyone knows how much world there is out there. And if they can swing it, they want to see. Can't blame 'em, but Pilot Point wouldn't be the first town to disappear off the map."

"That's hard for me to imagine."

"I'm sure, Miss Queen of Los Angeles."

Lillian scoffs. "Hardly."

With her attention elsewhere, I take a moment to look her way. She's lost in thought, taking in her surroundings. A curious fish out of water. I like this side of her. Not at all aware of the way she looks to others, something I'm sure is hard to shake in the City of Angels. "The town I grew up in," she says suddenly, "wasn't even that small. I can't imagine it disappearing either."

"Yes, but Michigan isn't nearly as remote."

Lillian blushes and drops her head, looking at her fingers as she pulls at her cuticles. "It felt that way growing up. Silly now to think of it."

I spot the gravelly beach up ahead, and point the skiff toward it. "It's all relative."

"I suppose."

A few moments of silence pass between us. "Have you, um, found anything yet?" I ask carefully.

"With my research?"

"Yeah. How's it looking?"

Lillian cocks her head. "Are you going to tell on me?"

"No! No, of course not, I . . ." I wave my free hand. "Forget I asked, I don't mean to pry."

She smiles. "It's fine. I trust you."

My heart swells.

"I mean, I have to since I'm out in the middle of nowhere with you. Could have turned out very badly for me, in hindsight."

I swallow. "Well, I'd never—"

"I know you wouldn't."

My eyes catch hers for a moment. I wish I had my pullover buttoned up, so I could dip the lower half of my face into it like a turtle, so she couldn't see my flushed face.

"I mean, some things are to be expected. Water temperatures are rising everywhere. So is the turbidity. Water's getting murkier, thanks to pollution. I'm still observing bacterial counts and pathogens. Those could suggest there's something in the environment impacting the decline in the fish population. Might also suggest an issue for humans too," she explains. "Of course, that's a leap at this point. There is some consistency with the data so far, but doing this on my own is a bit of a challenge, I won't lie. Especially when I have a makeshift lab."

I pull us into the shallows and hop into the water. Lillian starts to move, but I grab the end of the skiff and drag it up onto the shore with her inside. She squeals out my name in surprise, and I chuckle. Holding out my hand to her, I say, "Well, if you ever need an assistant . . ."

Lillian takes my hand. Her skin is soft. City girl. But it's her poise that strikes me every time I touch her. The exact way her fingers curl, elegant and graceful. "Are you offering, Matt?"

"Maybe," I reply before hauling her up to her feet and onto the shore. Her fingers are cold. I could keep them warm if I kept her hand in mine. Could even pull our clasped hands into my pocket to keep her both warm and close. But I don't. Of course, I don't.

We head up the rock-laden patch of beach and onto the tundra.

"Wow," Lillian remarks.

There's a strange sense of pride I get every time she takes in a new piece of scenery. Like I crafted it just for her, a new swath of beauty to encounter. If she likes Alaska enough, maybe she'll come back. "Pretty great, huh?"

Being out on the tundra is a different sort of magic. The magnificence of Alaska is unfettered out here. There are rolling grasses and bushes for miles, all under the shadows of the mountains. Here, you are as wild as the wildlife, which means being careful where you step and how you interact with the world around you.

In the distance, there are antlers just above the landscape. "Caribou," I say to Lillian.

"Where?"

"Shhh." I hate to tamper her excitement, but it's best to be careful around here, especially after her run-in with a bear. I pull her close to me and point over her shoulder so she can follow my finger. "All the way out there."

Lillian spots them. "Oh, my gosh. Look at all of them."

I take the moment of distraction as an opportunity to hold her a bit longer.

Lillian looks up at me with a big smile. "Did you know caribou are the only species of deer where both sexes grow antlers?"

I don't understand my brother's resistance to brains because I can't think of anything sexier than a woman who knows what she's talking about. "I did know that."

Lillian rolls her eyes. "Of course you did. You live here."

"I like your fun facts," I say. "Don't stop on my account. Now, follow me."

There's a path engraved in the tundra to the bountiful blueberry bushes from years of people coming here to collect the harvest. Lillian follows behind me slowly, caught up in her surroundings. "It's just amazing out here. Quiet."

"Good place to come and think," I say. "Although, that could be said for a lot of Alaska."

"I'm sure you do a lot of thinking out on the water."

"Naw, out on the water is the only place I'm not thinking," I say, then immediately feel self-conscious. "Not that I'm not paying attention or don't care, I just—"

"I get it," Lillian says. "I think I do at least."

After all my years as a fisherman, my actions are innate. Out there, I'm one with the water. I can slow down and just be. No family drama to deal with; no politics to argue over.

Just nature as intended.

When we arrive at the bushes, Lillian once again marvels. "There are so many!"

"That's what happens when you let nature do the work," I say, skimming my fingers along a clump of blueberries on the shrub, dusty and plump. I grab a couple off the branch and hold them out to Lillian. "Perfect time of year for them too."

She takes one of the berries and inspects it.

"These are called 'lowbush' blueberries," I tell her.

I watch her with rapt attention as she holds the berry between her unpainted lips. And while I try my best to be respectful, I am only a man. I am indeed jealous of that blueberry.

Lillian's eyes light up at the taste. "Oh, *wow*." She takes a couple more from my hand and chows down.

"Okay, okay, save some for me!" I exclaim through a laugh.

It doesn't take long for our hands to be full. I riffle through my pockets. "Let's see, I probably have a bag in here." I find a crumpled-up plastic bag, just as expected. "My mom had a nice wicker basket we'd use, but I'm not sure where it is now," I say, a pang in my chest.

We pick more berries, each one making the bag crumple as it lands against the plastic.

"Gwen mentioned your mom passed away."

"Yeah. Almost ten years ago now."

"I'm sorry, Matt."

It doesn't matter how long it's been. Every day without my mom feels like the first, even if the grief is easier to manage. "It's all right," I lie. "She had cancer."

"Cancer's a bitch," Lillian says.

I laugh despite the tenor of the conversation. "Yeah, it really fucking is."

We continue picking berries, and I find myself

compelled to say more, like a mounting pressure from the bottom of my throat to my mouth. "That's when I took over captaining my dad's boat. He was a total wreck. Still is, as I'm sure you noticed."

"Of course. I mean, she must have been young."

I swallow, accidentally squeezing a berry too tight, its juice staining my fingers. "Yeah. We all miss her."

Lillian's hand covers mine, loosening my fingers along the broken berry. I stare at our clasped hands for a moment, watching how hers caresses mine. She's just trying to be comforting. Of course she is. But, fuck, it feels nice. I take a deep breath and look into Lillian's eyes.

She smiles at me. Sweet. Without pity. Like a port in a storm. My god, she's a beauty.

"I bet she'd be really proud of you."

My brows lift in surprise. I didn't expect that.

"Especially because you've been so nice to the new girl," Lillian adds.

I laugh to keep from crying. Fuck, I haven't gotten so emotional over Mom's passing in years. I've learned to keep it down and quiet. "Thanks for saying that, Lillian."

"I believe it. It's not hard to say."

Fuck it. You know what? I'm going to do it. I'm going to kiss her. I'm just going to kiss her, and if she hates it, then I'll apologize and bury my head in the sand for all eternity. But I can't resist the draw anymore.

I lean in slightly, giving her an opportunity to move away.

She doesn't.

But before I can close the space between us and press my lips to hers, thunder rumbles long and loud.

I tear my hand from hers and turn around. The sky that has been robin's egg blue since this morning is darkening in the distance. And that darkness is encroaching fast.

"Shit," I mutter. "We gotta get back to the boat." I don't wait for Lillian to wake up to the urgency of the situation. I grab her wrist and pull. "Come on!"

We run all the way back to the skiff, Lillian's hand fisted around the plastic bag.

"Are storms really that bad out here?" she asks, breathless.

"With clouds like that, yeah," I say. I've been caught in a few tempests in my day. I point at the funnel of clouds. "Cumulonimbus. All the way up. Big storm. Lots of water."

As if on cue, there's another roar of thunder. The clouds aren't even over us yet, and the thunder is loud. I glance back at Lillian. Her face has gone slack with surprise. "Are we going to be able to get back to Naknek?"

I hold my breath and let it out slowly. "Maybe."

However, the clouds are cinematic, threatening the bay with lightning trapped in the grips of the storm clouds.

"Maybe not," I add.

As the skiff putters back down the river, neither of us speak. The damn thing can't move fast enough for my sanity. We make it to the mouth of the river just in time to feel a sprinkling of water. The waves thrum with the wind, and that wind is bringing the storm on faster than I'd like.

Naked in Naknek

But we're close. At least to the boat. Naknek is a different story.

The skiff crests a swollen wave. I think nothing of it. I've seen much worse in my days on the water; waves that make you worry your boat's about to do a barrel roll and never recover. However, Lillian screeches in surprise.

I hold back a laugh, reaching a hand back to pat her knee. "It's okay. You're in good hands."

My hand doesn't reach her leg, though. She grabs onto it for dear life, squeezing tight and not letting go. A hold that reaches all the way into my chest and wraps around my heart.

Chapter 16

I Need You to Climb Up

LILLIAN

I cling to Matt's hand. It is the only thing in the world other than the storm. The only thing that can keep me steady.

More than once, the skiff becomes almost perpendicular to the water, and I'm afraid we'll be thrown into Bristol Bay.

My only saving grace is Matt. He's coolheaded and seemingly unconcerned. I think back to what he said, that the only time he isn't thinking is when he's on the water. And the reason I understand is because I get it. When you know something well, it's a part of you, engrained in your every movement and thought.

So, I trust him to get me to the *Bristol Belle* safe.

Even if I see my life flash before my eyes at least three

times.

As we pass Pilot Point, the heavens open up above us and water pours in sheets. I can barely keep my eyes open. I want to curl closer to Matt and press myself into his back, but I can't move a muscle. I'm barely breathing.

When we emerge from the mouth of the Ugashik, the waters get even rougher.

I can see the *Bristol Belle* like a mirage on the horizon. She, too, is getting tossed on the water, and though she's meant for such things, I fear for her life as much as mine.

"Hold on!" Matt shouts out over his shoulder at me, water beading through his beard.

He has to remove his hand from mine, and I lose all sense of stillness. I grab onto my seat, bracing my feet against the bottom of the inflatable skiff. I realize that suddenly, the thing could pop, and we'd be lost to the sea.

Don't panic, I tell myself. I close my eyes and let my stomach settle into the rolling, unpredictable waves beneath us.

You'll be fine. Matt has it under control.

I keep my head down as I am pummeled by rainwater. The chill aches down to my bones. Sea water sloshes into the bottom of the boat, soaking my socks.

The skiff's motor starts to slow. I look up, thankful to find we are approaching the stern of the *Bristol Belle*. That's a difficult task when the skiff is bobbing and so is the gillnetter. But we're so close to safety . . . or some semblance of safety. Because the gillnetter might be bigger than the skiff, but it still pales in comparison to the research boats I've been on. I've never been on a boat so small. Never been in a storm this huge. Put them together, and what do you get?

Absolute terror.

With the throttle chugging low beneath the sound of the wind, Matt sits back on his haunches, reaching for the ladder. "I need you to climb up!" he shouts over his shoulder.

"What?" I shriek.

"You have to get up there and throw me the towline," Matt says. "Come on, quick."

I push myself up from my seat, my legs shaking, which isn't helped by the swaying of the skiff. I fall back into my spot. "I can't," I say, for the first time in a long time genuinely believing it.

"Yes, you can," he says. "The only other option is leaving you down here while I climb up, and I'm not going to do that."

Matt clutches the ladder so hard the veins in the back of his hands pop out. "Lillian, look at me," Matt says.

Through the torrent of rain, I meet his gaze. For a moment, the storm seems to let up. Whether it's reality or a trick of the mind, it doesn't matter. But staring at Matt, I'm hit with absolute calm. I believe him. I *trust* him.

"You're going to go up there and grab the black towline and toss it to me," he says firmly.

"What if I can't find it?"

"It's tied to a cleat. You can. You will."

"But—"

He doesn't give me another chance to protest. "Give me your hand."

Matt takes my hand and pulls me to my feet, placing it onto the rung of the ladder. No going back now. I grab a rung farther up just as the boat rocks under me.

I scream.

Matt's hand lands on the back of my thigh, squeezing to steady me. "I've got you. You're not going anywhere."

Something steels inside me. Giving into the fear means losing time, which means threatening not just my safety but Matt's. And I'll be damned if something happens to him because I'm a coward.

I'm not a coward.

I heft myself up the ladder, not even flinching when my shoe slips against the metal.

"There you go," Matt calls out after me.

His encouragement propels me faster as a strange combination of bravery and excitement washes over me. In seemingly no time at all, I'm on the deck, my sea legs stalwart under me.

I hear him shout to me again, but the words are lost under the sound of the storm. The black towline is just as Matt said, tied off to a cleat, even though the coiled towline has shimmied out of place like a snake. I grab it, nearly falling into the railing with the movement of the boat. "I've got it!" I scream, peering over the side of the boat.

"Throw it down!" he yells.

I toss the end of the towline down and watch as Matt manages to coil it around his arm, calm under pressure. Astonishing. The way he moves is like he's in a ballet. Tying off the boat, he manages to pull himself up the ladder, despite the fact the skiff has drifted to a strange angle.

I reach for him without thinking, clutching at his wet jacket and pulling. I'm probably not doing much, but I'm desperate to get him on board.

Matt manages to leap over the railing, right into my arms. He grabs my shoulders. "Are you alright?"

"Yes, I'm fine, I'm—" I can't seem to catch my breath.

"You need to get down below, alright?" he says. "It's not safe out here with the—"

"I'm not going to leave you up here alone!" I yell.

The weather takes that very moment to say, *fuck you.* Blinding lightning strikes close, and the thunder claps loudly in my ears. The boat rocks again, my grip slipping off Matt as I tumble backward.

But he's quicker than the tumbling Bristol Bay waters. He sweeps me up against his chest with a free arm, keeping us upright by steadying himself on the railing.

"Goddammit, Lillian, if you're out here, I'm going to have to worry about you, too!"

Our bodies are flush. And while I'm wet and cold and terrified, Matt's body pressed to mine is impossibly hot.

Through gritted teeth, Matt keeps his eyes on mine as he instructs, "Now, please go inside, okay?"

I agree through a trembling voice. "A-alright."

Matt's arm relaxes just a bit. "I've got it taken care of, I promise. Just let me do my job. I'll be able to do it better knowing you're safe."

I nod. It makes sense. I hate feeling useless, but now is not the time to assert my competence.

"This is what I know how to do best, Lillian. Trust me."

I take a moment to cross the deck and step up into the wheelhouse, sliding the door shut against the wind and water. There's an eating nook across from the steering wheel, two benches facing each other, and beyond that, down some small stairs, the sleeping quarters. Wooden bunks the size of coffins. I slide onto the bench and sit, clinging to the table as the boat rocks. Closer to the boat's center of gravity, the likelihood of seasickness is lower, but not zero. And after the ride in the skiff, and now being stuck on the rolling sea, I'm queasy. I spend the time willing my stomach to settle and focusing on Matt's footsteps overhead. Whenever he pauses, my anxiety flares until he moves again, reassuring me he hasn't been tossed overboard. Time passes. Grueling seconds turn into arduous minutes.

Suddenly, the door above bursts open, and the sound of the storm roars into the cabin. It takes me a second to realize it wasn't the wind. I look up, but before I can see clearly, Matt answers my unspoken question.

"It should be okay in a minute or two," he says, not looking up from the helm. He's tense with concentration, steering the boat through the last of the storm. His hair is soaked, flattened, and dripping water down his forehead.

As promised, things calm down. The boat jerks less, and the floor evens out beneath me. I hadn't realized just how tightly I was bracing every muscle in my body or how hard my heart was pounding, like the force of a fist against my chest.

I can breathe again.

I have more mental clarity for thoughts that don't have to do with survival now, and the first thought upon seeing Matt slick with rainwater is . . . damn, he looks sexy. Not only is he sexy for knowing what he's doing, but he's also sexy while doing it.

As if hearing my thoughts about him, Matt glances my way. I smile and look out the window, so as not to betray my wandering mind.

We've outpaced the storm just enough to get more visibility. I realize we're going down the river farther, not following the coast back up the bay. We move in silence, other than the sound of the storm and the taut, heavy breaths Matt lets out from time to time until he mutters, "Should be deep enough."

I'm not sure what he's talking about until the bow of the boat turns toward the entrance of a slim creek on our right. "We're going to go down *there*?"

He continues maneuvering the boat, already confident in his choice. "Safest option while we wait out the storm. I mean, we could stay on the river, but the reduced current will be welcomed if we remain here overnight."

Overnight. I hadn't even thought about that. The ride down here was already hours long, nearly half a day. Of course, there's no way we're getting back to Naknek. Unless Matt drives us through the night, and I wouldn't ask that of him. Still, though, staying on the boat overnight prompts many questions.

Navigating into the creek turns out to be much less dramatic than I anticipate. Matt stops and starts frequently, stepping onto the deck and returning several times before settling, only to decide it's still not quite right. I offer to help, but Matt only says, "Leave it to me."

He doesn't sound like a man who thinks a woman couldn't handle the work. It's just that he's got it taken care of. He's not going to let *me* struggle. He's got this.

I don't feel safe around men as a general rule unless I've known them for a long time. But Matt has earned my trust much faster than any man has before. It scares me a bit, but it's also thrilling.

When he's satisfied, Matt drops the anchor down into the creek bed with a sated, "Okay. We've done what we can."

I swallow. "What we can?"

Matt gets up from the captain's chair and heads down below, his steps confident despite the rocking of the boat. "It's safer here on the creek but not invincible. There's potential for the anchor to come unmoored," he calls out.

The storm catches up to us, the sheets of rain, cracking thunder, and lightning consuming our sightlines. And while the creek is certainly steadier, the boat still rocks, especially when the wind kicks up.

The seasick feeling returns, so I go below deck to join him and steady my stomach.

There are four bunks in the sleeping quarters. Two on either side. At the back is a small door, which I assume is the bathroom. I realize now that if Matt and I are stuck here overnight, we'll be sleeping in the same room. Which is meaningless, of course. But I can't ignore the knot in my throat at the thought.

Matt leans on one of the bunks, running a hand towel

over his hair and face, attempting to dry off. He looks up at me.

I swallow my tongue. There's a quality in his gaze like he doesn't know what to do with me. Like I'm . . . bad luck.

Maybe what Marina said was right.

His eyes flick down the length of my body. "You'll need dry clothes. Here." Matt turns around and reaches up above to a sliding panel. He pushes it aside, revealing stacks of folded clothing.

"It's fine, I don't—"

"You're not gonna catch a cold on my boat, Lillian."

Dry clothes *do* sound nice right about now.

"It might be kinda big," he says, pulling down a couple of pieces for me and holding them out. "I'll go up while you change."

"Thanks," I say, taking a long-sleeved shirt and some sweatpants from him. Tentatively, Matt squeezes past me and goes up to the wheelhouse. The aisle between the bunks in the cabin is not meant for more than one person at a time. I move slowly, trying to keep my bearings as the boat pitches and rollicks.

Matt calls out while I struggle to change quickly, "I'll set up a bunk for you. Best way to pass these things is to sleep through them. Calms the anxiety. Top or bottom?"

For the first time since the storm hit, my mind goes somewhere dirty. Sarah would be proud. *Naked, Alaska* . . . "Uh, what?"

"Bunk. Top or bottom bunk."

Duh. "Bottom," I answer. The idea of climbing into the

top bunk reminds my stomach that I'm not on solid ground.

"Good choice."

I emerge a couple of minutes later as Matt is laying out a blanket on the lower bunk, his big body contorted into it. "Okay. All set. Have to warn you, it's *rustic*."

"Trust me, I don't care. Laying down is all I need." Under a pile of blankets preferably. The rain has brought a chill to the air that seeped into my bones.

And he's right. It's rustic. A gray, scratchy-looking blanket, a pillow that looks like it belongs on an airplane, and an orange vinyl mattress.

"The boat's old, but I've updated most everything. 'Cept the sleeping quarters."

"At least there is a toilet," I say.

He smiles; however, it's fleeting because at that very moment, the boat rocks. Matt grabs onto the top bunk to steady himself while I fall onto the edge of the bottom one. The back of my head knocks against the top bunk, pain splaying out over the back of my skull. "Ow."

"Jeez, are you hurt?" Matt asks with urgency, his hand cupping the back of my head.

"I'm fine. I . . ." I reply, because it's the truth, but I trail off because he's so close, making sure I'm okay. I stare up into his face, waiting for his eyes to meet mine. He's so rugged and handsome.

Matt's brown eyes shift to mine in question. Warmth blooms across my chest.

"These bunks aren't up to snuff for an LA girl."

It takes him a moment to register my joke, but when he

does, he *beams*, a big grin spreading across his face. "Well, Lillian, you ain't in LA anymore."

To my chagrin, he releases the back of my head and pats the end of the mattress. "Swing your legs up here. I've gotta show you how to sleep on this thing."

"*Show* me?" I ask.

"I'm the expert, aren't I?"

That wasn't the question. "I didn't realize it was a skill to sleep on a boat."

Matt crosses his arms over his chest. Though the boat shakes and moves, he is completely stable. Forget professional, this guy is like Poseidon on the water. In control. "There very much is, Lillian. Now . . ."

He grabs my calves and swings them onto the bed. "What's with all the forceful maneuvering?" I cry out.

"You're being stubborn," he says plainly.

Anyone else, I'd be spitting curse words. But I welcome Matt's touch. His guidance and instruction. I spend so much time being on my shit that having someone else in charge, even for something as small as helping me down some stairs or making me lay down is nice.

Matt pats the lip of the bunk that rises a few inches above the mattress. "Lay on your side, top knee wedges against the lip here." He pats the wooden frame. "And stretch your bottom leg straight to push against the end of the bunk."

I do so and, though the bunk is small, I stretch to reach the end of it and keep myself in.

"Perfect form," he says, then grabs the blanket and

pulls it over me. "This is how you don't fall out. Get comfortable."

I attempt to snuggle into my bunk. The water no longer churns my stomach as much. In fact, the boat's movement feels soothing now that I'm lying down.

"Okay, I'm gonna keep an eye on things. But if you need anything, I'll be around," Matt says, knocking his fist on the top of the bunk.

"Sounds good," I reply.

Matt gives me a quiet smile before lumbering back up the stairs to the cabin, shutting off the light as he goes.

I can't imagine I'll fall asleep since it's still so early. However, between the darkness and the rolling water beneath me, it might be easier than I anticipate.

∾

I'M NOT sure how long I've been sleeping when I am flung from the bunk, a flummox of limbs as I tumble to the ground and ram up against the bottom of the opposite bunk.

"Jesus, Lillian, you alright?" Matt cries out from somewhere.

For a second, I think I'm dreaming. "What the *fuck?*" I groan, pushing myself up from the floor of the cabin.

A hand lands on my shoulder. I gasp and look up. Through the darkened cabin, Matt's face comes into focus above me. He's in the bunk across from the one I was sleeping in.

"You hurt?"

Nothing more than my pride. "Fine."

"I told you to wedge yourself in there."

"I was! I mean, I did. I guess, I—" A shiver runs through me. Not only is my body stunned from being catapulted from sleep, but I'm freezing. My teeth are clenched, and my nose feels so cold I'm not sure it's still attached.

Thunder rumbles through the boat. The storm is still raging outside. Damn, Matt was right. These storms are no joke.

"Come here," Matt says, helping me up off the ground.

I expect him to cram me back into my bunk and go through the motions he did earlier. However, that's not the case. He pulls me down onto the bunk next to him. "You claustrophobic?" he asks through a sleep-laden rumble.

I resist another shiver, this one not from the cold. "Not usually."

"You okay if we share a bunk then? I'll put you on the inside."

My stomach swoops. "What?"

"Not because—" Matt huffs. "I don't want you falling out again. That's it. If you sleep closest to the wall, I'll keep you in."

The bunks are *tiny*. There's no way you'd be able to sleep next to someone without touching them *completely*.

But I'm not sure I'll be able to fall asleep alone knowing how easily I can be tossed from my bunk. Not to mention, we could share body heat.

"I promise I'm not trying to make you uncomfortable or . . . take advantage."

I'm surprised I believe him. However, after all the time

we've spent alone, the plane ride to Dillingham, the ride down the Kvichak, and now all *this* time too, hasn't Matt proven he is safe to be around? "Okay. You're probably right. That's a ... that's a good idea."

"If you change your mind, just let me know. Even if I'm asleep, just wake me up."

My heart flutters. This storm has been such an intense situation, and he's *still* concerned with my comfort.

Matt helps me work myself up against the back wall of the bunk and then, once I'm settled, he crawls in next to me, his back to my front. We pull the blanket over our bodies, apologizing when our hands knock in the dark. But eventually, we're both tucked underneath and settled.

Yep, just as expected, there's *zero* room between us. My front is pushed up against his back like I'm his big spoon.

"You comfortable?" he asks.

Surprisingly, yes. My heart is racing, my body is tense, and I don't think I could fall asleep if I tried though. Not when Matt is so close, and I'm already sweating. But I'm comfortable. *So* comfortable.

"I'm sorry if I snore," Matt says after minutes of quiet.

I giggle into the pillow. "I'm sorry if I talk in my sleep."

Matt groans. "Oh, *no*."

"Hey! You're the snorer!"

"And you're going to monologue me awake."

I laugh, settling further into our closeness. It's a necessity. Survival.

Yeah. That's what it is.

The boat rocks with a motion I've grown used to, but now the hull creaks ominously, as if in protest. I tense, gripping the back of his shirt. I can't let myself get too comfortable—we're still in a dangerous situation.

"It's okay," Matt says, reaching back to touch me, his hand landing on my thigh. "Just a sound."

I don't reply, letting myself sink into his touch. To my delight, he doesn't draw away. And with each passing moment, I allow myself to unwind into sleep. Except this time, I am warm and safe, pressed up against Matt. I know he won't let me fall or grow cold.

I'm afraid I could get used to this.

Chapter 17

I Don't Really Buy into That Stuff

MATTHEW

Something tightens on my chest, pulling at the fabric. I snap my eyes open.

Then, I realize what it is.

It's Lillian's hand. She's clinging to me.

Despite the gales outside, the rolling waters, and the anxiety of being trapped in a storm, I haven't slept so well in a long time. Her body pressed against mine and the touch of her hand brought me a peace I didn't know I needed.

Not to mention her breath tickling the back of my neck, so close she could kiss me.

The boat lurches to the side, and reflexively, I clutch her hand against my chest to steady her.

Lillian gasps awake. "What the . . ."

Her arm tightens around me as if she's afraid I might roll away.

Like it was nothing, the boat rights itself again, steadied and aligned, so there's no reason for me to be grabbing her anymore. I release her hand, tingling with disappointment. "Um. Sorry. Didn't mean to wake you."

To my surprise and delight, Lillian laughs. Her hand unfurls the front of my shirt. "It's fine."

We lay there in silence a bit longer. "I should probably go check on—"

"Can I ask you something?" she interrupts.

"Yeah, of course." I wish I could turn over and face her, see how her mahogany hair is mussed from sleep, how her eyes pinch at the corners.

Lillian hesitates. "Do you—do you think I am bad luck?"

I frown. "What?"

"I just . . . I was told it's bad luck to have women on boats."

"Oh. That." I breathe out through my nose. I sit up on the edge of the bunk and glance back at her. "I don't really buy into that stuff."

Lillian smiles. "Oh. Good."

I ruffle a hand through my hair. "Did—uh—Did someone give you a hard time about that?"

"No, I just . . ." She raises herself up on her elbow, her head almost brushing the bunk above her. "I met that female sea captain. Marina?"

My brows lift in recognition. "Oh, yeah?"

"Yeah, she was out fishing on the riverbank and—" Lillian shakes her head. "She mentioned the superstition."

"Storms happen, women on board or not. If I chalked everything up to mere superstitions, I'd be a shit captain." I push myself up to stand and lean on the opposite bunk to face her. "But I have to admit, it crosses your mind now and then. Been hearing shit like that since I was a kid."

"I'm sure."

"These superstitions run deep, but I have a hard time believing most people still think that way."

Lillian doesn't argue. "I am glad to hear it."

I had a preconceived notion about her being a city girl. That she'd be judgmental and lack the capacity to understand or broaden her horizons about Naknek. However, she's a great listener. She's open to learning more. I like that a lot.

She sighs, shimmying to the edge of the bunk and sitting up. "I wouldn't blame you for being superstitious after that storm."

"That's true. I should have thrown you overboard," I reply, teasing.

Lillian laughs, smiling up at me. I'd like to swallow her laughter with my mouth against hers.

"Anyway, I should go check on the boat and the weather, and then if all's well, we can head back to Naknek and—"

Lillian presses her hands into the mattress. "Can I help? I'd like to."

Just as she stands up, the boat rocks again. Her legs are still weak with sleep, so she pitches toward me, landing against my chest. I don't have my bearings to keep both of us upright, instead catching her against my chest. Our bodies are as close as they were in the bed, except now we're chest to chest. I'm towering over her. She's breathless with her mouth parted.

Fuck me.

Lillian rests her hand on my arm tentatively, trying to find her balance. I help her stand back up, away from me before I can do anything stupid, something that can't be undone. "You can help by staying inside and listening to the radio for any weather updates, okay?"

She bites her lower lip, coquettish and teasing. "Okay."

I turn away as quickly as I can, launch myself into the galley, and up the stairs. Away. I need to be away. "Be back in a minute."

I'm up and out of the wheelhouse before I can hear her response. I inhale deeply, the fresh air a welcome change from the stuffy cabin. I'm not going to acknowledge the sweat and deliciousness pouring off Lillian.

The sun is peeking through the clouds, and the darkness has turned into a thin layer of gray. It only gets dark in the summer around here when there's a storm, like we're microdosing nighttime.

Other than a few things blown about on the deck, everything looks above board. No pun intended.

Now that it's not raining, I get a good look at our surroundings. We're in the narrows, swaths of grass covering the landscape on either bank. The sky is wide open here with ranges of mountains in the distance, doing

Naked in Naknek

their best to make themselves known through the hazy sky.

The expanse of Alaska never fails to humble me. It reminds me how I'm only a small part of all this beauty, and that long after I'm dead, the mountains will remain. Majestic and constant.

I hear the door slide open and turn to find Lillian standing in the doorway to the wheelhouse, the gray blanket wrapped around her. Her auburn hair is tied back into a ponytail, messy and sprigging in different directions.

"No activity on the radio," she says.

I tuck my tongue into the corner of my mouth, chuckling. "We're all good out here. Just need to check a few things, and then we can start back to Naknek."

She tentatively steps out onto the deck. The cool ocean breeze rustles her hair as her shoulders drop and head lifts.

That's what this place does to people. Releases us from the constraints of the complications of being a human. It's a beautiful thing to feel, but even more beautiful to watch come over a person.

I glance at Lillian as she raises an arm over her head and sniffs her armpit. I chuckle despite myself, and she immediately turns red when she realizes I saw her checking her scent. "Oh, my god. Sorry."

"Don't be sorry."

"I just haven't showered since yesterday morning, and I hope I don't stink," she says sheepishly.

You definitely don't.

I clear my throat. "Um, well, we don't have a shower on board."

"Ah, so *that's* why women don't want to be on board. Evidently, all the men go nose-blind," Lillian says with a smirk.

"It's just a part of the job. Having a clean boat is important, of course, but you kind of forget about smell after a while. We usually wash up with seawater or—" My heart pounds in my chest, quick and excited as an idea dawns. I smile. "You want the full Alaskan experience, right?"

She tilts her head to the side, her eyes dripping down my body and taking in the sum of all my parts. My insides stir. "That depends . . . what do you have in mind, Matt?"

My smile grows into a grin.

Chapter 18

I'm Going to Get Naked

LILLIAN

I stand amidst pampas grass and cattails, unsure of what to do with myself now that we're at this small inlet off the creek. The skiff waits nearby, except this time I'm not collecting samples or measuring the temperature of the water.

I'm supposed to be taking a bath.

"How's it going?" Matt asks, a few feet from me.

I glance his way. He unbuttons his overshirt farther and farther down as he looks at me as if we didn't just sleep next to each other. Clearly, I'm the only one with my mind in the gutter. "Yeah, I'm just . . ." I hold up the soap on a rope in my hand. "Still shocked soap on a rope is a real thing."

"It's a lifesaver," he says, shucking his shirt off and

folding it masterfully and quickly. "Look, you don't need to be nervous. This is some of the cleanest water in the world."

Is that true? I don't have the wherewithal to check the Rolodex of facts in my brain because Matt chooses that moment to lift his undershirt up over his head, and *god almighty*. I'm not a religious person, but a body like that would have me worshipping on my knees. His chest is as finely sculpted as a Greek statue and covered in a perfect layer of dark hair. His peachy nipples prick in the air. How I'd love to run my tongue down—

No. He's just trying to get clean. And so am I. Guess I should get started on that.

I turn away and finger the zipper on my sweater, immediately fearing what the air will feel like when I take it off, let alone when I'm . . . naked. "Aren't you cold?" I ask.

Matt laughs. "This is nothing. You should see me during the Polar Plunge at Thanksgiving."

"Polar what?" I balk.

"Hey, it's a tradition in Naknek. I wouldn't expect you to get it since you're a Californian."

I glance over my shoulder at him. He's down to his boxers. "Michigander."

"Yeah, still got nothing on us Alaskans." A moment passes. "Um, I'm going to get naked."

"I won't look."

"I just don't want to offend you." He clears his throat. "I don't want to make you uncomfortable."

Oh, I'm uncomfortable alright. Not for the reasons he's implying, though. No, I'm getting hot all over, and I don't want to think about what's happening in my panties.

Matt's treating this as something objective, something we're just doing. I want to do the same, but I haven't ever bathed in a lake, much less with a man nearby.

As if reading my thoughts, Matt says, "I'm not looking, I promise."

There's a weird sense of relief mixed with disappointment. Part of me just wants to get this over with, but the other part wants him to look, wants him to see me, wants to know if he likes what he sees.

"I'm going in. You're gonna want to be quick about it," he says with a wink.

I don't turn back until I hear movement in the water. I peek over my shoulder and nearly scream out at his naked form moving into the water. The man is completely naked, and while I can only see his backside, it's an incredible backside.

His back is just as muscular as his front, a rippling topography of strength. The man has a perfect body, which is usually obscured under his bulky clothes. If he lived in Los Angeles, he could be a model. And I'm not innocent. Not by a long shot. Of course, I'm going to admire his ass too. 🍑 Does he do squats? How does a fisherman have a butt like that? It sits atop tree trunk thighs covered in swirls of that same dark hair.

More impressive than his body, which is hard to overshadow, is that he's walking into the chilly water without any hesitation whatsoever. It's like the cold doesn't impact him. Like he has a layer of blubber over his body.

Although, I know that's not true. I don't think that man has *any* body fat.

Suddenly, Matt dives forward, his entire body disappearing under the placid, sparkling water. I wait for him to come up with bated breath. When he emerges, breaking the surface of the water, it's just his head.

"Woo! That's fucking cold!" he cries out, shaking the water out of his hair like a wet dog.

I laugh. "You're not selling it!"

"A good kinda cold!" he calls back to me. "Toss me the soap, would you?"

I lob the soap on a rope toward Matt. He manages to catch it midair with a triumphant, "Ha-ha!"

For a few moments, I watch him lather his arms and chest. This is like porn for me. I'm objectifying the poor man, but I can't help it, he's so—

Matt's eyes meet mine, catching me red-handed as I stare at him. "So, are you coming in or are you too chicken?"

I gape. "I'm not *chicken*."

"That's why you haven't even taken off your sweater?"

My mouth stays hung open as I attempt to figure out something to say. There's no use arguing. I either do it, or I don't. And . . . I don't want Matt to think of me any differently. He's already taken such a chance by supporting me when the rest of Naknek wishes me dead.

Naknek . . . more like Naked.

Wait until Sarah hears about this.

"Fine. But turn around. I don't want you . . . *yeah*."

Matt holds his hands up out of the water. "Of course,

Naked in Naknek

wouldn't dream of watching." He turns around to face the open expanse of water.

As I undress, I keep my eyes on him, waiting for him to take even a little look over his shoulder at me, which he doesn't. Because of course, he's a perfect fucking gentleman. Why does he have to be so perfect? He's hot, he's nice, he's smart. And he's *respectful*. That's a quadrangle you never get in Los Angeles.

I get down to my bra and underwear. I could go in with them on and it'd be okay, though I wouldn't be able to wear them under my clothes. But I'm out here in some of the most untamed land in the world. It wouldn't be right not to match it with my own nakedness. First, I swing the bra off. Then, let my underwear slide to the ground. I pile it up on a rock not nearly as nicely as Matt has his organized. I'm too nervous to fold my clothes properly.

"You still there? Or did you run away?" Matt calls out.

"I'm here!" I peep, wrapping my arms over my chest. It's cold out and the sun isn't quite up. It's still early morning, but the midnight sun makes it feel like the middle of the day.

"Don't be tentative about it, okay? You just gotta go in all at once or else you're going to change your mind."

I go up to the water's edge. He's right. Just my toes feeling the frigid water makes me want to run the other way. "If I freeze to death, it's your fault."

"I'll carry your death on my conscience forever. But I promise I would never let that happen."

How would he never let that happen? He'd wrap me up in all the blankets and towels he could possibly find, then wrap me in his big arms, press me up to his warm chest and hold me until my lips turned from blue to pink again?

I don't hate that idea.

At his advice, I rip off the coldness like a band-aid, running into the water and letting myself be consumed by the frigid temperature before my brain catches up. I dive under the water, letting it baptize and welcome me into its chilling embrace.

It's a shock to my system, so when I emerge, I gasp for air, my eyes wide, and my body fully awake. "Holy shit! I did it!"

"You did!"

My eyes find Matt's as I catch my breath. It's impossible not to smile, though my body is still in shock. "It's fucking cold!"

Matt laughs and nods. "You got that right!"

I can breathe here. Actually breathe here. Whether it's the freshness of the air and the distance from LA smog or the endlessness of the sky, I can't be sure. But something about Alaska has captured my heart. It's a place I won't easily forget.

With people I won't easily forget either.

There's a splash in the water, and I let my feet drop to the silty riverbed as I look up. The soap floats next to me, its rope trailing in the water behind it. I grab it, glancing over at Matt. "Thanks."

He moves toward the shore, water up to his neck. "Lather up, rinse, and come on out. If you stay out here too long, you'll get hypothermia."

As he goes, I wash. I keep myself under the water while

Naked in Naknek

I wash, unwilling to expose myself to the cold air. When I'm done, I wriggle back toward the shore. Matt has already toweled off and pulled his sweater and boxers back on. But he pauses to hold out a towel for me.

"Don't worry," he says, then cinches his eyes together. "I won't look."

I'm too cold to have the wherewithal to worry. I emerge from the water and sprint toward the towel, letting the terry cloth envelop me in a semblance of warmth.

However, it's Matt's arms around me that really do the trick. It feels like we've done this a million times. I fit into his chest perfectly and his warmth settles into my skin like I've known it for years. I resist the urge to burrow into his chest further. That would cross a line.

But he doesn't let go.

"You surprise me, Lillian," Matt says.

I look up at him, a flush creeping onto my cheeks as our eyes meet.

He smiles. "Every time I think you're finally going to say 'no,' you say 'yes.'"

"Is this all some big hazing ritual?" I ask with a cheeky lilt.

"No, not at all," Matt answers. He rubs the towel over my arms to dry me off, then lets me go, much to my disappointment. We both go about putting on our clothes, me wrapping my hair in the towel, gratefully burrowing into my sweater, eager to get back to the boat.

Matt speaks as we dress. "I'm just surprised. You know, people around here don't like when things are different. I guess I expect, more often than not, people to stick to what they know. And when they're met with something strange to them, or out of their comfort zone, they run away from it rather than just . . . try it on for size." A moment passes. "I admire you for that."

"Admire? That's silly. I'm just . . ." I shake my head, zipping up my sweater with finality. "Just doing my best to be respectful."

"By agreeing to wash in a river with a man you barely know?" Matt teases.

"Not *barely*," I correct.

Matt pauses. The corners of his eyes soften, a look of serenity overtaking his face. "No, you're right. Not barely."

∽

WHEN WE ARRIVE BACK in Naknek, it's almost noon. I mention I'm going to do some work the rest of the day, but not before I make some pancakes with the fresh blueberries we picked yesterday, hoping Matt will invite himself over.

He does not, because of course he doesn't. He's a gentleman. But I'm not going to beg him to spend more time with me after overnighting on the boat together.

Still, the rest of the day I have a distant ache in my chest. For *Matt*. Not even my text exchange with Sarah can fill the void.

I put the Naked in Naknek today.

Her response is quick, but disappointing.

!!!?? crazy day 2day, phone call SOON

Sarah's busy. I can't blame her. But being up here is so

isolating sometimes. And I haven't had a crush in *years*. I forgot how preoccupying they are.

I like being around Matt more than I like being apart, which is unusual. I expected my time in Naknek to be solitary other than my work. Now, though, when things get dull and I'm left with my thoughts, my mind turns toward Matt.

Matt. Fisherman Matt. Whose last name I don't even know, do I? This would be a recipe for disaster for the old Lillian.

But for the new Lillian, because *yes*, there's a new side of me being born the longer I spend here in Naknek— I'm just living my life. One moment at a time.

In the evening, as I try to muster the strength to microwave a frozen meal, there's a knock at the door. Without a peephole, I peek through the front window. My heart leaps into my throat when I see Matt. And he's looking right at me as if he knew I'd check the window before opening the door.

He smiles, like he's got citrus candy on his tongue, his eyes pinching closed.

I go to the door to let him in. "Well, hello!"

Matt's brown eyes widen. "Hi, yeah, I just—um—" He glances into the cabin. "Have you had dinner?"

My heart thuds. Is he about to ask me on a date? Did he feel me watching him in all his naked glory? Does he know I'm foaming at the mouth for him? "I was just about to make something," I say.

A smile of relief spreads over his face. "Oh, good. *Good.* Caught you just in time then." He lifts his thumb, gestures toward the truck. "I'm meeting the guys for some food. You want to come?"

Not a date. A night with the guys. I'm one of the guys. Which would be flattering if I didn't want to be one of the guys, but the *only* girl.

Still, though. Being out with Matt is better than being alone with my microwave dinner. "Would they be okay with that?"

Matt shrugs. "I don't give a shit. I want you to come."

My heart swells. Stupid heart. You've just basically been called "one of the guys," and you're still swooning?

And yet, I can't resist. "Let me get my purse."

Dammit.

～

THE SEA WITCH has a different energy at night. It's not necessarily busier. Just messier. Like a bar more than a diner. The communal table fills up bit by bit as the night goes on. The guys know everyone, and, surprisingly, I know *most* everyone. Or at least have crossed paths with a lot of them. They give me the side-eye and try to ignore me, but Matt doesn't let me go unnoticed.

"Marina, have you met Lillian?" he says when the female captain posts up a few people down.

Marina pauses, her beer lifted halfway to her mouth. Her eyes flick from me to Matt and back. A smile spreads over her face. "I've had the pleasure."

I hold back a giddy laugh. Maybe I'm not as much of an outsider as I thought.

"Good to see you," she says, holding her beer out toward me.

"Good to see you too, Marina."

Marina takes a sip of her drink. "How's Gwen been? I haven't had a chance to get to the Hitch the past couple days."

Matt frowns. "You know you could just text her and ask."

In the dark lighting, it's hard to tell for sure, but I think Marina's blushing. "I know, I could, but I don't want to bother her. She's so busy with everything."

I glance at Matt to see if he sees what I see. Marina's nervous. Bashfully so.

I think she has a bit of a crush.

Matt, though, seems unfazed by it. "She's doing fine, but I'm sure she'd love to hear from you."

Marina's eyes brighten. "You think?"

"Absolutely. Gwen loves keeping up with everyone."

Marina's smile falters. "Right. 'Course she does." She looks askance at me and then lifts her hand. "Don't let me keep you." She gets up from her recently claimed spot and disappears into the din of the Sea Witch.

"You totally broke her heart," I murmur to him.

He scoffs. "What are you talking about?"

I decide not to push it. I don't know these people that well. I shouldn't assume anything. However, people are people wherever you go. If someone asked me to bet money on Marina's feelings, I would. "Nothing, I just thought . . . well, never mind."

Matt leans in a little closer, placing his hand on the bench behind me. "You sure?"

His hand is so close to me that if I lean back, his hand might brush up against my tailbone. And his face is so close to mine that a few inches of movement would result in a kiss.

I draw away before anything can happen. "Yeah, it's nothing."

One of the guys, Lil. You're just one of the guys.

Speaking of the guys, Tuma is as friendly as he has been since we met. And Jesse, while preserving his hardened exterior, isn't treating me with the same scorn he used to. I mean, he may not be starting conversations, but he's not being actively rude. I'll take that as a win.

Tuma licks a splotch of ketchup off his thumb, then asks Matt, "You still cool with us flying with you for No-See-Um?"

Matt doesn't miss a beat, giving his answer as he picks up his beer and swigs, "Obviously."

"No-See-Um?" I interject looking between Tuma and Matt.

Matt shifts on the bench and it creaks. "Festival in Dillingham. Named after those tiny bugs that end up biting you before you can see 'um. That's where the name comes from."

Now that he mentions it, I've felt bites but haven't seen too many mosquitoes.

"And," Matt goes on, "that's where the fish-filleting contest is."

"Oh, yeah! The competition your wife is the champion

of," I say, snapping my fingers at the memory of that conversation.

Tuma shakes his finger in the air. "Not champion. *Reigning queen*. I have to correct you because she will correct you, and I'd rather you hear it from me."

"Because he's nicer," Jesse says.

Tuma elbows Jesse in the side. "My wife is *nice*."

"To you," Jesse spits in return. "She'd slice me up with an ulu faster than she can fillet a salmon if I say the wrong thing."

"Have you ever considered you deserve it?" Matt heaps on his own insult to the pile.

Jesse grits his teeth toward his brother. "Bite me."

I laugh into my hand. Are all little siblings like this? I bet Sarah and Jesse would have a field day together. They'd either tear each other's heads off or be a duo as dynamic as Team Rocket from *Pokémon*. "What's an ulu?" I ask.

"So many questions," Jesse responds.

"I'm curious! So what?"

His lips twitch. Is that a smile? Did I make the ice king *smile*?

I'm not the only one who notices. Matt does too. His hand lands against my thigh, and he squeezes it. My stomach swoops in response. He's making it difficult to keep my feelings at bay.

Tuma, thankfully, circles back to the subject at hand. "It's a traditional Alaskan knife with a curved blade. It's perfect for filleting fish and dressing other animals, but you can use it for other stuff too."

"Tuma gives great haircuts," Matt says.

I laugh.

Jesse gives a small shake of his head. "He's being serious."

My jaw falls open, and my eyes fly toward Tuma. The Aleut man gives a small shrug. "I'm still learning how to do layers," he says as if it's not impressive enough he cuts hair with something other than shears.

Our conversation is interrupted when a bottle lands harshly at the end of the table, and a man with a pompous chest and scratchy-looking facial hair looms over us. "I'm going out for Dolly Varden tomorrow."

Matt chuckles. "How about a 'hello,' Lefty?"

Lefty's lip curls as he appraises Matt and then me. "Been hearing you've been taking this one out on your boat."

"This one has a name, *and* she's right here. So, you can be an adult and treat her with some respect," Matt says without batting an eye.

I don't demure except wanting to giggle and flush at Matt's defense of me. "Lillian," I say, holding out my hand to Lefty.

He isn't happy about shaking my hand, but he does it. And when his hand retreats, he wipes it on his pant leg. Wow. "You two going out tomorrow? I could use some extra hands."

"Are you trying to poach my crew?" Matt balks, leaning his forearms on the table, his hands turning to fists.

"You've been out doing God knows what with Little Miss Climate Change," Lefty says with a sneer. "You're not using your men. They need to eat, don't they? And they don't make money when you're off doing . . . whatever you're doing out there."

"Hold on," I interrupt. "What do you think we're doing out there?"

Lefty scoffs. "I know what it means when you take a woman out on your boat and don't come back until the next day. Wasn't born yesterday."

"It's not like that," Matt says, calm, but agitated. "She's working."

"Sure, she is," Lefty says under his breath.

Suddenly, Matt gets up from his seat and squares up with Lefty. "You want to say that a bit louder?"

My eyes are so wide they might fall out of my skull. I glance at Tuma who is just as surprised, and Jesse, whose hand is flat on the table, no doubt ready to launch himself up to intercede if he must.

"Oh, come on, Benton, you're being a drama queen," Lefty says, smacking the back of his hand against Matt's chest.

"Look, Lefty, you're the last one I'm gonna let get away with being a fucking jagoff about her, because she's trying to help us."

Lefty groans. "That's what they all say. You know how they are."

"I do! Because I've had a firsthand account of what she's doing. She's smart. She'd run circles around all of us. And she cares, she's a—Lillian's a good person. And you can take that back to your cronies," Matt says, tossing his hand down toward one of the other communal tables.

When Lefty says nothing, Matt turns back to us. "We'll go out tomorrow for Dolly Varden. On *my* boat."

"Ah, dammit, Matt, don't be spiteful!" Lefty exclaims.

"And you—" Matt points a finger at me, his fiery gaze meeting mine. "You're coming with us."

I realize the entire diner is quiet. They're listening in, wondering what kind of drama the *outsider* is causing. "A-are you sure?"

Matt scrubs his hand down the lower part of his face and doubles down with a firm nod. "Yeah. Yeah, I am."

If I wasn't just one of the guys, I'd leap up and kiss this man. In fact, I'm not convinced I can resist kissing him much longer.

Chapter 19

You Don't Have to Apologize

LILLIAN

Despite how things went down last night, there is a good energy going out on the water today. We go up the Kvichak, the same river I ran right into the bear. Great for me because I need to recollect my samples. We do that at the mouth of the river, then go farther down the Kvichak, so the guys can put out their nets.

Dolly Varden trout aren't actually *trout*. They're a type of char. They're named for their pink underbelly, which is comparable to a colorful cloth from the nineteenth century of the same name. Funny how things like that stick.

Overhead, a bald eagle splays its wings, majestic and

terrifying, its talons tucked under itself, waiting to strike food in the water.

I write in my notebook as I watch the surroundings, keeping my eyes peeled for any anomalies in the landscape. Beyond the tree line, rolling hills and tundra stretch out, covered in a tapestry of mosses, lichens, and dappled with colorful wildflowers. *Fireweed.* In the distance, the rugged peaks of the Alaska Range rise, their snow-capped summits staggering.

It's heartbreaking that a place as remote as this, seemingly untouched, is impacted by humans the way it is. It's not just the way fishing has affected the fish populations. It's corporate greed, rising temperatures, pollution; the list goes on and on. I wish it didn't.

If only the residents could see how I'm trying to *protect* all of this.

"Hey."

I look up to Matt, who's standing at the top of the ladder to the flybridge. I put down my pen, smiling. "Hey. Everything okay?"

Matt sighs, leaning on the low flybridge wall. "I just feel like I should apologize for yesterday."

"Apologize? What for?"

Matt ducks his chin, looking away from me. "I'm not that kind of guy. You know? I don't start fights or anything like that."

I pause, trying to figure out the correct tack to take. "You don't have to apologize. You were defending me."

"I know, but I could have kept my temper, I just—" He stops again. "Fuck, I don't know. I'm just sick of their ignorance. And it's one thing to be ignorant, but another to be so fucking aggressive about it. And then to imply you and I are—or that *you* are . . . yeah."

I swallow. Lefty did imply about the type of woman I am. I didn't say anything in the moment because it was so shocking. "I know myself and my integrity. What he says or thinks doesn't really matter to me."

Matt's forehead wrinkles. "Are you sure, Lillian? Don't put on a smile just to make me feel better."

"I'm not trying to make you feel better. I'm just telling you who I am," I say with a shrug. "The only person whose opinion I really value around here is yours."

His eyes widen.

"And mine," I correct. "Of course."

Matt ducks his head and laughs. "Of course."

Except, I do care about what he thinks of me because I have a high opinion of him. Sarah would have a field day with me. I'm not one to let my hormones drive my actions, but Matt brings it out in me.

It's not just biology, not just chemistry. It's emotional. I want to be closer to him, open my heart, and let myself be vulnerable. He proved last night he's willing to step up and protect me, and I want to do the same for him.

Matt has made me feel worthy of his attention, and now, I'd like to be worthy with benefits.

"I think you're pretty damn brave," Matt says.

I let out a nervous laugh. "Oh? I'm not really."

"You are though. You know that people don't like that you're here—"

"Okay, you don't need to rub it in."

Matt grabs my knee. "Not at all my point."

His touch makes me hot. I hope it's not showing.

Matt's mouth tips up in a soft smile. "What I mean, is—"

Suddenly, there's a splashing sound down below, the rumbling of feet, and a whole lot of cursing.

"What the—" Matt turns.

Before he can finish, there's a sound like an antique car horn. Except to the trained ear, it's unmistakable. Hell, even the untrained ear. If you're from coastal California, you know exactly what that sound is.

A seal.

"Shit," Matt mutters. He disappears down the ladder, and I scramble after him.

Tuma and Jesse are bent over the stern of the boat. Their argument is quick and aggravated, and I can't make heads or tails of what they're saying. I rush to the railing next to Matt and look down into the water.

There's a harbor seal trapped in the net below, amongst a bevy of fish. As it flounders and thrashes, red pools out into the water. At first, I think it's because the seal is hurt, but then I realize the blood is coming from the fish. The seal was feasting and got caught in the net. Its big black eyes shine up at me.

"Oh, poor thing," I say, looking for a way to help.

Jesse lets out a dark laugh. "Poor thing? More like a pest."

I shoot him a look, but he's moved on, focusing on his older brother.

"You want to do it, or should I?" he asks.

"I . . ." Matt stops, unsure. A rarity for him.

Jesse throws his hands up and heads toward the wheelhouse door. "I'll get the gun."

I nearly jump out of my skin. "The *gun?*"

"They can ruin an entire catch in record time," Tuma says, his voice kind but firm. "It already has."

They've done this before.

"You'll have to fix the net anyway. Why would you kill it, if you can—"

"It's the difference between fixing a net and having to make a completely new one," Matt interrupts. "We'll have to cut the seal out of the net to free him."

I grab onto the edge of the boat, my head growing light. Matt and Tuma work to winch the net up toward the deck. As the net lifts from the water, the seal squirms more, trapped in the netting. The seal keens. A painful sound.

Jesse barrels back onto the deck with a rifle in his hand like it's the most normal thing in the world.

Tears spring from my eyes. "Matt! Matt, you can't kill it," I say. I grab onto his arm, even though he's in the middle of trying to pull the net up. I can't let him kill the seal. I won't be able to live with myself.

Matt looks down at me, shaking his head. "It's what we do, Lillian. There are thousands of harbor seals."

"It doesn't matter. I mean, *look* at him," I say, wiping at my face as I try to keep my composure. The thought of hearing the gun go off followed by the stillness of the water is too much for me to bear. I gesture toward the net where the seal wallows, slippery and desperate to free himself. "He's struggling. He's in pain. You can't just—"

"Put him out of his misery then," Jesse says from behind me. The click of the gun chamber is a slap to my face.

"Matt, please." I grip his arm tighter. "Please don't. I'm begging. I'll buy you a new net. I don't care what it costs, but you can't. You just *can't* kill him." I'm sobbing now. I can't help it. The seal is innocent. It's just trying to protect itself.

Matt stares at me and says nothing, his forehead wrinkled in the middle and lips pursed.

Jesse rumbles up beside me, pointing the gun at the seal at such a close range I wonder if the seal knows what's about to happen.

"Oh, my god. No, no, no, please don't," I beg, too afraid to reach out to Jesse and stop him. I turn away, burying my face in my hands. I can't watch. But I hear the spring of the trigger, the beginning of it being pulled back.

"*Wait*," Matt speaks up, cutting through everything.

I turn in time to see Matt's hand on the barrel of the gun, guiding it downward.

"Are you crazy, dude?" Jesse says.

Matt doesn't reply, instead going toward the winched net. Tuma pulls Jesse back and mutters, "Just let him do it."

"Let him lose hundreds of dollars for a fucking seal?" Jesse retorts. "For a fucking—" His eyes land on me, practically black thanks to how dilated his pupils are from the intense situation.

"I'll pay," I say again, strangled.

"Tuma! Help me out," Matt cries out from the stern. There's a flash of silver in his hand, a knife.

Naked in Naknek

Tuma looks between Jesse and me before rushing to help Matt.

Jesse stares me down like he could incinerate me where I stand.

"I'll pay," I say again. "I promise, I'll—"

"This is why we don't have women on boats," Jesse interrupts, his fist tight on the barrel of the gun. "Bad fucking luck."

I swallow. I don't have it in me to argue with him.

Jesse blows past me, back into the wheelhouse, his feet thudding in time with my heart.

With him out of the way, I get a better look at what Matt and Tuma are doing. They are bent over the railing as close to the net as they can get. Tuma is doing his best to hold tight to the flopping, flummoxing seal.

Matt stops for a moment, places his blade between his teeth, and rolls up the sleeves of his sweater. Then, he tries again. "Easy, *easy*," Matt says in a kind, husky voice to the seal. "You're making this harder on all of us."

I want to interject and see if I can help, but I know I'll just be in the way.

The seal is heaving, tiring out the more he thrashes. Tuma and Matt stay the course, slicing the net until the seal comes free.

I glance over the side of the boat, watching half-eaten fish bob in the current. Hard to believe one seal can do so much damage.

"That's it. I'm helping you. Don't freak out, okay?" Matt coos sweetly to the seal.

More tears well in my eyes. I knew he had a good heart.

I just knew it. I probably shouldn't judge him for the work he has to do on the boat, but I can't let an innocent animal die for the sake of a net. That's just not me.

I don't think it's really Matt either.

"Careful," Tuma says.

The seal brays and Matt swears. He lifts his knife, a glint of red on the end. "I didn't mean to."

"Just a nick. Keep going," Tuma encourages.

Matt huffs, pausing long enough to get his bearings before working the net again.

Watching them work is a beautiful thing. Together, they are a dynamic duo. But their strength, tenacity, and focus give me a new appreciation of what the fishermen in Alaska are capable of.

I'm suddenly mortified that I begged them to free the seal when I truly don't understand the gravity of what they do.

Not at all.

Matt and Tuma lurch back, and moments later there's a splash. When they step back from the net, it's empty.

Empty and destroyed. It's been shredded to pieces.

Tuma turns to look at me, his lips strained as he attempts something like a smile. Matt leans over the stern of the boat and exhales. "Go check on Jesse," he tells Tuma.

Without another word, Tuma rushes past me and into the wheelhouse, leaving Matt and me alone on the deck.

Matt's left examining what's left of his net. And I'm left to examine the carnage I've caused.

I move tentatively beside him. "Shit. That was terrifying."

Matt glances at me, a distant look in his eye that he tries to veil with a smile. The smile, though, doesn't reach his eyes. "Yeah, it happens."

"I'm sorry."

"It's not your fault."

"It is, I shouldn't have—you didn't—" I blink, another tear rushing down my face. "I should have let you do your job. I should have just let you."

Matt doesn't respond for a long moment. "Yeah. You probably should have."

The Alaskan wilderness is so quiet, interrupted only by the water lapping at the hull.

"But I don't blame you," he says quietly.

"You don't have to say that."

"I don't. It's never pleasant killing a seal."

I wonder how many times he's done it to protect his nets. "I meant what I said. I'll pay for the new net."

"I won't ask you to do that."

"It's my fault."

"It's your fault you protected the life of an animal? Am I supposed to punish you for that? When you did the right thing?" Matt's nostrils flare. He taps his chest. "The *right* thing."

I can't tell if he's mad at me. Everything is so tense and confusing that I wish I could go back to my cabin and hide.

Matt looks down at his feet. "You're looking at me different."

I shake my head. "No, Matt. No. Look at me."

He doesn't.

I take matters into my own hands, grabbing his arm and pulling him closer. "*Matt.*"

He gives into my plea, his gaze full of anguish. "I shouldn't have gotten involved because no one knows better about what is happening here than you all. Your way of life is different than mine, but I respect it, and I should know when to step back and—" My throat constricts. If I hadn't interceded, the seal would be dead. And it would have felt wrong, and I would have had to live with the guilt.

But this isn't my world.

Matt places his hand over mine, his touch grounding. "It's never something I want to do, I promise."

"You're just trying to survive. I understand."

Matt's expression softens enough that he doesn't seem to be in pain. "It didn't used to be so hard."

"It won't be forever, I promise. That's my promise to you, Matt." I mean it with every fiber of my being. My work here in Alaska will mean nothing if the change I bring doesn't reach those who need it most. "Please believe me."

His fingers caress mine. "I do."

My lips lift in one of the most difficult smiles I've ever given.

Matt looks away. "I should go check on Jesse and Tuma."

I let him go, though it's the last thing I want to do. Alone on the deck, I take stock of my topsy-turvy emotions. I lean on the railing and look out at the expansive tundra.

I have to get this right. For Matt's sake.

Chapter 20

Two Can Play at This Game

MATTHEW

With a deep breath, I force myself out of the cab and go round to the truck bed to retrieve the bags of groceries. Gwen usually keeps an eye on dad, making sure he has what he needs. Jesse and I help out when we can, especially when the season is slow. The man is only in his late fifties, but he went from being taken care of by his mother to being taken care of by *our* mother. And since she passed, he's been helpless and drunk more than he's sober.

The house where we grew up has seen better days. The wooden boards have turned silver with patina and the metal roof has taken a beating from storms over the years. Wild grass has nearly taken over the path to the front door and could stand to be trimmed back. Still,

Naked in Naknek

through everything, it sits proud against the rugged, windswept plain.

Dad's door is unlocked when I go to put my key in. I tell him every time he's got to keep it locked. The wildlife around here is unpredictable. Today, though, I'm trying to keep the peace. Get in, get out. No problems.

He's sitting in his usual chair in front of the television, watching a baseball game with the volume too loud.

"Hey, Dad," I say as innocuously as possible.

He glances at me and grunts. Better than the silence I normally get when I walk in.

"Got your groceries," I say as I lumber into the kitchen, which is only separated from the living room by the long island where we used to sit for breakfast as kids.

The house smells like cigarettes and body odor. Needs more than a deep clean. Needs to start from scratch. New paint, new carpets, the works.

I start unloading the grocery bags. Frozen dinners, canned vegetables and soups, and snacks. A fifth of whiskey. I can't convince Gwen to stop buying him the stuff because she doesn't like upsetting him. Dad doesn't go at her like he does Jesse and me, probably because she's a girl, but she's always been sensitive to his disappointment.

The room is quiet, other than the rumbling of an announcer on television. Halfway through my unpacking, I hear the thump of his recliner footrest coming down and the squeaking rock of the chair's axis. The voices on the television go mute. I pretend not to notice.

"Need to talk to you," Dad grumbles, his voice gravelly. Probably hasn't said a word all day.

"'Bout what?" I ask, balling up the plastic grocery bag and putting it under the sink for later.

"Don't play dumb."

I lean back against the sink, facing my father. He's at the bar, already eyeing the bottle of amber liquid. Behind him, the baseball game still plays without sound. "Say what you mean, Dad. Gotta be specific."

He scratches his cheek, his beard overrun and probably unwashed. Gwen usually can cajole him into a shower. If I tried that, he'd bite my head off. "You're thinking with your dick."

I laugh. "Okay, well, this has been fun, but—"

"Cutting up a net. What the hell were you thinking?" Dad asks, shaking his head.

"My boat, my rules," I say. "You don't have to worry about that anymore."

Dad's chin dips. I know I've wounded him. He's not too old to be out on the water the way his buddies are. He just doesn't have a grip on things since Mom died. "I taught you better than that," he says, hardening his gaze on me.

I shake my head. "Taught me differently, that's all."

Dad's nostrils flare. Looks exactly like Jesse when he does that. "You're smart, Matt. Smarter than this."

Dad doesn't call me smart. He thinks the dwindling salmon numbers are my own fault. That I'm not as good of a fisherman as he is. Or was. It's an insult to himself, really. He's the one who taught me everything I know. No matter how many times I tell him I have better numbers than most, he's always looking for something to be disappointed about.

"She's using you," Dad says.

I scoff. "For what?"

"For her own personal gain! You don't know what these people are like."

"And you do?"

He screws his lips up in aggravation. "Been around a lot longer than you, and don't you forget it."

"She's a scientist, Dad. She's not a politician or a lobbyist or—"

"She has an agenda!" Dad shouts, spittle flying from his mouth. It's zero to sixty with him. "She wants to change our way of life because it doesn't suit—"

Two can play at this game. "Have you even spoken to her?"

"I *have*, actually."

I roll my eyes. "Other than cornering her outside of Half-Hitch?"

He hesitates. "I didn't *corner* her."

I laugh, looking down at the tips of my boots. "You're so fucking lost, Dad."

"You're the one who's—"

"You haven't been out there the past two seasons," I say. "You have no fucking concept of what's going on out there."

Dad narrows his eyes. "Don't talk to me like I'm an idiot. I've been alive a helluva lot longer than you and—"

"You don't—"

Dad steamrolls me, doesn't stop to let me get another word in, just clenches his teeth and goes on, "*I've been around a lot longer than you,* and I won't stand to be talked to like I don't know what I'm talking about!"

I rub my hands over my eyes.

"You don't waste nets for a fucking seal! And I know you did it to get into that girl's pants."

I push up from the counter, holding my ground. "Don't you fucking talk about her like that!"

"I'll talk however I fucking like! I'm your father. You're the one who has to watch your mouth."

"Just because you don't understand what she's doing doesn't mean—"

Dad waves his hand through the air. "Gah! It's all bullshit."

It's like talking to a brick wall with him.

"We don't need people who don't know a thing about us coming in here and telling us what we're doing wrong. You think things are tough now? You just wait until she brings her research back to California. That's when the real shitstorm begins."

I don't say anything. I don't know enough about what Lillian has done or discovered to throw any information back at him with any sort of mettle. I don't have hard facts or proof that I can trust her.

But I haven't forgotten her promise. Her hand on my arm. Her tear-stained cheeks. Our eyes *locked*.

None of that is proof of anything, and yet, I can't shake the feeling I can trust her. The way she approaches Bristol Bay with an open heart—despite having every reason to close it—inspires me to do the same for her.

"You don't know her, Matt," Dad goes on, his voice softening. "You think you do because you're thinking with—"

"Maybe the way things are around here doesn't work anymore," I say, lifting my chin. "Maybe they haven't for a long time."

Dad is silent, his lips forming a tight line and darkness clouding his hazel eyes. I said it to hurt him, and it worked. Nothing offends an Alaskan more than the suggestion we can't handle ourselves.

"We aren't immune to change, Dad," I say, trying to bring down the heat a little bit.

Dad shakes his head slightly, then swipes the bottle of whiskey off the counter before returning to his seat. He kicks the footrest up again, then cracks open the bottle. He pours it straight into the glass on the side table. Pours far too much, if you ask me.

Dad's the old way of doing things. No change. No nothing.

He unmutes the game and doesn't give me a second look. Conversation over.

Fine with me.

∼

FAT FRED'S is quiet tonight. I nurse my beer at the bar. People leave me alone. Maybe it's because I'm acting standoffish. Or maybe it's because they're tired of me being an apologist for the scientist they abhor so much.

I finish my third beer, starting to get a little buzzy and

sparkly in the head. Fred catches my eye from behind the bar, and I lift my finger for another.

Maybe I'm an idiot for being open to what Lillian has to offer. She's convinced me she can help, and I've been swayed. If she needs a champion, it'll be me. And if I'm made a fool for it, so be it.

"All by your lonesome tonight?" Ian asks, bellying up next to me at the bar.

I glance at Ian. "Something like that."

Ian grabs the stool beside me and yanks it out to take a seat. He doesn't say anything more, thank God. The company is nice, but I don't need the chitchat.

Fred comes back with my beer, and Ian tells him he'll have the same.

I have to admit, it's nice not to be alone. I came here after that awful conversation with my dad and haven't said a word to anyone, other than to order my beer. I've been running circles in my brain, trying to make sense of how I feel. Except I'm all knotted up like a necklace, not sure how to untangle the chain.

"Heard about your net," Ian mutters.

I let out a bitter laugh, looking into the head of my beer, the white cream interrupted by popping carbonation. "The whole town has heard."

"Yeah, well, it's not often someone goes soft on a seal," Ian says with a chuckle.

"I'm not soft," I reply, sounding more juvenile than I'd like. "I made a choice."

Ian nods. "That you did."

Naked in Naknek

His beer arrives, and we drink for a bit without interruption.

"Your brother's telling everyone you've turned to the dark side," Ian says eventually. I can tell by his tone that he finds Jesse's claim as funny as I do.

"Jesse is an idiot."

"We all are sometimes."

I reposition myself, elbow on the bar, looking over at Ian. "Things are changing around here. You have to admit that."

"I know, mate, I know. But I also know it's best to keep your head down and not make a stink, unless you want to become subject to the rumor mill." An incredulous hum rumbles in his chest. "Then again, it took me years to be accepted and fly under the radar after I got here."

"I remember that," I say, thinking back to Ian's arrival in Naknek. I heard his accent for the first time when I was with my mom at the grocery store. I couldn't believe people actually talked like that off of the television.

Ian looks around, as if trying not to be overheard. "Listen, I'm with you, mate. I think people are coming down too hard on her."

This is something he won't say in the public forum. He's loaning me his solidarity in private, and that's as much as I'll get. Still, it's good to know I'm not the only one who sees the good that Lillian can do.

"But we don't *really* know what she's all about at the end of the day."

"No one's given her a chance to explain," I say defensively.

"You have. Has she explained it to you?"

I divert my gaze to my beer. "No. Not exactly. But I haven't really asked."

Ian chuckles. "Hard to focus on science when you're soft on her."

"I'm not—" I stop right there.

Yes, I obviously am.

"I'd never begrudge you your feelings, Matt. You just have to make a decision whether you're going to let it eat you alive that people are talking about her, or if you're going to follow your gut," Ian offers. "And maybe your heart too."

I grimace. "Corny ass."

Ian throws his head back with a big, boisterous laugh that has some people glancing our way. "If that's the worst thing I am, I'm alright with that."

I drum my fingers on the bar. "It'll probably get worse if we don't let anything change, right?"

"Probably. Things don't change if nothing changes." Ian gives me a solemn smile. "But you're not doing anything being angry in the corner by yourself. You're getting angry because you feel like you're on fire, and no one is willing to join you. And hell, why would we? We've got our own shit to worry about. We can't afford to be on fire, too."

I slump forward onto the bar. "So, what the hell am I supposed to do, Ian?"

Ian puts his hand on my back and leans closer, more like a father than my own. "You worry about *your* own shit."

"I'm not just going to bend to Jesse's will, because—"

"I don't mean that. Don't mean fishing. Forget about fishing." Ian's eyes find mine. "What aren't you taking care of, Matt?" He extends a finger and points toward my chest. "What aren't *you* taking care of?"

If I strip away all the logic, all the frustration over my fellow fishermen and their lack of open-mindedness, I'm left with Lillian. Left with her pretty smile and wonder-filled eyes. My heart swells with every thought of her. She's not just a scientist to me; she's not just an outsider.

She's Lillian. And I want to be closer to her.

"You get what I'm saying? Go for what *you* want."

Chapter 21

I Think You Look Perfect

LILLIAN

It's been a few days since I've been out in the field. A few days since I've left the cabin, honestly. I'm running low on supplies and need to make a run this afternoon.

But after the seal incident, I'm not sure I want to show my face around town. I don't want people looking at me sideways, not that they haven't been already. But it feels different now that I don't have Matt on my side.

I don't know that for sure. However, we haven't spoken since, and the boat ride from the Kvichak was long and arduously quiet.

Without Matt, the road to the end of my research trip is going to be long and lonely. I can handle it. At least I think

I can. But the idea of staying in a town that hates me just for existing makes my chest hurt.

There's a knock at the door, and I jump. It's so quiet out here most of the time. Mostly, I hear the sounds of birds or tires driving down the gravel road.

I go to the window and peek tentatively through the curtain. I'm half-expecting pitchforks and torches.

Instead, I'm surprised to find Matt standing outside the door, holding a bouquet of flowers. He gives me a little wave through the glass, his smile a mixture of apology and hope.

I'm still in my pajamas and haven't showered yet, but I open the door anyway. "Hey, what's up?" It's hard to ignore that bouquet in his hands. Also, hard to ignore that he's wearing nice clothes. Not clothes he'd wear out on the water but a fancy pullover and khakis. I didn't even imagine he had khakis in his closet.

Matt swallows, then licks his lips. "These are for you," he says, holding the bouquet out to me.

I take the bundle of flowers. It's composed entirely of purple, yellow, blue, and white wildflowers. "Thank you. They're beautiful."

Matt slides his hands into his front pockets, evidently unsure what to do with them. "Um, I guess I'll just get to the point."

I hold my breath.

"Would you like to spend some time together that isn't research, or on the boat, or—" Matt closes his eyes, wincing. "Like a date. Not *like* a date, but an actual date. Would you like to go on a date with me?"

Something like helium fills my entire body, threatening to make me float away. I smile, not wasting time or mincing words. "I'd like that."

Matt smiles back. "Good. How about today?"

"Today?" I gape.

"Yeah, is that . . . I know you're not here for a long time, so no time like the present, right?"

I've been trying to use the fact I'll be leaving in a couple of months as inspiration to forget my crush on Matt. It's not easy since he regularly haunts my dreams and waking thoughts. However, not for a second do I consider saying no. "Seize the day," I say with a delicate lilt.

"Yeah, something like that."

A moment passes between us, our eyes locked. Instead of questions, there's the electric pulsing of potential between us. Creating sparks. Threatening to start a blaze. I pull my gaze away, so I don't get caught up in the moment. "So, today. Like now?"

"Sooner the better," he replies.

The man is going to make me pass out by being so sweet. "I'll have to take a shower and get changed first. Put on some makeup and—"

"I think you look perfect," Matt interrupts. The only reasonable thing a man should interrupt to say.

I curl my hand through my ponytail, unable to keep from blushing. "Well, I want to *feel* perfect too, then."

Matt lifts a hand. "Of course. You take however long you need. I'll be in the truck, and there's legitimately no rush. I could wait all day if I have to, and—" He stops, and I giggle. "If you can't tell, I haven't done this in a while."

"You're doing great," I reply. "If it's any consolation, no one's asked me this nicely ... ever."

"Well, that's unacceptable," he says.

"Points in your favor." The corners of his lips bend down, and he gives a thoughtful nod. "You know what? I'll take it."

"I won't keep you waiting too long," I say before disappearing back into the cabin with a final, parting look.

"I'm good at waiting. Take your time," he says before the door shuts.

When I'm alone, I bundle the flowers up to my face and inhale their brilliant, fresh scent. And every worry, every fear I had the past few days fades away to nothing.

~

I'VE NEVER TAKEN a plane ride on a first date, but then again, I've never dated a man with his own plane.

I didn't pack any date outfits. Why would I for a research trip? Not to mention, I don't really have date clothing for this type of climate. So, I opt for a green cashmere turtleneck and a pair of jeans, complemented by some heeled booties and a cream-colored vest.

We fly east to Brooks Camp, a part of Katmai National Park. The campground boasts a wooden boardwalk that overlooks the Brooks River and plenty of bear activity. And this time, there might be Grizzly bears. This detail freaked me out at first until Matt told me we'd be watching them from a viewing platform. I've had enough up close and personal with bears for a lifetime.

It's not particularly busy since the tourist season is having its last breath.

On the viewing platform, the sight is tremendous. We can see Brooks Falls, crystalline water cascading and churning into a froth of white foam against the rocks. Along the edge of the falls, two grizzlies stand poised, focused on the rushing water below as they wait for fish to leap.

"Alright, from here, they're amazing," I tell Matt.

He chuckles. "Yeah, because they look smaller from up here."

I punch him on the arm playfully, and he laughs some more. He keeps his hand on the place where my fist landed.

The conversation grows stilted. It's a little awkward, but in that pleasant first date way when you know you both want to say something, but you can't figure out how.

As if reading my mind, Matt says, "I'm sorry. I'm not good at this kind of thing."

"Dating?" I press.

Matt nods, his swooping dark hair falling over his forehead. He cleans up nice, that's for damn sure.

A tawny grizzly ducks its snout under the water and lifts its catch into the air, the scales of the fish glinting in the sunlight.

Matt moves his arm behind me and grabs onto the railing, boxing me in without pushing against me. "This okay?"

I look up at him, my head grazing his chest. "Yeah, more than."

Naked in Naknek

Matt's lucky he has facial hair so he can cover up his blushing cheeks, but this time his blush creeps up to his nose, making it impossible to ignore. "Um, you know, trying to make it feel a bit different than other times we've spent together."

"Well, the bear doesn't help set a different scene," I tease, leaning my back against his chest.

"Yeah, I'm realizing that."

He smells great. A pine and cypress cologne that's sharp and tingly in my nostrils. Heavenly.

"I have an idea of how to make it feel *really* different."

Matt lifts an eyebrow. "You do?"

He's so innocent. So, *so* innocent. "Yeah, I do." I lift a finger, encouraging him closer. "Let me whisper in your ear."

Matt warily leans down, and I rise onto my tiptoes. I bring my mouth toward his ear but divert my lips to land against his scruffy cheek.

He inhales in surprise but doesn't draw away until I do. I smile, biting down on my lower lip. "What do you think?"

He hesitates, and I wonder if I've crossed the line. "I have an idea too. To make it feel different."

I turn around in his arms, leaning up against the railing and tilting my head back for him. "You do?"

Matt's uneasiness fades into a smile. "Yeah, I think I do."

"Go for it, then."

I expect him to go in for a kiss, eager and insistent. Instead, he takes his time, cupping the lower part of my face, his thumb aligning with my chin. His warm gaze explores all my features for what feels like an eternity, but a welcomed one.

"I got cut off the other day when I was complimenting you."

My insides lock up. "Oh, you don't have to—"

He shakes his head. "I want to."

So, I'll let him.

"You're brave to fight for what you believe in. But you're also brave because you have hope."

"I do?"

Matt smiles and nods. "You do."

I never thought of myself like that. "I just want to leave the world a bit better than I found it."

"And that's another beautiful thing about you," Matt says.

And then, when I least expect it, he closes the gap between us, pressing his mouth to mine in that insistent kiss I had hoped for.

Matt tilts my head into his hand, letting his fingers skim through my hair.

My heart thuds in my chest and blood rushes to my face. Warmth brews in my belly. I cling tighter to him. If we weren't out in the open, I might not ever stop kissing him. How could I when my body feels infinite despite being enveloped in his arms?

The world doesn't stop. It keeps going.

Which is somehow more beautiful than if everything halted for us. We are a part of the landscape. Something that was meant to be. Something natural, innate, and

Naked in Naknek

important. We fit into the shape of things. From just one kiss, I feel that rightness inside me.

What's between us is unique. Is *rare*. And I am right to run toward it.

Matt ebbs the kiss, rolling his lips off mine, then pressing another kiss to my cheek and then my temple.

I wind my arms around him, pulling myself tight to him. He engulfs me in his strong arms, nuzzling the top of my head with his nose.

I haven't lost him. Far from it. Because with one kiss, I know.

Matt has chosen me. Against the odds.

And boy, are there a lot of odds.

∽

FOR DINNER, Matt flies us into the town of King Salmon, midway between Brooks Camp and Naknek. "One of my favorite places," he says when we approach Eddie's Fireplace Inn.

It feels a bit like a cluttered basement. Dimly lit with a warm nostalgic charm. There are vintage photos and art on the walls, a big yellow model plane in the corner of the ceiling, and leather seats line the bar and tables. There's even a wall of DVDs and VHSs. Who said physical media is dead?

You can feel the stories in this place, humming like the jukebox in the corner. Eddie's Fireplace Inn is indeed emblematic of the fireplace in the title. A place for people to gather, stay warm, trade stories, and enjoy the comfort and safety of the fire's embrace.

"Hope this is okay," Matt says as he pulls out a chair for me.

"Definitely. Reminds me a bit of home," I say. And it does.

"LA home or Michigan home?" Matt asks, a twinkle in his eye.

"Michigan, obviously," I reply as he settles into his seat across from me.

He grins. "Well, I'm glad to provide you with a piece of home away from home."

I scan the restaurant, taking in the people scattered around sharing drinks, conversations, and food. None of them know who either of us are. "Did you bring me here for dinner so we wouldn't see any people we know?"

Matt's brows rise. "I know plenty of people here," he says.

"You know what I mean. I don't blame you."

"I didn't bring you here to hide you, but I'd be lying if I didn't say it's a bit more private out here in King Salmon than back in Naknek," Matt concedes.

I pick at the corner of my nail. "You know, Matt, I like you. A lot."

"I like you too. That's why we're here, isn't it?"

I smile, though it's cut with a tinge of sadness. "You know how you say I'm brave? I think you're brave too. To support and help me, when people wish I wasn't getting in the way."

Matt watches me and waits for me to say more.

"You and I both see a lot of beauty in the world, despite its cruelty," I tell him, surprising myself with the poetry.

"I agree," he says. "That's another thing I admire about you."

"We're not talking about me. We're talking about you," I reply.

Matt scratches the back of his head. "Yeah, I hate that."

I grin. "You need to let me give you flowers, Matt. I already got mine."

We're interrupted by the server. I follow Matt's lead and order a beer to match his. When we're alone again, I continue. "You didn't have to stick your neck out for me."

He crosses his arms over his chest and leans back in his chair. He repositions his feet under the table close to mine. "I wanted to."

"Why?"

"Because you're pretty, obviously."

I scoff. "Hey!"

Matt smiles, cocking his head to the side and sizing me up. Warmth snakes down my chest to my belly. When he looks at me like that, I think he could eat me up and swallow me whole.

I wouldn't mind that at all.

"Because you've made me acknowledge something we're all too scared to," Matt says. "And you do it in a way that makes me want to act. Not shrivel up and die."

"You're complimenting me again."

Matt leans forward, grabbing my hands on the table. "It's too easy, Lillian."

Fuck. If I keep waiting for the right way to say what I

mean, Matt's going to keep trying to take the spotlight off him. I have to say what I mean now. "I just don't want you to lose anything because you're choosing to . . . explore *this* with me."

His smile falters.

"You know, your brother isn't my biggest fan. And your dad just might think of me as his mortal enemy," I go on.

Matt looks away, but his grip on my hands doesn't falter. "They're not bad people."

"Oh, I don't think that they are," I say, pulling on his hands. "Please don't think I—"

"Life around here doesn't change much," Matt says. "It's not like a big city. Or even Michigan. It's wild out here. And the only way to tame wildness is to be prepared for it. But it's sad, right? Because we live in a place that's so free, and yet, we're all so rigid."

"I understand it though," I say. "At least I try to."

His eyes scrunch at the corners. "I'm honestly sick of it."

An unexpected laugh bubbles out of me. "Oh God, I'm sorry, I—"

He laughs. "You think my pain is a joke?"

"I just didn't expect that . . . you love it here."

"I do. But Alaska is nothing if I don't feel free. And you, Lillian, make me feel free."

~

WHEN WE LAND IN NAKNEK, it's still light out, but I wish we could be bathed in darkness.

We're silent as we return to his truck, the question of what's next heavy on my mind. Will he take me home? Kiss me and say goodnight? Or is the night not close to being over?

I haven't gone home with a man on a first date in years, mostly because I've never desired anyone that quickly.

Matt is a totally different story. One I'd like to read.

"Alright," he says as he shuts his door, though I'm not sure what he's saying alright too. "I'll take you home now, then."

I can't tell if that was a statement or a question. My gaze flits to his. We stare at each other for a few moments, and then it's *game on*. I'm not sure who moves first, me or him, but we have a month's worth of tension to break, and we've been too polite this entire time.

Not anymore.

Our mouths collide and our hands find any purchase they can.

Want undulates through me; want I know I should temper so as not to rush this any more than we already have. Yes, we have limited time, but that doesn't mean we need to be gluttonous.

Still, though, I'm not going to say no to Matt's chest pressed to mine.

Matt's hand strays to my lower back, while I comb my fingers through his hair, delving my tongue into his mouth.

The man moans. *Moans.* I feel it starting in his chest, traveling through his throat, and against my lips.

You've got to be fucking kidding me.

He rips his mouth from mine, though I want more. "We should stop."

"Why?" I reply, then kiss him again.

Matt's lips hum against my mouth. It takes effort to pry himself away from me. "Because if we keep doing this, I'll be forced to take you home with me."

"And that's a bad thing?"

"No, not at all, I just . . . " His hands sit on my lower back, feeling like they're *itching* to move lower. "I don't want to rush or—or—"

"Do you want me to stop?"

"No!" he says. "I mean—"

I laugh. The combination of his eagerness and shyness is adorable. "Do you want to take me home tonight?"

Matt's Adam's apple bobs. His nervousness melts away, leaving his delicious brown eyes boring into mine. "Yeah. Yeah, I do."

I scrape my hands through his beard, up through his hair, and give him one more momentous kiss.

The night is far from over.

Chapter 22

This is a Good Start

LILLIAN

I don't know how we manage to behave between the Naknek airport and Matt's house, but we do. Conversation is limited, but that doesn't bother me one bit because the anticipation is building. The tension is threatening to break.

And I can't wait to crack it in two.

This connection has been building since the second I laid eyes on him at Half-Hitch. Of course, I didn't know then what I know now. That the feeling is not only mutual, but the desire to act on it is, too.

Now that we're here, though, it's impossible to ignore just how deep my feelings are for him. How long I've wanted this moment. Even as I pushed it away, tried to keep it professional, and assumed that he'd want nothing to do with me since I'm an outsider, I still wanted him.

Each time I steal a look at Matt, he's more and more tense, shifting his hands on the steering wheel and rolling his shoulders back.

With every passing mile, eagerness builds.

We turn off the highway onto a steadily inclining gravel driveway, flanked by trees that open up when we get to the house. Matt's house. Which doesn't look anything like I expected it to. It's dark red with white trim, almost like a farmhouse. The black-shingled roof looks rustic and durable. But what surprises me most is the wood-carved bear by the front door, holding a sign that says, "Welcome."

"Never took you for a lawn ornament type of guy," I say.

Matt clears his throat. "Yeah, well, Gwen had it made for me when I bought the place and—"

"It's cute. I love it."

My eyes linger on his for an extended moment. He looks nervous, like a scared deer waiting for its predator to make the first move.

"Shall we . . . go inside?" I offer.

"Yes! I mean, yeah. Good idea," Matt says before climbing out of the truck as swiftly as he can.

I hold back a laugh. Do *I* make him this nervous, or does *sex* make him this nervous?

Matt buried the lead with the carved bear, because the inside of his house is darling. Wood-paneled walls, oriental rugs, and a unique collection of art and photos on the walls.

Of course, I'm much more interested in the doorway at the end of the hall that leads upstairs.

Matt, on the other hand, is surprisingly not. He ducks to the left into the kitchen. "You thirsty? Want some water? Let's have some water."

I hold back a giggle. God, he's darling when he's nervous! The steady sea captain is actually a bundle of nerves when he...

When he really wants something.

I follow him into the kitchen and watch as he shuffles from the cabinet to the sink, his shoulders rippling through his jacket.

Which reminds me, I should make myself comfortable. I unzip my fleece and drape it over my forearm.

Matt fills the cups with water and returns to me. "Here."

"Thanks." I take the glass, though I'm thirsty for something else.

"Yeah, sure." Matt lifts his glass like we're about to toast or something, his lips pursed in an awkward line. He drinks his water. Almost all of it in one go.

I'm about to explode from the laughter I'm holding in.

Matt takes a moment to catch his breath, running his hand over his mouth and beard. "Uh, let me take that," he says, gesturing toward my jacket.

"Matt—" I try to interject, to slow him down, if only for a moment.

But he doesn't wait, probably can't even hear me with

all the thoughts stampeding through his head. He dips back into the front hall, his footfalls heavy, and his actions quick and precise. Moments later, he appears again in the doorway. "I—um—"

I stare at him, waiting.

Matt runs his hand over his head, messing up his signature black toque. His dark hair is ruffled and glorious, begging to be pulled by my fingers. "I haven't done this in a while. If that wasn't completely obvious by my . . ."

We both look at the glass of water in my hand.

"Yeah," Matt finishes, trying to smile.

I let out a sigh, place the glass of water down on the counter, and go up to him. With steady, tender hands, I take hold of his biceps. "Kiss me," I tell him.

Matt laughs breathlessly before giving me a soft kiss. His lips are just as tentative as his hands, and, god, how I want him to *not* be tentative. To haul me up the stairs and have his way with me.

I know he can. He just needs a little boost of confidence.

I settle my teeth into his lower lip and relish the frustrated huff he releases as I let go. "Now, would you show me your bedroom?"

Matt hesitates just long enough for me to worry he's gotten into his head again. But before I can go in for another kiss, he ducks down, wraps his arms around my thighs, and hauls me over his shoulder like I'm a sack of potatoes.

I scream, laugh, and wiggle the entire way out of the

kitchen and up the stairs, but there's nowhere I'd rather be. Well, other than his bed, of course. But this is a good start.

When we make it to his bedroom, Matt sets me down. "This is my room."

I spin around and take in the master bedroom. A king-sized, or should I say Matt-sized, bed dressed in a dark gray duvet and framed by ancient, hearty wood. There's a matching wooden dresser against the wall. I bet it's full of wool sweaters and old jeans. More important than any of the furniture, though, is the view. There's a series of three windows across from the bed that look over the treetops toward the serene Naknek River in the distance.

"Oh, my gosh. What an incredible view!" I exclaim and go to the windows.

"Thought you might like that."

It's a view I could get lost in. The swaying treetops and the clear sky would already be dark at this time in Los Angeles. Not in Alaska, though. In fact, I see both the moon and the sun at the same time. Celestial bodies that are two sides of the same coin. Can't have the moon without the sun. And yet, we act like they're polar opposites. That's just not true, is it?

My trance is broken when I hear the squeak of mattress springs. I turn to find Matt seated at the end of the bed, bent over to untie his heavy work boots. I lean back against the windowsill, letting the view of Matt overtake me.

He finishes removing his shoes and places them at the foot of the bed, side by side. "There we go. I usually take them off first thing when I get home, but I don't really have my head screwed on right now, so . . ."

I grin and toe off my sneakers before going over to him, his knees grazing mine. "Why are you so nervous? It's just me."

Matt smiles. Handsome. Easy. "Is that supposed to be some kind of joke?"

I rest my forearms on his shoulders, softly straddling him on the bed. "No?"

He laughs, shaking his head. Cautiously, he touches my waist, then lowers his palms to my hips. He squeezes. My insides flip. "You have no idea how nervous you make me, Lillian."

"Don't be ridiculous. I'm just Lillian," I say as I lower my mouth to his.

"You've never been 'just' anything to me," Matt mutters just before our lips connect.

I swoon into the kiss, my body melting into his strong, accepting arms. Matt's hands sneak under the hem of my shirt at my back, his palms grazing my skin. I hum into his mouth, nestling myself into his body.

Now, I'm the one feeling nervous. His stare is consuming and electrifying. Goosebumps spark across my skin.

"You are beautiful" He touches my cheek with his big hand. Again, his touch is so much softer than expected. The calluses and hard ridges of his hand don't hold a candle to the gentle energy he uses to *touch*.

Our eyes meet briefly. They're wide, and for some

reason, unsure. Like we're both doing this for the first time. We are, in a way. The first time with each other. We both want to make it good. Make it count.

At least, I hope he's thinking that, too.

Chapter 23

Flying Always Takes It Out of Me

MATTHEW

I peek one eye open to see the color on the woman's paintbrush.

"Close your eyes!" Winnie snaps, as vicious as the tiger features painted on her face.

"Jeez, you're watching me like a hawk," I say, shutting my eyes tight.

The face painter chuckles. "Almost done."

I'm impatient, ready to be out of this chair and look at the damage Winnie's done to my face.

"Any regrets yet, Matty?" Gwen asks from somewhere to my left.

"We'll see when I look in the mirror."

Winnie laughs, and I smile. That's why I subject myself to this silly form of torture. All for my niece and her enjoyment. When she caught sight of the face painter but felt too shy to go over alone, the answer was simple. Go with her and get my face painted, too.

I feel a final swipe on my forehead. "Alright, all done," the painter announces.

I blink my eyes open to find myself face-to-face with my reflection. From the nose down, I look the same. Bless the beard for preserving some of my dignity. But on the top of my face, I'm a unicorn with a rainbow horn. "Oh, I should have known," I say, giving Winnie a look.

Winnie bursts into a fit of giggles, and Gwen pats my shoulder in sympathy and gratitude.

We settle up with the face painter, and I take a deep breath. I'm going to be facing a lot of teasing today.

"Well, look at you."

My head whips around to see Lillian and Marina standing just a few feet away. I try to respond, but my mouth has gone dry, and my face is hot. Partly because I'm embarrassed for them to see me like this, and partly because Lillian looks so damn good. She somehow manages to outdo herself every time I see her.

Now that I know the feeling of her mouth and her body on mine, everything about her is exponentially more beautiful. Not only do I know the look of each of her features, but I also know the *feel* of them now. Her auburn hair isn't just hair, it's silken and soft, her waist isn't just a polite contour, but hot and womanly in my hand, and her lips...

"Winnie's idea," Gwen clarifies due to my prolonged silence.

"Ah, she's got good taste," Marina says, ruffling her hand through Winnie's hair.

My niece grins up at her. She might be a member of the Benton clan, but given how small Naknek is, children are such a rarity they end up being adored by everyone.

Lillian's eyes linger on me, waiting. I'm so out of practice with how to behave around a woman I've got eyes for that I'm embarrassing us all. "Uh, how was the flight?"

"Not bad," Lillian says with a polite smile. "Although Marina's not as smooth of a ride as you are."

I swallow. Blink.

"Plane! Your plane. I mean . . . I'm talking about your plane," she says with a sheepish smile, blushing.

"I'm sorry we didn't have room for you," I tell her. Before Lillian found out about the No-See-Um festival in Dillingham, I'd committed the seats on my plane to Tuma, Katoo, their kids, and, of course, Gwen and Winnie.

"Don't worry. She made it in one piece without throwing up once," Marina says, holding back a smirk while glancing over at Lillian. "Didn't you?"

Lillian pats her hands over herself. "I guess so."

"I think we're going to go get a corn dog or something," Gwen says as Winnie pulls her toward the food trucks. "Anyone want anything?"

Marina stretches her arm up. "I'll join you two. Flying always takes it out of me."

My sister's eyes catch on mine. "You two want anything?"

Ah, my sister's a sneak. She's trying to get me and

Lillian alone. Can't say I'm mad about that. I glance at Lillian. "Um, I'm good. Are you?"

She nods. "Yeah, I'm good."

"Come on, Gwendolyn. Let's leave these kids alone, huh?" Marina says, ticking her head toward the thoroughfare of food.

Kids.

That makes me feel so small, but not in a bad way. In an . . . innocent way. You never really leave behind the feeling of butterflies and yearning and anticipation. Pulls the rug out right from under all those feelings of "manning up."

I don't actually mind it, though. Not when I know the object of my affection feels the same.

"We'll see you guys at the fileting competition!" Gwen calls out over her shoulder as Winnie pulls her to follow Marina.

"Yeah, see ya," I respond, then turn to face Lillian. I don't know what to say. Maybe give her a kiss. We're surrounded by people though, and that would be a pretty big move. I'm not sure either of us are ready for—

Lillian points at my face. "I mean it. It's cute."

Shit. I remember the fucking unicorn on my face and blush even harder. "Oh, god. Don't remind me. Winnie picked it."

Lillian touches my arm, leans in, and pecks me on the cheek. She's lucky she didn't get any paint on her lips. "It's sweet," she murmurs.

Before her hand can fall away, I grab it in mine and

pull her away from the busy food trucks. "Come on. I'll show you around."

Her hand tightens in mine as we walk and talk. I take her to where the salmon fileting competition is rearing up to get started. Entrants are already practicing, and salmon filets are hanging from the Spartan wooden racks.

"I never thought I'd enjoy the smell of fish," Lillian remarks, her eyes dancing across the vermillion filets.

I inhale the sweet and salty air. "Fresh is best," I say with a smile. The way fish smells when it's freshly caught and sliced is nothing compared to the smell people normally associate with fish. As with most things, time is the greatest enemy to fish. "There's an enzyme in the fish that breaks down and causes it to smell . . . fishy."

Lillian's eyes widen, and she smiles. "That's right."

"Right, you know that, of course." Who am I to explain science to a scientist? Especially when my knowledge is so limited.

"I like when you tell me about it, though," Lillian says, causing my heart to swell.

We continue past the drying racks to the tent where the fileting competitors are preparing. I see Tuma watching his wife sharpen her knife.

Katoo's long black hair hangs down her back while her colorful beaded earrings sway with the force of her work.

Tuma looks up and gives us a wave over.

"Ready to meet the queen of salmon fileting?" I ask Lillian.

She grabs at her chest. "Is it weird that I'm actually nervous?"

I laugh and lead her down the rows of others preparing for the competition. "Katoo's a sweetheart as long as you don't get between her ulu and a salmon."

"Duly noted," Lillian says.

When we reach them, Katoo holds her blade up and examines it in the light. A proud smile twinkles on her face. She pushes some hair out of her eyes with the back of her hand and looks up at us. She grins, the line tattooed from the bottom of her lip to her chin stretching. "Ah! Is this your girlfriend?"

I sputter. "What? Girlfriend?! I never said—"

Lillian laughs. "Is that what you're telling people?"

"No, I didn't—I wouldn't—"

Katoo's dark eyebrows waggle. "That's what Tuma told me."

"I never said girlfriend," Tuma says, folding his arms over his chest.

Katoo throws her head back with a tinkling cackle. "Your face, Matthew! And I'm not talking about the unicorn. That is a nice touch, though."

I ignore her. "Katoo, this is Lillian."

Thankfully, Katoo gives me a break. I've known her as long as I've known Tuma, and she always gives everyone shit for simply breathing. Part of her charm. She hands her ulu to Tuma before reaching out to shake Lillian's hand. "Good to meet you."

"You as well. An honor to meet the queen," Lillian says with a mock bow.

"My reputation precedes me, hm?" Katoo asks, lifting an eyebrow.

"Yes, I've heard so much about you from these two," Lillian says, gesturing to Tuma and then grabbing my arm. I love it when she touches me. The casual way her hand lands on me as if we've been at this a lot longer. "I'm looking forward to seeing you defend your title."

"Yes, I don't want to get overconfident, but I have a good feeling about it."

"Is this your ulu?" Lillian asks, pointing at the half-moon-shaped knife in Tuma's hand.

"You've done your research," Katoo says with a grin, taking it back from her husband.

Tuma slinks over to my side, and I immediately relax. I didn't realize how tense I was, watching Katoo and Lillian interact. Katoo is a hardass, but it's only because she's fiercely loyal and loving. She's like a dad threatening the boy dating his daughter with a shotgun.

I want Lillian to make a good impression, for all our sakes.

"They mentioned it, and I watched some videos online," Lillian says, shoving her hands into the pockets of her fleece. "I got curious. It's cool to see it up close."

Katoo lifts the ulu and holds the handle out to Lillian. "You want to try?"

"Kat, they were just stopping in to wish you luck. Don't put her to work," Tuma interjects.

Katoo rolls her eyes. "Relax. She can say no."

"I'd love to try, but don't we need a fish?" Lillian asks.

"Don't you worry. I can swipe a fish as well as I can skin it," Katoo says, patting her knee as she gets to her feet. "Be back in a minute."

"What can't she do?" Lillian retorts.

Tuma glances around to make sure we're not overheard. "Laundry."

We all laugh, and I take advantage of the moment to place my hand on Lillian's shoulder.

As promised, Katoo returns quickly with her pilfered salmon and invites Lillian to join her.

Tuma and I stand back as Katoo teaches Lillian how to filet the fish. There is an art to it, one that I have never mastered. But Lillian does a great job, letting Katoo guide her hand down the first flank of fish, separating the meat from the bone.

"Not bad," Katoo exclaims as Lillian rocks the ulu over the fin to separate it from the meat.

"Hardly," Lillian says, without drawing her eyes from the fish.

She's a natural, though. At everything she does because she *tries*. People don't make an effort the way she does. She likes to get her hands dirty and know as much as she can. I admire that about her. Too often people are afraid of trying something new. Myself included.

Tuma moves closer to my side to say something. I lean down, so he can get closer to my ear. "I think you found a keeper," he says.

I glance at my friend as his mouth glimmers into a grin, and I try to shrug it off. But my heart is pounding because I know he's right.

To LILLIAN'S SURPRISE, the fileting competition is finished after just a few minutes. Each contestant fillets two fish consecutively and is judged on their speed, the quality of the filet, and the amount recovered in the process. No use being a quick filet if you're going to waste the meat.

"What happens with all the fish now?" Lillian asks in a whisper.

"They get smoked and divvied up among the community for winter food," I whisper back, not wanting to break the heavy concentration of the competition. "Nothing goes to waste."

We wait with bated breath as the judges tally up the times. Tuma's knee bounces, though he maintains a calm demeanor for the kids. Amka is almost fifteen, which is hard to fathom given that I still feel so young. She's a spitting image of Katoo, and even draws the black line on her chin since she isn't allowed to get the traditional Aleut tattoo of maturity for women until she's eighteen. Lusa is ten, and Toklo, the only boy, is seven.

Tuma might be my best friend, but in this one place in our life, our paths diverged immensely. Katoo and Tuma married right after we finished school and babies followed swiftly. Meanwhile, I kicked the can around as a bachelor, worked hard, and built up my business.

We all have struggled through the changing of the seasons together. The poor fishing seasons and the strange weather patterns.

But when we go home at night, our lives are completely different. I am alone, and he has a family. Those were our choices.

Naked in Naknek

I didn't envy him until I turned thirty, though. I heard all about the hardships of being a parent and a husband on long boat journeys. Not to mention the weight he carries as an Aleut man. Their history is tragic, marked by oppression from settlers on all sides. It's a tale known throughout Alaska. Only white people like to pretend it doesn't exist.

Lillian's hand wraps around my bicep. "I'm nervous," she whispers.

I smile. It's hard to keep an even keel when she's touching me, but I manage it. "Don't need to be nervous for Katoo. She was the fastest."

"This is my first time! I don't know what to expect," she says, elbowing me.

I tilt my head down to meet her gaze. "Yeah. Your first time?"

Lillian's eyes widen. She smacks my hand. "Get your mind out of the gutter."

I start to laugh, but the mic feedback cuts me off. One of the judges is ready to announce the winner.

"Ada, *Ada*— –" Toklo exclaims hurriedly, thwapping Tuma on the thigh.

Lusa shushes him and wraps her arm around her little brother to calm him.

The judge, an Aleut elder, clears her throat into the mic. "It should come as no surprise for the fifth year in a row—"

We're up on our feet cheering before she can even announce Katoo as the official winner. And with the filleting competition finished, the barbecue begins. The smell of smoke permeates the air as fillet after fillet is cooked up for the festivalgoers.

Lillian and I break from the rest of our party to eat together. We chat and flirt while a band of Alaskan musicians—dressed in their traditional leather and fur tunics—strikes up on a stage overlooking the water. Lillian pauses to listen and watch as the drummers begin, each of them holding their paddle-like skin and wood drum.

"Gosh, that's just . . ." She trails off, allowing the melodic drumbeats to speak for her.

A funky beat emerges from an electric bass and an organ sound from a keyboard as the song opens up.

Lillian does a doubletake. "Traditional?"

"Traditional adjacent?" I say with a shrug. "They're a popular group around here. They take traditional songs and transform them by combining with other genres. The group is called Tribal Funk, after all."

Lillian taps her foot, her head grooving with the beat.

"Yeah, you got it," I tease.

She looks away with a laugh. "I like it."

I glance over at the band. Some singers have come forward, and they're moving and grooving in their traditional Aleut attire, singing new melodies and lines along with the ancient instruments. Festivalgoers swarm the stage, some of them jamming out on their own, others taking partners and dancing together.

I'm not much of a dancer on a normal occasion, but I've got a gorgeous girl sitting next to me, who clearly would like to get on her feet and dance. "You wanna . . ." I tilt my head toward the musicians.

Her forehead scrunches. "Wanna what?"

"Um, you wanna dance?" I manage, though it feels a bit foolish coming out of my mouth.

Lillian bites her tongue, smiling. That does something to my insides. Oh *no*. Not here. I can't start getting horny here, all the way in Dillingham, a plane ride away from Naknek where we have nowhere to go. Hell, she didn't even fly with me.

Don't act like you haven't been thinking about it all day, dumbass.

"You dance, Matthew?" Lillian asks, leaning toward me.

"I dance," I say, unsure. "Not well, but I do."

"You can follow my lead then," she says and gets to her feet, pulling on my hand.

I follow her onto the dance floor, my eyes trained on her ass despite my best intentions. Once we're amidst the crowd, she turns to face me, drops my hand, and sways her hips, lifting her arms into the air.

I watch, forgetting that if *we're* going to dance, I have to dance too. But I'm entranced by her body, how free she looks, and how her auburn hair falls in and out of her face as the music flows through her.

"You're not dancing," she says in a sing-song tone.

I guffaw, pulling at the front of my shirt as if I've just been struck by a hot wind. "Ha! Sorry, sorry, I just don't know how to—where to start."

Lillian spins around and steps back until she's pressed against my front. She lifts her chin up, locking her eyes with mine, and . . . holy shit, her eyelids waver low and wanting. I'm really regretting that plane ride now. "You know how to move your hips. I've seen it. On the boat. You move with the water."

She takes my hands and places them on her hips. Swinging them back and forth, they brush up against my crotch, not in a lewd, obvious way, but enough for my body to get the message. "Felt it, too."

I am immediately inundated with the memory of our first night in bed together. God, I want more of that. Soon.

She spins back around, facing me again. Throwing her arms around my neck, she glances down at the space between us. "There, you got it now."

And I do. I'm moving without thinking too hard about it, letting her guide me. But that space between us makes my heart pulse with the anticipation of closing that gap. Makes me want her more than I can possibly say with words.

"You nervous?" Lillian asks.

I scoff. "What?"

She glances over her shoulder, scanning our surroundings. "To be seen so close to me?"

I don't respond. Not with words at least. I fondle a skein of her hair and move it off her shoulder as we move together, the throbbing bassline threatening to send me into overdrive. Then, I situate my hand on the back of her neck and lean in to kiss her.

Her body slows, now merely wavering as my lips overtake hers.

Lillian's hands grip the front of my shirt as the kiss ebbs and our mouths break. She smiles up at me, licking her bottom lip.

"Does that answer your question?" I ask. I decide not to tell her some unicorn paint has transferred onto her cheek.

It's Lillian's turn not to answer with words. She rises on her tiptoes and brings her mouth close to mine but does not kiss me. Her breath coasts along my mouth as her hands slide lower, lower, lower, until her fingers slip into the belt loops of my jeans. With a single tug, our bodies are flush.

And there's no question.

It's fucking on.

Chapter 24

Forget Me Not

MATTHEW

I couldn't wait any longer to get Lillian home, so I struck a deal with Marina: if she took Gwen, Winnie, and Tuma's family back to Naknek, I'd pay for her plane's next fuel up. Once everything was set, Lillian and I jetted back to Naknek, went straight to my house, and locked ourselves inside to take full advantage of being alone together.

The next morning, I have to pinch myself when I wake up and see Lillian in bed next to me for the second time. I still can't believe it's real.

But when I pull her into my arms and she awakens with a sharp intake of breath, I know I'm not dreaming.

After breakfast, we take advantage of the clear morning and head out for a walk along the river. The crisp air carrying the earthy scent of damp soil, wild sage, and the quiet murmur of the water is almost meditative. The sunlight filters through the trees, casting dappled shadows across the path as our footsteps crunch softly on the gravel trail. Ahead of me, Lillian stops and crouches down. She reaches out her hand and strokes the flowers in front of her. Little blue Forget-Me-Nots. "You can find those things everywhere," I say, distracted.

Lillian glances at me. Her makeup is gone from her face, save for some mascara rubbed into her lower lash line. "They are so pretty," she says. "Your state flower."

"Another fun fact," I say, crouching down next to her.

She smiles, her fingers still tenderly caressing the tiny petals. "The name is almost like a prayer. You know, all of you being so far north and so—"

"Forgettable?" I offer.

"I wouldn't say forgettable," Lillian says, her shoulder lifting. She touches my knee, her knuckles curled softly like she's afraid to grab me fully. "Far away, maybe."

I tip her chin up and give her lips a soft kiss. "Not *so* far away," I murmur.

"No, not anymore."

I clear my throat and divert my attention back to the flowers. I pull a sprig off and tuck it behind Lillian's ear. "Now, you can't forget me."

"Flirt," she says, pushing me on the shoulder and jumping back to her feet.

My heart expands in my chest. This is so dangerous. I keep forgetting the reality of our situation. Lillian makes it too easy. "So, um, how's the research going?"

She laughs. "Research talk? This early in the morning?"

I look at the toes of my boots as we walk. "We don't have to talk about it now. But I'm curious."

"I know you are." She squeezes my arm. "I like that about you. It seems genuine."

"Well, I do have a vested interest in what you're studying," I say, taking her hand in mine. "But I'd listen to you read the phonebook."

Lillian giggles as I press a kiss to the back of her hand. "I assure you, that'd get boring after a while. But anyway—" Her tone shifts away from sweet and sappy to a more businesslike tone. "Nothing about my research is exactly *surprising*. I mean, we're seeing this story play out around the globe. Pollution and environmental stressors are causing declines in fish populations, combined with fishing habits of the past century—"

My ears go deaf for a moment. It's one thing to be confronted with the reality of what pollution does to our environment, but the impact my livelihood has on it is uncomfortable to sit with.

"Of course, I'm interested to see how the changing of the season might impact my data, and contrast it with studies of other species," Lillian goes on. "Observe the conditions that may or may not harm populations in autumn versus summer, compare fishing behaviors, and—"

"You seem to think fishing is a big part of the problem," I say. I don't mean to sound as edgy as I do, but it's hard to ignore the knot in my throat this conversation caused.

"I—" She pauses. "That's not what I mean to imply. But nothing exists in a vacuum."

I'm quiet.

"Yes, it's unfortunate how much Alaska and the more remote locations suffer from the impacts of metropolitan areas. It's unfair, to put it plainly. The ecological impact here isn't proportional, I suppose," she says.

"Suppose?" I press.

Lillian's touch slips away from me, and she puts a gap between us. She tries to laugh, but it comes out raspy and unsure. "You asked for my theories. I'm just indulging your curiosity."

"And I'm asking questions," I say.

"If you give a mouse a cookie . . ." she mutters, looking up at the overcast sky.

I shove my hands in my pockets. I know I've made it awkward. I just can't ignore the feeling that I'm tangled up with . . .

The *enemy*.

"What happens when your research is done?" I ask, my voice gravelly.

"Matt—"

"I'm just asking a question."

"I know, but I don't want to think about leaving," she says.

I can tell she's trying to bring the conversation back to us. "We should think about it, though," I say. "Because you'll go back to Los Angeles, to your life at PMI, and relay all your research—and then what happens after that?"

"With us?" Lillian asks.

"No," I answer too quickly. "I mean, I guess, yes, but—"

She stops walking. "You want to know what's going to happen to you and Naknek."

I stop a stride ahead of her and let out a heavy sigh. "Yeah, I do."

Lillian licks her lower lip, her eyes falling to the river. "If I were to hypothesize what kind of recommendations I'd be making, which would be based on a shaky foundation mind you, I'd probably encourage the state and local governments to start making more mandates around clean energy."

I laugh. "You can't be serious."

"Why wouldn't I be?"

"That's expensive. You think anyone around here can afford solar-powered anything?"

Lillian's expression doesn't change, which for some reason, makes my blood boil. Her recommendations don't impact her. Not on a personal level. Not when she'll be thousands of miles away in sunny fucking Los Angeles.

God, how was I so stupid? So naïve? We'll always be too different.

"That's why PMI tries to get involved on a governmental level. We can introduce grants and bills and—"

"That's all well and good, but what do we do right now? The government takes forever anywhere, but this is Alaska, Lillian."

Lillian blinks. "Matt, I don't think this is a productive conversation." She starts off down the beach, faster than before. The crunch of her shoes double-times.

"Come on, don't walk away."

"You're asking me questions that I don't have good answers for. And I can't help but feel you're trying to play some sort of 'gotcha' game."

"Gotcha? No gotcha. I'm just—"

"Curious. Right. Except people don't act like assholes when they're genuinely curious."

I'm stunned by her choice of words. "I'm not trying to be an asshole, Lillian. I swear. But this is my life. You can't blame me for wanting to know as much as I can."

"It feels like you just want to be upset with me the way everyone else has been. I don't know what I did between last night and this morning to deserve that," Lillian says, her eyes fixed ahead. Hardened, and . . . maybe trying not to cry.

I don't say anything. I know she wants me to apologize, but I just can't. Not when I'm so uneasy about everything she's said thus far.

"So, what do you want me to say? That I'd recommend fewer fishing permits? That the only immediate course of action to increase fish populations would be controlling the fishing until we get some movement on the government level?" she rambles, words clipped and quick. "Is that what you want?"

"Of course not," I grumble.

"Well, then, sorry to disappoint you, but with everything I know and given that I'm being forced to make predictions based on the scant information I have, that's what I'd say."

Ice runs through my veins.

"If you don't start making sacrifices now, it will destroy the bay. That's the truth," she goes on.

"People won't survive if they—"

"You're being shortsighted," she snaps.

"So are you," I return. "Does the community mean nothing to you?"

Lillian rubs her forehead. "You're twisting my words. I never said that. I know how important fishing is for all of you, but you won't be able to fish much longer if drastic measures aren't taken."

"Your idealism is showing, Lillian. You can't just swoop in here and act like you know better."

"Then why the hell did you ask?" Her voice bounces off the water, disturbing the peace of this morning.

I stare at her. "Because I need to know if I'm making a mistake."

Lillian's jaw drops open. The insult landed right where I wanted. It doesn't feel good though. Not like I hoped it would. "Well, fuck you for that."

I scrape my hand through my beard. I can still smell her there, her essence deep in the wiry hair, despite washing my face. Fuck. *Fuck.*

"I can walk myself the rest of the way," Lillian says, then turns on her heel and heads off down the beach. "I'll take my chances with the bears."

I stand there, wanting to chase after her and apologize. And knowing it would be hollow. Unearned. Because while I care for her, I've known her for a fraction of my life. This town, these people, *Alaska,* has been mine since day one. And I owe something to all of that, don't I?

I owe Naknek much more than I owe a scientist I met in July. A woman who comes from a completely different world, who sees this all as a novelty, rather than a reality.

As Lillian walks away, I back up, step by step, until the distance between us is great enough to justify turning around and going home.

Maybe that distance was too great from the start.

Chapter 25

Just Callin' It Like I See It

MATTHEW

I stare at my plate of food. Haven't been hungry in days.

"You don't like it?"

I look across the table at Winnie, her little face distraught at the idea I'm not enjoying her dinner. "Love it, Winnie. Taking my time. Savoring it. See?" I dip my fork into the mashed potatoes, the ones she loves that come from a box. I put the bite of food in my mouth and feel my stomach turn, reminding me I'm not hungry. Not at all.

I manage to swallow it down. "Mmm...wow...incredible."

Jesse snorts while Gwen gives me a small shake of her head. However, Winnie smiles, and that's all that matters.

My insides churn with anger. Two days without Lillian, and I'm losing my mind.

Yet everything about it feels wrong. And if it feels wrong to be with her and wrong to be without her, what's right?

The dinner table falls quiet again, save the snapping of the tab on Dad's Dr. Pepper. He doesn't drink on days we have family dinners at his place. For Winnie's sake. That is until we all leave for the night. There is a customary rush once the dishes are washed to get us out of the house.

As he pours his third can of Dr. Pepper into his glass, he clears his throat and eyes me.

Fuck, what is it now?

"You getting the most out of your summer fling, Matty?" he asks.

Jesse laughs into his glass of water. I glare at my brother.

"Dad, not while Winnie's here," Gwen says in her soft, placating tone.

Dad swirls the ice in his glass like it's whiskey on the rocks. "Just making conversation."

I put my fork down. "Why don't you just say what you want to say, instead of pretending you're 'just making conversation,' Dad?"

Gwen lets out a long sigh. "Oh boy . . ."

"Are you guys going to fight?" Winnie pipes up. She's used to it by now, sadly.

"Probably," Jesse says with a mouthful of food.

I purse my lips together, cross my arms over my chest, and wait for the attack.

"I warned you." Dad chuckles. He's not drunk, so he's not ornery. I'd almost like that better than him being a smug smartass. "Warned you not to get involved with her."

"Who?" Winnie squeaks.

"Why do you care, Dad?" I ask.

"I care because people are talking about my son behind his back," Dad replies. "Calling him nasty names I won't repeat near sensitive ears."

Winnie's big eyes roll toward each of us, desperate for some modicum of understanding.

Poor kid.

"They think they're gonna lose their jobs over her," Dad goes on.

I hold my tongue. He might not be far off with that.

"And then they see you taking her out on your boat, out to dinner with her, trading spit in public—"

"Trading *spit*?" Winnie gasps.

Gwen guides Winnie's fork-holding hand toward her plate. "Eat your dinner, Winnie."

"You're a regular Benedict Arnold around here," Dad says.

I rest my thumb on the bridge of my nose. "Okay. And?" They'll all be baffled not to see Lillian and me around town anymore, then. They'll all tell me I did the right thing.

Doesn't feel right.

"They like each other, Dad," Gwen interjects. "Just let him have it."

Dad narrows his eyes at Gwen. "We all know how 'liking' turns out for this family."

Naked in Naknek

My sister swallows, her jaw hardening. Everyone avoids looking at Winnie, and Winnie is pleasantly distracted with her boxed mashed potatoes.

"Don't do that," I snap at him. Bringing Gwen into this and what happened with Winnie's father isn't fair.

Gwen holds up a hand. "It's fine." Too strong for her own good. "Look, Dad, Lillian's not coming here to turn Naknek upside down," Gwen says. "She really cares about the town. I mean, she's getting to know people and learning about the way we do things around here. She's not just a suit or someone looking to be a hero. She's really trying to make a difference."

"Who said anything needs to be different around here? Goddammit," Dad growls.

"Grandad!" Winnie admonishes.

"I know, I know. I shouldn't say words like that," he mutters.

Jesse and I exchange a look. Dad said whatever he pleased when we were kids. It's nice he tries to turn a new leaf when it comes to Winnie, but it's a hollow thing to watch, especially when we know the real him.

Gwen picks up Winnie's plate from the table. "Go turn on the TV and eat there, alright?"

"Okay!" Winnie takes the plate and runs out of the dining room.

"Now, why'd you do that? She's a big kid. She doesn't need you pussyfooting around her, Gwen." Dad sneers.

"I don't care if she's a big kid. She's a kid, and I'd like for her to feel that way for as long as possible," Gwen snaps back. "You don't even know Lillian. It's not fair for you to judge her without—"

Jesse steps in now. "He doesn't need to know her. He's got her pegged."

I glare at my brother. "Seriously?"

My brother is nonplussed by my attitude. "Just callin' it like I see it."

"You're such a fucking—" I stop myself. Why do I feel so incensed? I could just tell them Lillian isn't an issue anymore. Isn't a problem. We realized our differences were too great just in time. Or maybe a little bit too late. And yet, I can't bring myself to let anyone else know.

Maybe I'm not done. Maybe I was rash, letting the voices of my dad and brother infiltrate what Lillian and I were building.

"A fucking what?" Jesse nags.

"Quit it, Jess," Gwen tries to interrupt.

Dad's turn to get in on the fun. "No, let him. A fucking what, Matt?"

You're just like him, I want to tell Jesse. Just like Dad. Stubborn and angry, and if he's not careful, he's gonna wind up just like him in the end. I won't do that. Not right now. "So, what do we do if we just ignore what's happening?" I ask as calmly as I can. "What do we expect to happen?"

"We handle our shit," Jesse says. "Same as always."

Dad nods. "Exactly."

I laugh disdainfully. "But we're not handling our shit. We're going broke trying to make ends meet every season!"

"And that's because—" Dad tries to interrupt.

I point in his direction. "Don't you act like you know a goddamn thing about what's going on out there while you're drinking yourself to death, alright?"

Dad's nostrils flare, but he says nothing.

Jesse shifts forward in his seat. "Jeez, Matt, what the hell is that about?"

"You know the definition of insanity is doing the same thing over and over, expecting a different result. Well, that's what we're doing. All of us go out there and act like the coho season is somehow going to get better. Newsflash, it's not. Because climate change, and—"

Dad makes a strangled sound. "Not that liberal garbage. You're better than that, Matt."

"Dad, be reasonable." Gwen tries to step in. "Everyone is struggling. Not just Matt and Jesse. And not because they're doing a bad job. They're working harder for less."

"Thanks, Gwen," I murmur.

She throws me a fleeting, apologetic smile.

"So, all the more reason you shouldn't be distracted. That's all," Dad says, the vinegar in his voice muted now.

"But that's not all. Because you're talking out of your ass. You have no idea what she's working on or what she's trying to do, and—"

"So, you leaving with her? When she goes back to La-La Land?" Dad stares me down and waits until our eyes lock. "Has she poisoned you so much against your own blood that you gonna get the hell out of town too?"

I shake my head in disbelief, unable to speak. If he

only knew how I had betrayed *Lillian* just two days ago in favor of my home, in favor of the place and people that raised me, because I believed I couldn't have both. I chose *home*. And I'm still being treated like a turncoat. I'm thirty-five fucking years old, and I'm still under the thumb of my father, who can barely stand up straight most days. "She's trying to help. That's all."

And that's the truth.

Dad sniffs. "You can't trust everyone, Matt."

"Neither can you, apparently. Can't even trust your own son," I say, then push myself out from the table. "I'm gonna go."

My brother and father don't stop me, but Gwen follows close behind. I leave the dining room and head into the front room where Winnie is sitting in front of the television, eating mashed potatoes with her hands.

"Matt, wait a second," my sister says.

I'll always stop for her. "What?"

Gwen grabs me by the arms and smiles at me. She's so tired. I can see it on her face. I can't believe I'm piling my antics onto everything else she has to deal with. "Don't listen to them, okay? Dad doesn't know what it means to care about anyone anymore, and I don't think Jesse has ever learned."

My ribcage threatens to split open.

I cared for Lillian. I still care for her. I know what that word means, what it feels like. And I let all the noise get in the way of that.

"You know what you're talking about, Matty. I believe

you. I believe *her*. And I know that my opinion doesn't mean much in the scheme of—"

"It means everything, Gwen. You know that," I tell her.

Gwen smiles gratefully. I touch her cheek, giving it a gentle pinch. My little sister. Too often left to pick up the pieces for everyone else. "Thanks, sis."

She goes to the door and opens it for me. "Say bye to Uncle Matt," Gwen instructs Winnie.

"Bye, Uncle Matt," Winnie says.

I laugh at how she doesn't even look away from the television. "Bye, Win."

I head out the door and only get a few steps before Gwen calls out after me, "Tell her 'hi' from me."

∾

As I drive down the highway, I count the seconds until I pass by the turnoff for Lillian's cabin. And once I do, I don't get much farther before I pull my truck over and try to settle my racing heart. I rub my hand over my chest and lean my head back, cinching my eyes closed.

I fucked it up. I fucked it all up.

I should just go home. But the thought of going to that empty house right now and having to hear my own breathing makes me want to drive my truck into the river.

Fishing has *nothing* to do with Lillian and me. We can exist apart from that. Can't we?

Before I realize what I'm doing, I pull my phone out of the cup holder and tap on her contact. The phone rings and rings. And in the middle of the third ring, she answers.

"Hey." Her voice is unsure but not unfriendly.

"Hey," I reply, my brain frozen.

"Is . . . everything okay?" she asks.

"Yeah, yeah. I mean, no, but, uh—" I swallow. "I was just with my family, and my dad and Jesse were being idiots. And it made me realize what an idiot I was being the other day."

Lillian lets out a timid soft laugh, and the weight lifts off my shoulders. "Well, at least you know it."

"I owe you an apology."

"I owe you one, too."

I place my hand on the steering wheel and tap my thumb against it.

"Do you want to come over, and . . . apologize in person?" she asks.

I pull back onto the road before I say, "I'll be over in five."

When I pull up in front of her cabin, Lillian already has the door open. She leans on the doorframe, waiting for me in a pair of plush sleep pants and a sweatshirt, her hair clipped back out of her face.

I try not to run to her. But god, does it feel nice to see her with a smile on her face again.

"That was less than five," she says as I ascend the steps of her cabin.

"Sorry about that," I say. "I can wait in the car if you need the extra three."

Lillian shakes her head. "Don't be ridiculous."

She reaches for me and I for her. We hold each other in

the doorway. Two days was far too long. I've become so accustomed to her that my body craves her.

I kiss the crown of her head, inhaling her scent.

"I missed you," she whispers. "Is that stupid?"

"Only because I was a jerk."

Lillian laughs, her breath on my neck. "Did you miss me?"

I kiss her in answer.

Chapter 26

New Kink Unlocked

LILLIAN

I've never slept well next to anyone. But sleeping next to Matt, especially after two days of thinking we were done, has given me the most restful night of sleep in years. He doesn't snore, doesn't toss and turn, and he's the perfect temperature and size to cuddle up against when a chill cuts through the air in the night.

He smells good in the morning, too. A perfect mixture of his musk and a little bit of sweat. Pheromones that go right to my core.

I cuddle up next to him, pressing a kiss to his neck. Then his jaw.

He stirs when I reach his cheek and is fully awake by the time my mouth is on his.

"Mm," he hums against my mouth, a limp hand wrapping around my waist. "What time is it?"

"Don't know," I tell him, nudging my nose against his. If I were to guess from the light sneaking in past the dark curtains, it's probably earlier than I think. Still haven't gotten a grip of how time works out here.

"Hold me. I'm cold."

Matt obliges, wrapping his big arms around me and kissing my hairline. "You *are* cold," he whispers, touching various parts of my body to check my temperature. "Why don't you use the fireplace?" Matt asks.

I glance over at the metal fireplace with the stove pipe. "I don't know. I don't want to do it wrong."

"Aw. That's adorable."

I shove his chest. "Shut up."

"I mean it!"

We tussle and fall into another languid series of kisses. I thought when he came over last night, I'd keep my distance. I'd be more rational about this. We could see each other again, but I wouldn't let the head-over-heels feeling set in again.

Joke's on me.

"Let me build you a fire," Matt says.

"I don't have any firewood."

He rolls out of bed, and gestures out the window. "This is Alaska. There's firewood everywhere."

I move onto his side of the bed and soak up all the leftover warmth. "Well, I don't have an axe."

"You rented this place from Ian, right? No way this guy doesn't have an axe around here somewhere." Matt patrols the floor for his boots and socks. No pants. No shirt. Just underwear and boots.

New kink unlocked.

He heads for the back door, bare chest and all.

"You're not going out there like that," I say in disbelief.

Matt clutches a hand to his chest, covering up his nipple as if he's been scandalized. "Are you trying to ruin my reputation?"

I laugh into his pillow. It smells like him. "No, I mean—yeah? Do people just go out to chop wood without clothes on here?"

"Baby, this isn't LA. You're in Naknek. It's our right to be naked out here."

"Won't you be cold?"

Matt shakes his head, pulling the door open. "I'm Alaskan," he replies before disappearing out the door. As if that's an appropriate answer.

Which I suppose it is.

I pull myself out of bed and hurriedly make a cup of tea before rushing back to the window. I need to see this with my own eyes.

To my surprise, he has indeed located an axe. He wields it like a rogue going into a medieval battle, with ease and so much confidence I'm a little freaked out he's going to hurt himself.

With tea steaming into my face, I watch. I'm more excited than I ever thought a situation like this would make me.

Matt throws a look to the window, eyes locking on me, and he smiles like he's a fucking model and I've got a camera trained on him. He *knows* how good-looking he is, and now he's showing off for me.

I love it.

He positions the axe over his shoulder and lets it fall with an ease that makes my thighs clench. He slices the log into two and quickly sets one up to cut it into fourths.

I never thought I wanted a "manly" man. Then again, in cities, there seems to be way more cultural divide, especially when you're dating on the apps. Algorithms show you what they want you to see, and I haven't matched with many who work with their hands, muscles coming from labor rather than vanity. And yes, my ex, Cal, was a surgeon, so technically he worked with his hands. Refined movements based on years and years of education. But there's a posturing that comes with that.

Matt's work is inherent to who he is. Not something he puts on and takes off, depending on how he wants people to see him.

He finishes his work quickly and comes inside with a pile of logs, not a goosebump on him. I watch him build a fire in the stove, crouched over, his tight butt staring me in the face.

"You ogling me?" he asks, as he strikes a match.

The match is a symbol of my insides right now. "Yeah. I'm objectifying you."

He lights the fire, stoking it with delicate, directed breaths before it's fully ignited. Once that's done, he gets to his feet and dusts off his hands. "You have my permission to objectify me any day."

We crawl into bed again and cuddle, the room filling

with an embracing warmth. Matt keeps his hands under my sweater, against my belly. So simple and yet, so intimate.

I don't want to hurt him.

The thought appears out of the blue. And it goes deeper than not wanting to break his heart. I don't want to ruin his life.

"I'll figure something else out," I murmur. "For my recommendations."

Matt is quiet at first. "You do what you think is best. That's . . . that's your job."

"But if it hurts you and your job, I don't want to do it," I say, lifting my hand to touch the side of his face as I gaze up at him.

Matt touches my wrist and moves his mouth to my palm, kissing it tenderly. "Won't hurt me."

"Yes, it will," I say. "I mean, that's what you said and what everyone thinks, isn't it?"

With a sigh, Matt furrows his brow. "It's complicated. What they think."

"I wish they'd let me talk to them rather than trying to bite my head off any time I'm in the room. That way, I can know how to direct my research in a way that will help them not feel alienated." I roll my eyes up in thought. "Maybe you could talk to them. They trust you, right? I could give you my questions or thoughts and—"

Matt pulls me closer. "I have a better idea."

"Oh, you do?"

He kisses the side of my head. "I do. But first . . ." Matt yanks me on top of him.

"No, tell me your idea!" I exclaim, trying to get away from him, but once he drags his lips along my neck, I'm done for.

∼

MATT'S IDEA, it turns out, is a barbecue. On paper, it sounds like a nothing idea, but after he explains it to me, I let him take the lead.

Apparently, Matt is known for his barbecues. Or at least he has been in the past. This year, he hasn't scheduled one, so what better time than when the girl he's dating needs to probe his friends for information?

He doesn't see it quite like that, though. He's excited. We go to the supermarket together to get supplies, ignoring prolonged gazes from passing patrons. I help him clean and set up the backyard for guests. It's all so domestic, and I hate how good it feels. Well, I don't hate it. It just scares me. Because I don't belong here. Naknek has made that clear. Hell, Matt even made me realize my lack of belonging when we had our fight.

There's a piece of me that *wants* to belong. So bad.

The gathering is small but mighty, about six fishermen, not including Matt. Tuma and Marina are both friendly, familiar faces. Ian too, but I'm not sure where he stands with me. One of Marina's crew also came along, a guy named Rio. Baldy, whose actual name is Paul. And an older gentleman named Kirk.

Baldy, Kirk, Marina, and Rio all eye me warily as Matt works the grill. I try to stay out of their way at first, letting them mill, seethe, and enjoy themselves before I say anything that might raise the tension. I'm getting that out-of-place feeling, my hands tucked awkwardly in the pockets of my jacket, but I'm here to learn and listen. There's a hum of conversation, laughter blending with the crackle of the fire Ian tends in the middle of the yard.

"Uh, hi."

I turn to find Jesse. "Jesse, hi."

"Brought some beer," he says to me as if I'm hosting the party. He lifts a six-pack.

I didn't expect him to come, let alone bring beer. "Thanks so much. Matt will appreciate that."

Jesse lifts his eyes across the yard to Matt and Tuma at the grill. There's a hesitance in his gaze and in the way he holds his body. From what Matt told me, they didn't leave things on the best note the other night. They haven't talked since.

"I'll take this," I tell him as I accept the six-pack. "You go say hi. I'm sure he'll be happy to see you."

"Yeah, okay," Jesse mutters, like a little boy who has been told by the teacher to apologize to a kid he pushed down on the playground.

"I'm glad you're here," I tell him, which is the truth. I knew an invite had been extended to him, but Matt wasn't sure he'd come.

Jesse eyes me warily. "Sure thing."

I head over to the cooler near the back door to put the beer inside, which brings me closer to a conversation between Kirk and Marina.

"You're too old for that shit, Kirk," Marina scolds him.

"Don't fucking remind me. I haven't gone out for King Crab in over a decade."

"It's too dangerous," she says.

"Bah, there's fucking nothing out there near the islands anyway. Everywhere else, they've ended seasons early or quit them altogether."

Marina hums. "Can you fucking imagine? And we think we have it bad."

I slowly put the last bottle in the cooler and close the lid. Of course, coho isn't the only season touched by environmental shifts and overfishing. I don't know how I didn't see that before. "That sounds frustrating," I say as I inch toward them.

Both Kirk and Marina look at me. Kirk's expression is affronted while Marina's is more surprised.

"Frustrating. Yeah. Understatement," Kirk says before swigging his beer. He looks away as if I might disappear if he doesn't acknowledge my presence.

"Being pushed out of your livelihood. That doesn't seem fair," I go on, emboldened that I haven't been told to fuck off.

Marina nods while picking the corner of the label on her IPA. "Yeah, it's not fair."

"You're right."

"What do you know about it?" Kirk snaps at me.

I'm about to kowtow to his anger when Marina elbows him in the ribs. "Hey, lighten up. It's supposed to be a peaceful night."

I'm not sure how much Matt told them about the purpose of tonight. However, they're here, and I'm here, and I haven't yet been told to shut up yet. "It's not fair," I continue. "Because there are so many factors out of your control."

"Yeah, it's not our fault," Marina says.

Not entirely, I want to say. But I'm looking to make friends, not lose allies. "I mean, you've got issues with habit deterioration and rising water temperatures and pollutants. And you're the ones who have to deal with the fallout."

"And we've got issues with pike," Kirk grumbles, not agreeing with me but unable to keep silent.

"Yes!" I say with a smile. "And, you have the growing presence of elodea, which is—"

"The hell is that?" Kirk asks with an upturned lip.

I snap my fingers, looking for the common name. "Waterweed!" I exclaim.

Marina and Kirk both make sounds of agreement.

"And what about the green crab? That's not something to worry about yet, but given how they've infiltrated other bodies of water, it's a definite possibility."

Our conversation has gotten the attention of Baldy—sorry, Paul—and Rio who are seated by the fire. Now, I have an audience.

"Shit. I was just worried about pike," Kirk says.

"Well, how can you worry about everything when you also have to do your job?" I say with an emphatic flair.

Kirk looks at Marina, who smiles lopsidedly. "She has a point."

Yes, I have a fucking point.

"There's a lot on your plate already," I go on. "The last

thing you need is an outsider coming in and making you feel bad when so much of this is out of your control."

"So, what are you here to do then?" Paul grunts.

I take a step closer to the fire, opening up the conversation. "My job is to observe and record the data, so I can make recommendations to encourage the coho population to increase again."

Paul and Rio exchange a look.

"But I understand it can't be at the expense of the community here. At the end of the day, protecting the coho population means protecting Naknek. It's a delicate balance, though, right?"

"Right!" Ian exclaims.

I give him a smile of thanks. Maybe he's more on my side than I realized. "So, how do we encourage the salmon population without cutting you all off at the knees?"

"Sounds like it'll cost money," Rio mutters.

"Probably, yes." I go over to one of the seats by the fire and plop down. "Definitely will cost money. However, the more information I have, the better recommendations I can make. Do we get grants to curb invasive species? Do we enhance restocking measures? Or do we create jobs to make sustainable aquaculture to allow the natural environment to recover and give fishermen jobs *here at home?*"

A moment. Then two. I'm almost expecting someone to raise a pitchfork and run me out of town.

"Why do you care so much?"

I turn to see Jesse. His chin is raised, and he looks down his nose at me like I have something to prove.

"It's my job to care," I say.

"But you'll leave here in a couple of months, right?"

My gaze flits to Matt. He looks away from me, suddenly very interested in whatever he has on the grill.

"It's easy to say you care right now, but then you'll be back in California, and all of this will be so far away." Jesse shakes his head. "How are we supposed to trust that you'll have our best interests *then* too?"

I look at Jesse when I speak, but it's all for Matt. "I've fallen in love with this place. I really have. It's utterly special. What happens when, um, or if, I go back to California? Well, that I can't possibly guess. But . . ." I harden my jaw, staring Jesse down. "I'm what you've got right now. And you can take my work as an opportunity, or you can keep pretending everything is okay until it's too late."

Jesse remains stone-faced for a few more moments before his tension softens. I check on Matt with a fleeting glance. He's still focused on flipping salmon onto plates, but he's smiling.

And to my delight, none of the fishers are hoisting pitchforks.

Kirk saunters over to Rio's lawn chair and leans on it. "Okay. Well, what do you want to know?"

Jackpot.

~

THE NIGHT GOES AS WELL as I'd hoped. Better, actually. They listen to me. They talk to me. And then, we talk about other things. Like I'm not some outsider who isn't deserving of small talk and joking around. I feel like I finally have an opportunity to make my work *count*.

Jesse is the last one to leave. He offers to help clean up, and the whole time I try to keep my smile at bay as I listen to the two brothers palling around together.

When it's time for him to head out, Matt and I follow him to the driveway. "You wanna stay over?" Matt asks softly, leaning into my ear.

"Like a sleepover?" I tease.

"Exactly like that. I have nail polish and everything."

"And rom-coms. Can't forget the rom-coms."

Jesse stops by his truck. "Okay, well." He stares at Matt and me side by side. "Have a good night," he says, looking away.

"Get home safe," Matt calls out.

"Yeah." Jesse climbs into the cab of his truck and revs up the engine.

Matt turns to go inside, reaching for my hand. However, there's an impulsive burst inside me I can't ignore. "Go ahead. I'll be just a second."

I start toward the truck, breaking out into a tiny jog before Jesse can pull away. I knock on the driver's side window and wave.

Through the glass, his brow furrows, but he indulges me by rolling down the window. "What?"

"Thanks for giving me a chance," I say. "Seriously."

Jesse looks over my head to Matt. "Yeah, well, I did it for my brother."

He still wants to put a wall up, I see. That's fine. I can handle it. "Well, I appreciate it. I really do."

Jesse smiles sadly at his hands on the wheel. "Listen, just don't hurt him, okay?"

"I won't," I reply, meaning it.

"No, listen. You're gonna leave eventually, right? That's going to hurt him. So, don't give him false hope." Jesse glances up again. "He doesn't deserve that."

I pat the side of his truck and step back. "Noted."

Jesse gives me a nod, rolls up the window, and drives away.

Chapter 27

Fuck Off to California

LILLIAN

Matt wakes me in the morning with a line of kisses in my hair until his mouth brushes my ear. "I have to go work on the boat."

"No," I whimper, grabbing him and throwing my leg over his hip.

He laughs and humors me for a bit longer, holding me like a koala and indulging me with sweet kisses. "You can stay here as long as you want, but the sooner I get this done, the better."

"Fine," I groan and flop into the bed facedown. "I have to do work anyway." I've been slacking. I need to update Dr. Harrison on my findings and start doing some write-ups on my first round of data.

I'm buzzing with excitement. But I'll try to sleep a bit more first.

Matt is quiet as he gets ready. I like his little sounds. His footfalls on the floor, the grunts he makes when he bends over, soft scratching of nails on skin, a ruffle of hair.

More reasons to adore him.

When he's ready, he comes over to the bed and kisses my temple. I wrap him in a goodbye hug, like we've done this a million times—him heading out early and giving me a kiss goodbye.

No one told me Naknek would make me turn to mush.

"I'll see you later," he says.

"Sooner rather than."

Matt chuckles. "I'll do what I can."

We hold each other for a while longer. I play with the button on the pocket of his denim jacket.

"You should stop by Half-Hitch and say hi to Gwen. She'd get a kick out of that."

I lift my weary eyes to his. "Yeah?"

"Yeah, she's a fan," Matt says, before kissing me hard as he grabs my ass.

I squeal with laughter and accept a dozen more kisses before he acts like the adult and says goodbye.

∼

"WELL, THAT'S A SURPRISE," I say, putting my hands on my hips as I stare up at the "Buy Your Friend a Coffee" board. My name is up there. A free coffee on behalf of Matt. Have

I really not told him I prefer tea yet? I guess we still have a lot to learn about each other.

"There you are!" Gwen cries out with a large grin. "Matt said you'd be stopping in."

I laugh. "Did he now?"

She glances up at the board with a cheeky smile. "You know, this isn't like him at all."

"To buy someone a coffee?" I say.

Gwen's face falls. "Oh, god. I should have told him you prefer *tea*."

At least one of the Bentons remembers. "No harm, no foul. I can take a coffee now and then."

"Don't be silly. Tea for Lillian, on Matt," Gwen says, grabbing a cup and turning around to get some hot water.

I glance up at our names again. "You were saying this isn't like him?"

"Oh! Yes, sorry. My mind is always in fifteen different places," she says, glancing at Winnie quietly assembling a scene of dinosaurs on a nearby table.

"What I mean is—" Gwen rips a tea bag open and pops it into the cup. "He just doesn't get a chance to be . . ." She turns back to face me, her lips turned upward as if she's eaten something entirely too sweet. "Romantic."

I'm totally blushing.

She slides the cup across the counter to me. "So, I shouldn't say it's not like him. He just hasn't had an opportunity to exercise that muscle in a long time."

"Well, he's doing a nice job so far," I say, taking the hot cup of tea carefully from the counter.

"That makes me happier than you know," Gwen

says. "Seriously. I can't think of anyone more deserving of, well, whatever you two are doing."

I try not to wince.

Whatever we're doing is a hell of a lot deeper than either of us are ready to admit.

"Well, thanks for the tea."

"You want to sit for a bit?" Gwen asks, gesturing toward an empty table. "It's slow today."

No wonder Matt told me to come visit. Not only did he want to start my day with a romantic flourish, but Gwen needs some company. I hate saying no to her. "I've got some work to do today, but I can try to come back later?"

After saying our goodbyes, I head out the door and walk to the truck. Out of the corner of my eye, I see a dark figure. I jump with a gasp, turning to find Matt's dad standing right next to the truck.

"Mr. Benton!"

Is he drunk? It's not even noon. My mind races, trying to think of something to say.

Wayne approaches me. He's in need of a shave, and from the smell of it, a shower, too.

"I told you to stay away from him," he says.

I swallow.

"You deaf?" Wayne growls.

"I don't know what you want me to say," I answer honestly.

Wayne leans in toward me again. "You think you can whore yourself out to my fucking son and—"

"I'm *sorry*?" I can't believe what I'm hearing.

"Use him to get your way—"

"I'm not *using* him," I say in defense. I'm cornered against the truck, afraid of him grabbing me and throwing me down.

"Like hell you aren't!"

"You don't know what you're talking about," I say.

Wayne leans further in, lifting his chin to intimidate me. He grits out, "I know your kind! And my son is much better than the likes of you."

I want to run, but I'm trapped. The only option is to fight. I drop the cup of tea as he comes in closer, fearing I might have to push him away. I can smell his breath as he snarls, "Go back to where you came from."

With my heart racing, I shut my eyes and thrust my knee into his groin as hard as I can. I wince, expecting him to come at me, but he stumbles back, crying out in pain.

With that small berth, I scramble into the cab and drive away as fast as I can, tires squealing across the asphalt.

My knuckles whiten as I grip the wheel, my heart threatening to punch out of my chest. What would he have done with another moment? Would he have hurt me?

And how am I going to tell Matt what happened?

I drive until I don't recognize the scenery. My head is reeling, and my stomach is in knots as I pull off to the side of the road. I feel like I'm going to throw up, like I'm out to sea, being tempest-tossed.

I slide over and open the door on the passenger side. I get out of the cab, shaking on the side of the road, bracing my hands on my knees. The fresh air steadies my stomach, thank god. But I remain bent over, catching my breath.

That was . . . insane.

With a sharp inhale, I look up at the sky. "What the fuck!" I scream at the mountains, almost laughing at how ridiculous this all is.

As if it could get worse, when I turn around, I realize there's something wrong with my truck. White spray paint spans the length of the truck to the back of the bed.

FUCK OFF TO CALIFORNIA

The words are too steady for Wayne to have painted, especially in the time between me entering the Half-Hitch and him following.

I blink, twin tears sliding down my face.

I can't handle this alone. I just can't. My hands tremble as I grab my phone, sealing myself back in the truck and locking the doors. It's a long shot that I have service, and a longer shot that Matt does too. But I need him.

The call goes through, but he doesn't pick up. I keep calling until he does.

"What's going on?" he answers, breathless.

"I—they—*someone*—" I pant through sobs.

"Woah, woah, woah. Lillian, what's going on?"

It takes a minute to get control of my tears before I'm able to come out with it. "Someone spray painted my truck while I was in the Half-Hitch, and—" I don't tell him about his dad. I can't do that to him right now. "They told me to fuck off."

"They spray painted that on your truck?"

"Yes, I- I—"

"Where are you right now?"

I look up, but the world is bleary. "I don't know. I just kept driving down the main road, and I pulled over, and—"

"Stay where you are. I'm coming to get you."

"Don't hang up. Please don't hang up. I can't be alone. I can't."

"I won't. I'm right here."

By some miracle, the call doesn't drop, not even once. And he drives like the wind until he finds me.

With trembling hands, I unlock my door for Matt. And when he opens it, he pulls me to his chest and squeezes tight.

"It's okay. It's gonna be okay."

I grab onto his jacket and weep into the collar of his shirt. And even though deep down I know it's not going to be okay, I try to focus on this moment in Matt's arms.

Chapter 28

This Has Gone Too Far

MATTHEW

I hold up the net and curse. This is the third shredded net I've found on board.

Crates are overturned and strewn about, and rotting fish litter the deck.

A fucking nightmare.

I should have known whatever's going on wouldn't end with Lillian and the message written on her truck. Yesterday, I had to take care of her and make her feel safe again. And that meant staying at my place, closing the blinds, and forgetting the rest of the world.

Yes, we were able to get lost in each other for a while, but the questions lingered and kept me awake late.

I could guess who is behind this, but I bet the reality is much stranger than anything I can conjure in my head.

There are plenty of people here who would want Lillian to "fuck off" to California, and only a handful who *might* be on her side since the barbecue.

Now, though, whoever is responsible for the attack is coming for me too.

Luckily, this isn't a big city. This is Naknek. It shouldn't be hard to find out who's behind this.

I clean up the boat as best I can, ignoring the money leaving my bank account when I think of replacing those nets. And then I head to the scene of yesterday's crime. My sister's place. I *know* Gwen didn't know something like that would happen. She's too kind of a soul to be an accomplice.

The parking lot is pretty full this morning which is a blessing and curse. Good for business, but bad for investigating, especially when I'm hopping with anger. But I manage to steady my nerves as I push open the door.

Gwen isn't here though. It's Josh behind the counter. No one notices me at first, which is how I catch wind of someone at Lefty's table muttering, "Won't take much to get her to go."

I purse my lips. Fucking idiots. I give Josh a nod, making my presence known with a booming, "Where's Gwen?"

The whole room shifts.

"She didn't come in today. Had to stay home with Winnie."

That's news to me. "She sick?"

Josh merely shrugs. I should know better than to think I'd get any info from a teenager. "Coffee?"

There's a creeping feeling down my spine. I scan the coffee shop, realizing there are a lot of eyes on me. "Yeah, coffee. Fine."

I turn back to the room. "What's up?" I pose to the room and wait.

All the faces are familiar. Lefty. Finton. Rio. Ian's here too, but he looks apologetic as hell.

"Someone want to say something?"

Nothing.

"Here's your coffee," Josh mutters.

I take it. "Thanks, kid." I sip it but don't taste it. "No one's gonna say anything?"

Still, silence.

I reach into my pocket for some bills.

"No, you don't have to—" Josh tries to stop me.

But I'm making a point. I don't bother to check the bills before I slam them down on the counter and glower at my brothers. My fucking *brothers*. And uncles and fathers. Apparently, we're only a family when it fucking suits everyone. "Who is going to fucking *talk?*"

"Relax, mate," Ian says, trying to keep his voice light. "Don't need to get your knickers in a twist just because—"

"Because you are all staring at me after someone trashed my boat? After someone vandalized my—" My *what?* Who is she to me? "You all know what happened. I don't need to spell it out."

Rio looks genuinely shocked. "Your boat was trashed?"

"Happens to the best of us, Matty," Lefty says, barely containing his snicker.

"Showin' your whole fucking ass," I snap in response.

Naked in Naknek

He holds up his hands. "You've become an ornery bastard since that girl came into town."

"She's not a *girl*, and she's here to save—"

"We don't need to be saved!" Finton snarls, his stupid, post-pubescent face red as a beet. "Not by some city girl who—"

I look at Rio and Ian. "Come on, guys, you were there the other night, you know how—"

"You tried to poison them against us, the way she's poisoned you?" Lefty cries out, pushing himself to his feet. He limps a few steps in my direction. "We're smarter than that, Benton. Smarter than you." He opens his arms up, gathering up the attention of the room like a smarmy politician. "We've all been there. Snowed by a pretty face."

I glare at him. I take umbrage with the use of the word "girl," of the mentions of her beauty, and of anything that devalues who she is beyond her exterior. But it's a lost argument.

Lefty sticks out a long, crooked finger. "But now, it's time to wake up." He pokes me in the chest.

"*You* trashed my boat, Lefty?"

His eyes bulge, the appearance of innocence absolutely failing him. "Me? No, I'd never. I just understand why someone might be inspired to get you to come to your senses. That's all."

"You're delusional." I look at Finton, at a few other faces that didn't come to the barbecue, and at Rio and Ian, who are too spineless to speak up. "Remember this moment. Seriously. Because this is a turning point. The longer you keep your heads up your asses, the less time you have to fix what's happening."

Lefty shakes his head and turns back to the shop. "Can't talk to someone not willing to hear."

"Unbelievable," I mutter, followed by a dry laugh. "That I'm the one not willing to hear."

I storm out of the Half-Hitch, not minding the coffee dribbling onto my hand. My blood is boiling anyway. A splash of hot coffee won't do anything to me.

My brain is a shitstorm of questions with unfulfilled answers: What do I do? *I don't know.* Where do I go? *Away from here.* Who do I have? *Lillian.*

I have Lillian.

I'll leave Naknek and go back to Los Angeles with her. Fuck it. There's fishing down there. I could work in a cannery if I have to. I'll do whatever. But I'm not going to stay here and listen to the chorus of "I told you so" for the rest of my life when it's *me* who should be saying, "I told you so."

It's *me*.

I go up to my truck and realize something is off. In the roil of my brain, I didn't see it until now. The door is lower than it usually is. Not by much. Just enough for me to realize something's wrong. I glance down at my front tire. It's flat. And not by accident. There's an obvious slice in the side of the tire.

All the tires have matching slices.

And unlike Lillian, I don't get scared.

I get angrier.

I prowl around my truck, then around the perimeter of

the property, looking for anyone hiding. Snickering kids, devious fishermen, a particularly cunning bear. Whatever it is, *whoever* it is, I'll take it on. This has gone too far.

When I get back to my truck, Lefty's leaving the Half-Hitch with his entourage. He grimaces at the tires. "Yeesh. Bad luck today, huh, buddy?"

I bite the inside of my cheek. Hard. Or else I might throw a punch, and that would be embarrassing for all of us.

Rio comes up beside me, puppy-eyed and quiet. Embarrassed. "Sorry, man. It's not looking good for your girlfriend."

I laugh humorlessly. "Yeah, whose fault is that?"

He diverts his eyes before scrambling away.

"Yeah, better fucking run," I say before whipping out my phone to call a tow.

Chapter 29

Whose Side Are You On?

LILLIAN

No matter how much I turn the knobs to focus my microscope, the sample remains blurry. My vision is totally clouded by my racing thoughts and high anxiety.

I can't shake the fear roiling in my gut. It was better at Matt's. When I wasn't alone. Being wrapped in his arms was my safe haven. But ever since I got back to the cottage this morning, I've been on edge. Waiting for someone to bang on my door and yell at me some more. Or worse.

I check the time on my phone. Who knows how many more hours I have here by myself until Matt's done working on the boat? I need to focus and get work done. I can't let my thoughts stew in the cacophony of my mind. Matt will come back, and I'll feel better. I just need to make it through each second, each minute, each hour.

Then, I'll be good.

I push the microscope away and rub my eyes. If I can just come up with a solution . . . they need to know that they're not going to end up like Egegik. That they're not going to shrink away because their livelihood is taken.

I blow out a breath and shake out my hands. "Come on, Lillian, *relax*," I say. My heart rate has been uncomfortably quick since my encounter with Wayne. I start rubbing my breastbone. "You're fine. You're safe. The door is locked. No one is going to come after you."

But what if they do come after me? What if Ian has just been friendly to appease me and actually gave out my key to the townsfolk so they could show up brandishing pitchforks?

Do they even use pitchforks in Alaska?

This isn't helping. I get to my feet and start pacing. I need to *do* something. Not just give myself a heart attack.

Grants.

I need to spend time looking at grants I can get for Naknek, so the fishermen have other jobs secured if they put more strictures on fishing. Maybe give them access to benefits they don't have when they're all working for themselves out on the bay.

Just as I start to formulate a plan, I hear the wheels of a truck on the gravel outside.

Oh no. They're here.

When I pull back the curtain to look out the front window, I see Matt climbing down from his truck. He's already done with his work?

No . . . something is wrong. The expression on his face isn't just angry—it's furious.

I open the door as he barrels up the front steps. "What's wrong?"

Matt nods his chin beyond me. "Let's go inside."

Great, now my heart is racing even faster. I don't need this. I can't handle this.

I need a tranquilizer.

Once we step inside, Matt shuts the door, locks it, and pulls off his black cap. His hair is a mess like he's been pulling at it.

"Matt, what's wrong?"

He rubs the lower part of his face and leans against the door. He's quiet for a long time as he gathers his thoughts. Finally, he lets out a long sigh. "They trashed my nets."

I frown, staring at him with confusion.

"And slashed my fucking tires. Just got them replaced down at—"

"Who?" I interject. "Who did?"

Matt looks away, shaking his head. "I don't know exactly. But if I were to hazard a guess, I'd say whoever spray painted your car had something to do with it."

My shoulders fall. "Oh, my god, *Matt*."

He says nothing, pursing his lips tight.

I go to him. "I'm so sorry. You don't deserve this."

"Neither do you."

"I understand why they'd take out their anger on me, but on you? That doesn't seem—"

"They think I'm a traitor."

I scoff. "And they don't see themselves exactly the

Naked in Naknek

same? They'd hurt one of their own just because you're—we're—"

What *are* we? Together? Dating? Fucking? I don't even know. And the fact that I don't know makes the entire situation seem even more ridiculous. Why would Matt be sticking out his neck for a temporary fling when he has a life in Alaska?

I don't know how to finish that sentence, so I throw up my hands and walk away. "God, I'm so tired of this. I'm so tired of trying to understand them."

"They're good people, they just—"

"They destroyed your nets! Slashed your tires! That's not what good people do!" I exclaim. I'm so mad. I can understand why they're coming after me, but to do this to Matt . . . that's a new low. "Those nets are expensive. Tires are expensive. A tow is—"

Matt shoves his hands in his pockets. "I've got the money."

"And you should still have the money!" I retort. "These people—your *family*! They're supposed to look out for you, and instead they're trying to ruin your life because they can't stand *change*." I'm unleashing every negative thought I've bottled up while trying to stay in Naknek's good graces. "The fucking ignorance is astonishing. Seriously, Matt. I don't know how you made it to the other side when everyone here is so fucking—"

"Stupid?"

I stop in my tracks and look at him.

"You think we're stupid?" Matt prompts.

I furrow my brow. "I didn't say that."

"You said 'ignorant.' That's the same as stupid in my book."

My mouth opens and closes as I flounder trying to find the right words. His gaze feels like the weight of mountains is on top of me. "Well, it's not in mine. If I meant stupid, I would have said stupid."

Matt tucks his tongue into his cheek and avoids my gaze.

"Are you . . . are you really fighting with me right now?" I ask, more out of heartbreak than anger.

"I'm just saying."

"How can you defend them when they've done this to you? To both of us?"

"Don't, Lillian."

"Don't what?"

"Make me angrier than I already am."

I claw my hand to my chest. "*I'm* the one that is making you angrier?"

"Yes. Now, calm down so we can—"

"Calm *down?*" That's my last fucking straw. I will not be told to calm down when I'm being threatened. If he doesn't want sympathy for his problems, fucking fine. But I'm not going to gloss over how scared I am. "Don't you tell me to calm down."

An angry little growl comes from the back of Matt's throat. "I didn't mean it like—"

"Spare me," I snap. "How dare you talk to me like that when I've been here all day trying to figure out what the hell to do to bridge the gap between my work and this stupid fucking town! How dare you even *suggest*

I'm the one overreacting when all I've done is try to help!"

Matt lets out a strained breath from between clenched teeth. "I misspoke, alright? I don't want to fight with you, Lillian, but I'm—" He lifts his eyes, and although his blood is running hot, I see something in his eyes akin to fear. Echoes of a little boy who's lost in the woods and can't find his way home. "This is my life! This isn't just a place I can walk away from. This is my whole fucking life."

"This is my life, too, Matt! Even though I don't live here, it's not like my soul's on ice."

"Dammit. I know that, but—"

"Then, don't fucking tell me to calm down! I'm scared. I'm terrified. And all I've ever done, tried to do, is to show these people I care. And now they're threatening us? What have either of us done to deserve this?"

Matt opens his mouth to respond.

"*Actually* done. Because, screw it, I'm tired of paying attention to their feelings. They're grown adults. I'm not responsible for them. And you aren't either."

Matt licks his lips. "They're not ignorant."

We're still on that, huh? "What would you call them, then?"

"They're scared. That's fair. To be scared."

"Just because they're scared doesn't mean they get to treat anyone the way they've treated me! Fuck! Whose side are you on?"

"Yours! I'm on your side!"

I shake my head. "You're not. You want to play both sides. That's why they're fucking with you."

Matt throws his hat down and crosses the room. "Dammit, Lillian. I'm not some sort of secret operative. I'm just trying to live my life."

"Then, it's probably for the best you take care of that," I say coldly.

Matt stops in his tracks and turns slowly. "What's that supposed to mean?"

"I mean, it's silly to keep doing this when we both know it won't last once I leave for California. Might as well just call it now. Then you won't be pulled in two directions," I say. I am not usually so cold, but it's clear this isn't working. Even if we weren't in shambles, what happens next? Matt's not going to come to LA with me, and I'm not going to stay where I'm not wanted.

What I've said lingers in the air.

"Besides, even if we were to try, your father wants me gone, too."

Matt's eyebrow quirks.

"Before I found my car all fucked up, he—" I stop. There's no need to give him the details. It will just make things worse. As if that were even possible. "He wants me gone like everyone else. And I don't want to put you in that position any longer."

Matt is quiet for a moment and then starts laughing. Not a real laugh, but a pained, disdainful laugh. "This some fucking joke?"

"No," I say without more explanation.

Matt's laugh peters out. I don't have the heart to look at him. It feels hot in here. "Hot" is not a word I use to describe my time here in Alaska, other than the times I've been tangled up with Matt amidst the sheets. But this isn't just *heat*. It's suffocation. My blood pumping, heart racing, and rage flaming down the sides of my face. I need fresh air. Need to breathe.

"You're done," he says. A limp fact hanging in the air.

"One of us was going to have to be done at some point," I offer. "We're too different. Let's just admit it."

The silence hangs. My temperature increases. It's like I have a fever.

Matt goes to my table of materials and observes them carefully. "Yeah. You're right." He makes no move to leave. And if he's not going to, I have to.

"I need . . . I need to go," I say in barely a whisper.

Matt says nothing, and I don't need him to. If I don't get out of here, I'm going to be burned alive. I open the door and leave, heading around the side of the cottage to the rocky beach.

As I walk, tears blur my eyes.

I don't want to admit it, but a part of me hopes Matt will come after me.

He doesn't. And why would he? I just ended things.

I guess I wanted him to prove to me why I shouldn't. Run after me, tell me he chooses me, say he'll fight for me.

I eventually slow to a stop along the shore. I'm not sure how long I've been walking. Long and fast enough that my calves are aching.

Turning, I look out over the Naknek river. Pain seizes in my chest. I've fallen in love with this place. With its remoteness, with its mystery, with its soul.

I've fallen in love with the people, too. When they

haven't been downright antagonistic, they've been kind and passionate. Thoughtful.

And, of course, I've fallen in love with Matt.

So silly and fast compared to every other relationship I've been in. I usually take my time. Have hypotheses, do experiments, get results, and *then* make decisions.

With Matt, all I did was feel. Because that's what Alaska calls for. Nothing to distract you from your inner nature. From aligning with yourself.

I'm not used to feeling so alive. In LA, despite the hustle and bustle, the world feels . . . suffocating. Now, I breathe for the first time. It's almost too much.

Finally, I turn back and walk the mile to my cottage. I say a soft prayer Matt hasn't left, and we can talk through what just happened. I don't want to lose him, but I don't know how to keep him. However, one of his embraces, a kiss to the top of my head, and a soft word or two would erase all my fears. I want to dive into him and remain there forever.

I'll tell him that I love him. Then, everything will be a real mess.

But at least I'll have him.

As I approach the cottage, I realize I forgot my keys. I'm cursing myself until I see the back door hanging open.

"Matt?" I call out as I approach. "You still here?"

I step into the doorway, seeing the mess inside. My worktable is flipped onto its side, and all of my equipment is scattered across the ground. Smashed samples, shattered glass, and tiny puddles of water are all over the place.

It takes a second to put two and two together.

Matt must have gotten angry and destroyed everything. He turned into one of them.

He turned on *me*.

Fine. It's as it should be.

Fuck him.

Holy shit. He was *violent*. What if I hadn't walked away? What would have happened?

My heart lurches. The samples are one thing, but was my computer—my research and findings— destroyed too?

I rush to the bed where I last had my laptop, and thankfully, it looks untouched. With trembling fingers, I turn it on. All of the information is still there.

Not all is lost.

But as I scan the scene left behind by Matt's tantrum, I wish I could get back all the memories we shared, all the beautiful times, all the love and respect I had for him.

Because all it took was twenty minutes to show me who he really is. And now that the curtain has been pulled back, I can't ever see him the same way again.

I secure the doors and grab my phone to call Dr. Harrison. It takes a few rings for him to answer. "Dr. Harvey, good to hear from you."

"The project—" My mouth is dry. I try to wet it with my tongue, but it's no use. I'm panicked, and there's no saliva coming. "It's over. I have to—I have to come back."

"What? I don't understand."

I stare at the mess Matt left in his wake. "I'm not safe here. They're—I have the data, but I need to get out of Naknek. As soon as possible."

"You're not safe?" Dr. Harrison sounds disbelieving. "What's happened? I'm sure we can—"

"I'm done. It's over. I can't stay here another day."

"Dr. Harvey, be reasonable."

"I've been scrutinized from the moment I arrived. I've been subjected to nasty comments, intimidated, and now I've just come back to my cottage to find all my samples destroyed. I'm not staying here a second longer!" I cry out, knowing it's not the appropriate way to speak to my boss, but not seeing another.

"Your samples? Oh my." There's some movement on the other end of the line. "Alright. We'll get you out as soon as—"

"Today. I need to get out *today*."

Dr. Harrison huffs. "That's probably not possible with—"

"Make it possible! I'm not staying in Naknek a second longer," I tell him. And that's the God's honest truth. If he's not going to help me out, then I'll get out of here myself. I grab my suitcase and fling it onto the bed. "If I need to spend another night here, book me a room in King Salmon. But Dr. Harrison, I'm done."

"Noted. We obviously don't want your safety compromised for the sake of the project." From his tone, I'm not sure I believe him. "Stay by your phone. I'll be in touch within the hour."

He hangs up, leaving me alone again. I focus on packing everything up.

I meant what I said. I'm not staying here.

Chapter 30

You're Gonna Have to Get Over Her

MATTHEW

I don't want to be around anyone but going home alone might kill me. So, I end up at Fat Fred's in the corner of the bar, where it's dark and I won't be bothered. It's the middle of the afternoon, and it's more crowded in here than you'd think.

She's done. That's that.

I don't want to be done. I don't want to carry Lillian's scar on my heart. This isn't how it was supposed to go.

Fred replaces my beer without asking if I want another. He's good like that. Clairvoyant or something. I don't know. A mind reader.

"Thanks," I mutter.

He gives me a half-smile. For what it's worth, he hasn't given me any impression *he* wants to fuck with me. But who knows, maybe I'll keel over and die from arsenic poisoning in an hour. All bets are off.

I swig the beer and look down at my phone, trying to catch it off-guard as if that might somehow manifest a text from Lillian. Still nothing.

After she stormed out, I waited for what felt like an eternity for her to come back. I imagined her tearfully returning, admitting she didn't *want* to walk away.

But she never did. So, I left.

I should have gone after her. Because now I'm left without knowing what comes next. Will she reach out? Do I reach out? Is it over? Over-*over*?

"For the best," says a familiar, gruff voice, a hand landing on my shoulder.

My spine straightens. "What are you doing here, Dad?"

He sits heavily on the seat beside me and gives Fred a wave. "Fred gave me a call you were out here drowning your sorrows by your lonesome. Thought I should check on you."

"I'm fine." I spin the base of my glass slightly, unwilling to look at him.

"It was never going to be easy with a woman like her. Better you cut it off now. It's for the best," Dad says.

I stare at him as Fred comes over with a beer for my dad. "How do you know?"

Dad takes a sip of his beer. It sickens me how his body responds to the drink. Unwinds. Settles. "Know what?" he asks.

"About Lillian and me breaking it off. How do you know?"

Naked in Naknek

Dad hesitates and then lets out a little laugh. "Well, I just assumed. After everything that's gone on the past couple days—"

"You mean, you intimidating her?"

"Aw, I didn't intimidate her."

"I bet you did," I retort.

Dad lifts a hand to the bar. "We're in public, Matty. Let's be civil, huh?"

"Oh, now you want to be civil?" I laugh wryly. "Pathetic."

His jaw hardens, but he doesn't reply in his quick, angry way. "Matty, I'm looking out for you. You get that, right?"

"It doesn't feel like you are," I tell him. It feels like a scorched-earth policy. That this town is looking to destroy everything I have, simply for falling outside the purview of what's acceptable to them.

"You'll thank me one day," Dad mutters. "I can wait for that."

If you live that long.

My phone buzzes, and my whole body jumps. I see Lillian's name flash on the screen, a text message. I scramble to pick up the phone, ignoring Dad's groan.

It takes me a few seconds to comprehend the message. My eyes jump from sentence to sentence without reading.

"You're gonna have to get over her, Matt."

I grit my teeth to block out the rest of the world and read.

Fine. You all got what you wanted. I'm gone.

I . . . what?

Lolu Sinclair

I cut my trip short, and I'm on my way to Anchorage.
My eyes sting. So fast. So quick?
I was trying to protect you, Matt. I loved you.
Loved. Past tense.
But for you to destroy my cabin. My samples. When you knew how much my work meant to me . . . that just shows me the person you've always been. It's easier to leave knowing I loved a man who never existed.

None of this makes sense. I don't know what she's saying. What is she talking about?

"She trying to sweet talk you?" Dad asks.

"No, I—there's—this is a mistake," I say. I type out a message hurriedly, telling her to call me, and that it wasn't me. Then, I wait.

"I guess it's only fair you get yourself twisted up over a girl now and then. Makes sense."

I ignore him. A moment later, a few photos appear on my phone. Photos from Lillian's cabin. Much different than the way I left it.

The table overturned. Vials smashed on the ground. Papers strewn about.

I shake my head. No . . . no, that wasn't me.

I press Lillian's contact and try to call her. Once, twice, three times. Each time it doesn't go through. She's either hanging up on me, or God forbid, she blocked me. "Fuck. Fuck, this is—I have to go."

Dad grabs my arm, pulling me back onto the stool. "Hey, slow down, okay? She's not worth all that."

I rip my arm from his grip. "What do you know about worth?"

Naked in Naknek

Dad holds up his hands in surrender, a rare sight for him.

My heart sinks as I look at him. He seems calm. Too calm to be angry at me or the situation. He knows something I don't. "How did you know that things were over between Lillian and me?" I ask again. This time, knowing his answer is going to be a lie.

His mouth falls open, and he forces a laugh. "I told you, Matty. I heard you were sulking. I thought—"

"Bull*shit*." I turn my phone toward him to show him the photos. "Did you do this?"

Dad doesn't look as affronted as he should be if he's innocent "I've done a lot of stuff, but I don't remember that one."

"Tell me the truth."

"Am."

"*Dad*, tell me the truth, *now*."

Dad picks up his pint glass and looks away. "You think I could do something like that? Sneak into the cabin and tear it apart in just a couple of minutes? Naw. I'm not spry enough for that anymore."

I push myself up from the stool, disgust twisting in my chest. He's not admitting guilt but isn't *not* admitting it. And the thing is, I believe he isn't capable of doing something like that. At least not so cleanly. But he knows too much. He's the brains behind the operation. I'm sure of it.

And I'm pretty sure I know who the muscle was.

I TEAR into the parking lot by the docks, traveling fast enough to kick up gravel loudly and make everyone look.

Including Jesse, who looks to be shooting the shit with Tuma and a few others.

He's the reason I'm here. I went up the highway looking for his car, and it didn't take long to find him after I checked Lillian's cabin. I thought maybe I could catch her. But her truck was gone, and when I looked in the window, so was all her stuff. I missed her. And I'm kicking myself for it.

But I'm done with this bullshit.

I'm not going to shoulder the guilt of doing something so unthinkable to Lillian. Even if we're never together again—even if I never fucking see her—I will not live the rest of my life with her thinking I did something so abhorrent.

I'm getting to the bottom of this. Now.

I park my truck so the front is pointing right at the group. My eyes lock with my brother. And for once, Jesse isn't his haughty self. He looks scared. He knows what his big brother is capable of when I'm being protective. I usually keep a cool head. It's why I'm the boss.

Which means the times when I go off, I'm a fucking volcano.

I climb out of the cab and storm toward the group. "You're a fucking piece of shit," I growl, pointing a finger at my brother.

"What else is new?" he asks, attempting a smile for the onlooking fishermen.

He knows what he did. I know it, too. I'm not pulling

any punches. Literally. I grab Jesse by the collar and punch him in the jaw.

Jesse's head swings to the side, and he lets out a gasp of pain.

"Wait, Matt!" Tuma cries out.

I ignore him, and all the other fishermen crowd around. Before Jesse can reset, I bend him over and jab my knee into his belly, knocking the wind out of him. Hands grab at my jacket to stop me. I throw Jesse down on the ground. "Get off me," I growl, shrugging off the hands.

Jesse coughs a few times and rubs his jaw. "What the hell?"

"Don't play dumb," I reply. "I know what you did to Lillian."

"Not her again," someone groans.

I send a seething glare in the direction of the voice. "You want to be next?" That gets them to back off.

Jesse is quiet. He won't meet my eyes—just like Dad. "It was for your own good," he says softly. "For all of us."

"Fuck all of you," I say.

Tuma appears in my periphery. "Matt, let's calm down."

"No, *fuck all of you!*" I shout, my voice echoing off the water. I don't care who hears it. In fact, I want everyone to hear. "You're all full of shit."

Jesse glowers up at me. "You've been fucking brainwashed, man."

"No, you're all brainwashed! You're all stuck in your echo chamber, telling each other what you want to hear, when the truth is we're digging our own graves if we don't admit things need to change. And Lillian—" My chest singes knowing she's gone. Knowing she left thinking I'm the villain in this story. That she believes I have a temper bad enough to destroy her work. I would never, *ever* do something like that. "You're my brother, Jesse," I croak.

Nothing comes out after that.

"Yeah, I am," Jesse says, pushing himself up from the ground, dusting dirt off his hands. Tuma goes to his side to help, but Jesse fends him off with a flat hand. "I'm fine." Jesse approaches me, his boots crunching on the ground.

I don't move a muscle. If he wants to square up, let's square up.

"Yeah, I'm your brother. And that means, sometimes I have to do the things you don't want to do . . . to protect you."

"I don't need protecting," I say.

"Sure, you do. You let her get in the way. You got distracted. And it's time you wake the fuck up."

I tilt my head to the side, my nostrils flaring. "Do I need protection from Lillian? Or do I need it from you and all the rest of this damn town? Because she's not the one who slashed my tires."

Jesse's jaw tics. That's his tell.

And yet, I don't move fast enough to avoid him socking me in the eye.

∼

"Here." Gwen shoves a bag of ice on my eye.

My whole body winces in pain. "Jeez, be careful."

"Yeah, says the man who got knocked out from one jab to the eye," she murmurs.

I try to argue, but she's right. All it took was one punch from Jesse to lay me out on the gravel. Next thing I knew, I was shaken awake in the passenger seat of my truck by Gwen. Apparently, someone went to get her during the fight. She was my rescuer, and now she's my nursemaid.

"Now, keep that on there. You need the swelling to go down," Gwen murmurs before moving away to check on Winnie, who's sitting in front of the television playing with some Hot Wheels, her new obsession.

Gwen's back before I know it. "Take these." She shoves a handful of Advil into my hand.

I throw them back, and Gwen brings a glass of water to my lips and tips it back for me. I side-eye her with my uncovered eye. "I can drink water on my own, Gwen."

"Sure," she says without much fuss.

A massive sigh pours out of me. "I can't believe they'd do this," I say softly.

From the carpet, Winnie makes an explosion sound and slams cars together. Ah, the innocence of childhood.

"And that she believes I would do that to her. How come this is so fucking dramatic? It's just—"

Gwen snickers. "What? Love?"

"I didn't say *love*," I grumble.

"Didn't have to."

I glance at my sister. She's smiling sympathetically at me. Her eyes travel to Winnie, her smile fading slightly. "You know, sometimes we humans believe so much in one thing that we end up circling to its opposite."

I glance at Winnie. She's oblivious to our conversation, rolling a car across the carpet with her eyes glued to the animated show on the screen. "Is that how you feel about what happened with..."

We don't say his name. He wasn't a good guy, Winnie's dad. At least, that's how we saw it. All it took was one fishing season for Gwen to fall so deeply in love with him that she almost left Naknek. Until he found out she was pregnant with his baby, and then he left her.

"I mean, don't tell me after all this time you regret me having Win?" she whispers with a knowing smile.

"Of course not. Winnie's my whole heart. You know that, Gwen."

"I know," she says with a nod. "But there was a time when you and Jesse couldn't fathom why I would want to have her on my own."

I haven't forgotten. My brother and I had planned out a whole trip to get her to a clinic so she could have an abortion. We assumed she wouldn't want to be a single mother. Wouldn't want the memory of a man who treated her so poorly. We thought she was giving up so much to become a mother. Her plans to become a pilot. All of her freedom.

And she did give those things up. For something so much greater.

"I'm sorry," I say, regret spiraling through me for how we handled Gwen when she needed us most.

"I'm not looking for apologies. I'm just saying you understand where they're coming from, more than you want to admit."

A stab of frustration shoots through me. "So, what? You agree with them? I thought you liked Lillian?"

Gwen tsks. "Jumping to conclusions, as usual." She places her hand on my arm. "We wouldn't have Winnie if I didn't tell you to fuck off," she says in a low voice.

"You're stronger than me, though," I say.

She rolls her eyes, pursing her lips. "Men. You all define masculinity as the thing that makes you strong. But when you have to step up to do the *actual* strong thing, you freak out and run the other way."

"Your point?" I ask.

Gwen pinches my arm, and I balk in pain.

"I'm injured! Go easy on me."

"Don't be stupid," Gwen says. "I'm trying to get you to realize this might be a time when you have to tell everyone else to back off because only you know what's good for *you*."

I bite the inside of my cheek. "I didn't push her away, though. She told me—"

"You were wishy-washy," Gwen says.

"I got my tires slashed for defending her."

"You got your tires slashed because they all knew they could get a reaction out of you. They kept dangling their approval for you, and you kept running after it like a horse with a carrot. All you had to do was stop giving a shit about all of them, stop giving them a reaction, and—"

"You know that wouldn't have stopped them."

Gwen's gaze hardens on me. "But she'd still be here, wouldn't she?"

I want to scream. Just scream. There's no other way I

know to express my feelings. It hurts so bad. I messed up so bad. "She was going to leave eventually."

"Did you ever think of asking her to stay?"

"Of course, but she's—"

"What? Totally in love with you?" Gwen shakes her head. "You make it work when that comes around." Her gaze travels back to Winnie. "I did."

"She thinks I destroyed everything. She's *gone*."

"And you didn't go after her? Lame, bro."

Chapter 31
Culture Shock

LILLIAN

I didn't consider the culture shock I'd experience when returning to LA.

The air hits me first.

It's thick, heavy, and carries the smell of exhaust and sunbaked asphalt. And I'd almost forgotten the way Los Angeles sprawls endlessly. Not a natural one, but a sprawl forced on the land, built up over and over again.

In Alaska, I'd grown used to the quiet—a quiet that has its own sounds: wind over water, bird calls, the distant crackle of branches in the forest. Here, the noise presses in, constant and loud as if everything is happening at once.

It's an entirely different world.

My Uber takes me to Sarah's West Hollywood apartment since my subletter is supposed to stay at mine through November. Sarah doesn't know I'm coming yet. I haven't had the heart to talk to anyone since I left Alaska.

Better late notice than no notice, I suppose. As he pulls out into traffic, I whip out my phone and call my bullish, lawyerly sister.

"What's up?" she answers.

It comes out in a torrent of word vomit. "Everything went sideways, and all of Naknek hates me, and now I'm back in LA on my way to your apartment."

"Woah, slow down. Start from the beginning. What?"

It takes most of my ride to unwind the tale for her. I've been keeping her updated, but not in much detail. Last she knew, Matt and I were knocking boots, and the research was going great. So, there's *a lot* to tell her.

My poor Uber driver stops in front of Sarah's apartment while I'm *still* telling her the story. He gives me a wary look as he unloads my luggage. It's mortifying enough that any of this happened, let alone having my freaking Uber driver overhear the tragic details in all their glory. I stand on the curb, staring up at the building, unable to move. "And then I left. I didn't even think about where I'd stay or anything, I just—"

"Okay, stop. Take a breath, Lil," Sarah tells me.

I do so, though my breath is shaky and strained.

"I'm coming home now."

Only now do I realize it's the middle of the workday. "Oh, my god, Sarah, you're at work. I'm sorry, I—"

She doesn't let me finish. "You think I can sit here and let you suffer alone? Absolutely not!"

I shut my eyes. I don't know which way is up and which

is down. My whole world has gone topsy fucking turvy since yesterday. I don't think I've even slept. But the idea of a big bed with crisp white linens sounds like heaven. "I'm sorry," I say meekly.

"Don't be sorry. You'd do the same for me."

I smile for the first time since I left the cabin. She's right. I would.

"What are sisters for? Other than being there when the chips are down?"

"And giving me shit."

Sarah snickers. "That, too. You have my key, right?"

I fish my ring of keys out of my purse. "I do."

"Head on up. I'll see you in twenty minutes."

I crash as soon as I get into Sarah's place. Her apartment is luxurious, the kind of condo you'd see on *Selling Sunset* with floor-to-ceiling windows and one of those walk-in rain showers. However, I bypass all of that to plant, face first, in Sarah's bed. I wake up shortly after Sarah arrives. She brings me greasy fries, burgers, and milkshakes in bed. We eat while Bravo plays in the background. There will be plenty of time for conversation about what happened.

Right now, I'm just happy to have my sister.

∽

THE NEXT DAY, I go into PMI to meet with Dr. Harrison, and when I walk into his office, his lack of reaction sends a shiver down my spine.

"Take a seat, Dr. Harvey."

I do, placing my laptop and the manila folder holding all my research on my lap.

Dr. Harrison says nothing, his beady eyes focused on me.

He wants me to talk first. Okay. Fine. "So, I've compiled most of my findings for you. While my samples were destroyed, I still have most of the data from the two and a half months I was in Naknek. I know it isn't the scope of four months we originally wanted, but—"

"No, it's not," Dr. Harrison bites out.

I grip my laptop harder. "I assure you my findings are conclusive, even with the limited timeline."

Dr. Harrison holds out his hand, and I give him the folder.

"I've yet to compile them into a cohesive research paper, but—"

He opens the folder and holds up his hand, signifying for me to stop talking.

What an asshole.

For far too long we sit in silence while he pages through my research. I'm incensed he's angry with me when my literal safety was being threatened. However, I have to keep an even keel. Naknek might have wanted to drive me away, but now I'm determined to help them, even if it's out of spite.

It will serve them right if things get better thanks to me. I bet they won't even send a fruit basket.

I bet Matt won't even call.

At first, I blocked him. And then, I unblocked him because I wanted to know if he could defend himself against the awfulness of destroying my samples. But then I blocked him again when Sarah arrived. I didn't want her giving me shit for hoping.

"Where do you see this going next with this limited research?" Dr. Harrison asks.

It's not limited. It's plain as day what's happening.

"Well, first, I'll draw up the report. And then, I'll submit it to the Alaska state government. I'd also like to start looking at grants and various projects that might be sustainable in the climate. Political and otherwise."

Dr. Harrison lifts his chin, eyes the folder again, and then tosses it across the desk to me. "I have to say, there's a lot more here than I anticipated."

I take the folder, trying to tread carefully through the things I want to say to him. "I promise, Dr. Harrison, if I had not felt so threatened, I would have happily stayed. But from the beginning, they were clearly unhappy with me being there. It probably would have been more sustainable if you'd sent a team rather than just me."

"Yes, if we had the budget."

I nod, but I want to ask why his office is so big if we're concerned about money.

"You have until the end of the week to get your full report in."

I gulp. That's not as much time as I originally anticipated, but I can make it happen. If I have to. And given how annoyed Dr. Harrison is with me, it's clear I have no wiggle room.

"We'll review it and see if it's worthy of publishing. And

then, you can explore the grants and related projects on your own time before your next project."

My stomach turns. Not that I'm not excited at the prospect of moving onto something else. It simply feels unceremonious. Write a report, find some grants, move on.

Dr. Harrison won't understand or appreciate how difficult it was to leave Naknek. He'd probably chastise me even more for mixing business and pleasure. With how everything turned out, I can't say I blame him.

"That's all for now," Dr. Harrison says, turning to his computer screen as if I've apparated from the room.

Chapter 32

Humans Are Weird

LILLIAN

Time passes. Both faster and slower than I'd like.
As promised, I have my report to Dr. Harrison by the end of the week.

However, being back in the thick of it reminds me just how nice it was to be away from LA. Just how much I'm really not made for this town. All the cars and wealth and everyone coming and going is so counterintuitive to my spirit.

No one looks up. Not even in Runyon Canyon. They're all having their insular conversations about the most trivial bullshit, walking their purebred dogs and sipping their Erewhon smoothies.

I don't belong here. It's obvious now.

At least I get to escape to PMI most days. I get there early and stay late, even after my report is done.

Speaking of my report, it's the best one I've written. It's going over really well with my peers and even Dr. Harrison, despite his clear disdain for me. Given how good it is, I'm not only applying for grants, but I'm also reaching out directly to institutions, donors, and fellow scientists I admire.

One morning in late October, Trudy knocks on my open door.

"Miss Ma'am, got a minute?" she lilts. Trudy is decked out in the Halloween spirit. An orange shirt with a jack-o-lantern face, white ghost clips in her box braids, and black lipstick to cap off the ensemble. "I've just signed onto a new project."

I lean my elbows on my desk. "Do tell."

She saunters into my office and sits in the spot across from me. "Coral bleaching in the Great Barrier Reef."

My jaw drops. "Shut *up*. You're going to—"

"Australia!" she squeals.

"Naur way!" I say in my best Australian drawl.

Trudy cackles. "Can you believe it? I mean, I've never gone farther than the Rockies for PMI."

"I'm so happy for you."

She grins. "Well, you're going to be even happier when I tell you they've asked me to bring someone else onto the project."

"Someone else . . . you mean?" I point at my chest.

"Duh, girl! You need a new project."

It's not meant to be a dig, but it makes my chest ache.

"Plus, after how your paper has gone over, you have your pick of what you want to do."

I look out the door to make sure no one is walking past, then say with a lowered voice, "Yeah, well, take that up with Harrison."

"He's an asshole."

"He's also the boss," I mutter.

"And that means he is not exempt from us talking behind his back," Trudy says, propping her ankles up on the corner of my desk and leaning back in her chair.

I glance back at my email. Nothing new has come in. I know it's only been a minute or two since I sent my last message, but I'm antsy. I'm desperate to make this work. Alaska deserves it.

And I deserve an apology from Naknek.

"Think about it, Lil. It would be incredible, right? We'd get to do science by day, and party it up with Australian dudes at night! I mean, those *accents*." Trudy waves her hand in front of her face.

I fold my hands under my chin. "I guess the Alaska project might take a long time to tie up anyway. With looking for grants and waiting to hear back from the government."

"Right. I mean, you can easily pass that work off to someone else."

I don't want to pass it off though. I want to see it through to the end. Although, that's what Captain Ahab said about killing Moby Dick.

"Or you can do that work remotely. It's not hard. It's just a few emails and maybe some phone calls."

Trudy has a point.

Later, at happy hour in a WeHo bar crammed with all the mirrors the decorator could find, I bring it up to Sarah. She claps her hands excitedly. "The *accents!*"

"That's what Trudy said."

"You have to go. You can find a husband, and then get dual citizenship. You can introduce me to his brother!"

I laugh, stirring my drink with my straw. "We can't be the sisters who marry brothers. That's ridiculous." I try to shake it off. I've been doing a pretty good job of not thinking of *him*. I've put a padlock on the door holding all those memories and thrown away the key.

Except no matter how far I throw it, I know exactly where it is. It taunts me.

"Besides, no more mixing business and pleasure," I say before taking a big swig of my drink.

Sarah flags down the bartender for another glass of wine. "Yeah, about that. When are we going to talk about it?"

"About what?" I don't need to ask. I know exactly what she's poking at, but I don't want to talk about it. Never will, probably.

"You know . . . sexy fisherman."

I roll my eyes.

"Oh, don't roll your eyes at me. You were obsessed with him."

"Not obsessed." *Totally obsessed.*

"How could you not be when he chops wood for you naked?"

"He wasn't *naked.*"

Sarah narrows her eyes at me. "You know I won't stop hounding you until you tell me how you're feeling about it."

"What's there to tell? I fell hard, and he turned out to be an asshole."

"Right..."

"What's that supposed to mean? *Right?* Don't be cagey."

Sarah shrugs. "I don't know. I mean, we don't know for sure he trashed your cabin, right? You didn't see him do it."

"You're a lawyer, Sarah."

"So?"

"So. Occam's Razor. The simplest explanation—"

"Sure. It's *usually* the right one. But humans are weird. They do weird shit all the time. Half of my client list would be subjects of great Reddit posts."

I'm suddenly very tired. Talking about Matt, *thinking* about Matt, is exhausting. "What's your point, Sarah?"

"I just mean, maybe you should talk to him. Get his side of things."

I don't know why I have to spell this out. "I left my cabin with him in it and returned to find it trashed."

"It could have been a bear, right?" Sarah asks, though it's clear she's not sold on that idea.

I shake my head. Although, it's not implausible. "It's over. Besides, it was just a fling. I mean, we barely knew each other."

That's a lie I'll tell myself until I believe it through and through.

Sarah puts her hand on mine, her eyes boring into

mine earnestly. "Will you talk to me about it when you're ready?"

"Sure," I say, determined to never be ready to talk.

"Okay. I'm your sister. You know you can say anything. I won't judge you."

I snort. "Yeah, right."

"I won't *actually* judge you. Even if I give you a hard time," she says, lifting her glass. "For now, a toast to your new project, right? Australia... that's exciting."

I lift my half-empty cocktail. "You're right. It is." Another adventure. Which will undoubtedly be followed by another adventure, and another, and another until—

I don't want to look back at my life and wonder why I never slowed down. I don't want to be alone. The last thing I want is to become a heartless institute head like Dr. Harrison.

We cheer, our glasses clinking.

I can only take one day at a time. I can't let myself be haunted by what-ifs of the future.

Especially not when the what-ifs of the past are chasing me.

Chapter 33

I've Got a Woman to Go After

MATTHEW

Despite the chill in the air, I'm sweating my ass off.

I unbutton the cuffs of my flannel and roll them up to my elbows, then toss off my hat. I've put off winterizing the boat far longer than I should have. I need to get the boat out of the water and into the storage center near the docks. Luckily, I'm old hat at this. I've had plenty of practice scrubbing off the salt, topping off the fuel tanks, and removing the batteries.

This is usually a celebratory time. An initiation of rest and hibernation for the upcoming cold months. But after my boat was trashed, I had to grind even harder to make up for the financial loss. I've been fishing up until the very last moment I can.

From outside my covered spot, I hear Ian's unmistakable boom, "About time you got her out of the water."

I peek over the bow and give him a meek smile. "Hey, Ian."

Ian walks closer to my boat and touches the side. "Damn, she sure shines, doesn't she?"

"Yeah, wanted to make sure she was in perfect condition for next season," I say before hefting myself over the side of the boat to the ground. "Considering I'm probably going to be working seasons back-to-back." I grab a rag out of my back pocket and wipe my hands off, busying my attention so I don't have to look Ian in the eye. Of all the fishermen, he's probably the one I'm least mad at. Even though he's been an innocent bystander in this mess, he's a bystander, nonetheless.

Ian crosses his arms over his chest. "Been worried about you, kid."

"I've been fine," I reply, mirroring him.

"Sure, you have," Ian says.

"I have."

Ian clicks his tongue. "I'm going to take Gwen's word on this one."

I lean against the hull of my boat. "What'd she say?"

"That you've been struggling since Lillian left."

I shove the rag back in my pocket. "That's not why I've been struggling," I say.

"You don't need to pull the manly-man bullshit with me, Matt. I'm not your dad, huh?"

I press my lips together. I couldn't give less of a shit about being a "manly man." If I think about Lillian for too long, my chest starts to ache, and it puts me in a state I can't get out of for days afterward.

"You cared for her. I know you did."

"Yeah, well. People care for people. Nothing special about it."

"Is that really how you feel?"

"Yep."

Ian pauses, tipping his chin up and looking down his nose at me. "So, if Lillian heard you say there was 'nothing special about it,' you'd be okay with that?"

Well, shit, he has me there. I'm almost cornered but not quite. "She's the one who left."

"You can't blame the girl, can you?"

"No, but I can blame her for not picking up the phone or answering my texts." I've thrown my phone more times than I care to admit.

"You could go after her," Ian says, waggling his eyebrows.

"Make a fool of myself by running to LA and having a door slammed in my face? No thanks. I've already had my ego bruised enough for one summer." For one lifetime, really. "Besides, I have to get through the winter." Ian nods quietly. I take that as a cue to go back to hanging nets.

Normally, I would hire out this task. My mother had a real knack for hanging nets, but I always found an excuse not to do it. This winter I'm doing it myself to save money.

It's actually a very meditative process. The rhythm of sewing the lead lines to the bottom of the net, and the cork lines to the top. The movement is methodic and relaxing.

"You have to decide if it would be worth it, regardless of her answer."

"Sorry?"

Ian clears his throat. "You have to decide if it's worth the risk of looking foolish if you went after her to LA. And if it's not, then you need to build a bridge and get over it. You know what I'm saying?"

I furrow my brow. "Ian, listen, I really don't want—"

"The whole reason I ended up in Naknek was because of a woman. You know that, don't you?"

"Well, yeah, but . . ." It's sort of a sad story, actually. No one mentions it for fear of making Ian get that far away, wistful look in his eye.

Ian opens his hands in front of him. "You think I regret it?"

"No," I say immediately. "I mean . . ."

A wry smile appears on his lips. "Of course, you'd think that. I mean, I don't blame anyone. I wouldn't have settled here if it hadn't been for her."

The story is one that's been passed around Naknek, but I only know bits and pieces of it. I've never heard it from Ian's mouth directly because I assumed he didn't like talking about it.

"I was only going to be in Naknek for one season. And then, I came back for another one, and another one, and you know what they say, third time's a charm." Ian hums. "Stuck around that time."

I watch the older fisherman, his expression thoughtful as he remembers.

"If I'd stayed with her after that first summer, we would

have had more time together. Maybe that would have changed the trajectory." Ian lifts his hand. "You know the rest."

Ian had fallen in love with a local woman, a widow whose husband had died out on the gulf. She had two kids and worked at the cannery to make ends meet. And then, after Ian decided to stay in Naknek for that fateful third fishing season, they lived together until her second child moved to college down in Washington.

Then, her heart gave out.

"I could have left Naknek right after she died, right? But I didn't," Ian continues. "I could have avoided being looked at by all those sympathetic faces if I had just left. But I fucking didn't."

"That's different, Ian. You didn't have any control over—"

Ian laughs. "I'm trying to tell you that love isn't without risk. It can hurt like hell, but . . . but I would have regretted not having those good years."

"But you knew she loved you. I don't know if—"

"What *do* you know, Matt? What do you feel?"

I'm quiet. I'm not sure if I can say it aloud without feeling foolish.

"Sometimes loving something is going toward it. And sometimes love is letting it go. You need a little bit of both," Ian says. "But if you lose it, it hurts like a bitch."

I sigh. I know he's right. The pain is proportional to how good it felt to be with Lillian. "I don't want to spend my whole life thinking about her."

"You won't have to as long as you do everything in

your power to fix things. Besides, if it does work out, then you'll be happy to think about her the rest of your life."

For a moment, I let myself forget how things fell apart. And I remember all those warm moments between us. Moments that made it easy for me to see a future with Lillian. I'd gladly spend all my days thinking of her, putting her first, and giving her my all.

But I can't do that if I'm not actually with her. It would be horrible to pine for her the rest of my life without even trying. "You're right."

"I am," Ian says.

I chuckle, rolling my eyes.

Ian backs away. "Anyway, good talk. I'll see you soon, alright, Matty?"

He disappears out of my port, and I stand there, staring at the pile of net and cork line I've started to hang.

Damn the nets. I've got a woman to go after.

~

WITH MY DUFFEL THROWN INTO the back of my truck, I pull into the Half-Hitch for a quick coffee before I head to the airport to fly to Anchorage.

Inside the café, I'm surprised to find Jesse at the counter quietly talking with Gwen. At first, they don't notice I'm here, which is just as well. I don't want to see Jesse.

I start to back out until I hear Gwen whisper, "Just go see him. He'll listen."

"He'll try to start a fight again," Jesse replies. "I need you to come with me, so he won't—"

"You're the one who clocked him in the eye!" Gwen replies.

They're talking about me. That much is obvious. Plenty of people have been talking about me since July. Since the second they found out I was taking Lillian out on my boat. Well, fuck it. I'm done running from it. "Ahem."

Jesse whips around, and Gwen's eyes widen at the sight of me. "Matt!" she exclaims. "What are you doing here?"

"I'm headed out of town and wanted to grab a coffee first."

"Out of town?" Gwen tries to smile, but her eyes are still wide, darting from me to Jesse and back again. "I didn't know you had to travel."

I stare at Jesse. He won't look at me. It's for the best because I'm like a dog right now. If he looks me in the eye, I'll attack. "Spur of the moment trip."

"Where are you going?" she asks.

"LA."

Jesse's head shoots up. "LA?"

I go up to the counter, keeping a few feet away from Jesse as I dig in my pocket for my wallet. "Going after Lillian."

"Took you long enough!" Gwen says.

"Yeah, well—

Jesse cuts me off. "I didn't know you were still talking to her."

"I'm not," I say pointedly. "She won't take my calls."

Jesse scratches his cheek. "Matt, I—"

"Coffee to go. Gwen, would you?" I ask, putting some cash on the bar.

Gwen takes the money, throwing Jesse a nervous smile before grabbing the coffee pot.

I drum my fingers on the counter as I wait.

"You're really going to LA?" asks Jesse.

"Yep."

We're silent again. Gwen returns with my coffee.

"I'll leave you guys alone," she whispers.

"No need." I pick up the cup and give her a small wave. "I'm off."

I turn to go.

"Matt," Jesse calls out after me. "Wait."

I stop. I don't know why I stop. I want to keep going and get my plane in the air. Because the sooner I get to Anchorage, the sooner I can catch a flight to LA. "I have to get going, Jess."

"Just give me a minute," he says, coming over to me. "Just one."

I hold back a growl from my throat.

My brother approaches me, for the first time in a long time, with hesitation.

"I, uh, I'm sorry," Jesse says.

"For what?" I ask. I'm going to drag this out as long as I can.

"For... well, you know."

I stare at him expectantly.

"Jesse!" Gwen calls out from behind the counter. "Be specific."

Our younger brother rolls his eyes but nods. He knows

what he has to do. "Look, I let Dad get in my head. I mean, it was such a group mentality by that point; it was easy to get caught up in it. I shouldn't have . . . well, shouldn't have done any of it, but especially the cabin. That was—"

"All of it was you? The tires, the message on the car? The—"

"They weren't all my idea!" he says in defense. "But I thought if I did it instead of someone else, then at least no one would get hurt. I mean, you know how some of these guys are. They barely have two brain cells to rub together after drinking," Jesse says. "I didn't want Lillian to get hurt. That wasn't the point."

I shake my head in disbelief. "I'm your brother, Jesse."

"And that's why I did it. I mean, that's why I told myself I was doing it. Protecting you from yourself. From her."

I want to be angry, but the pain in my chest just makes me sad.

"I could just see her breaking your heart, and you don't deserve that, Matt," Jesse says, voice trembling. I never knew he could be so emotional, especially over relationships. "I saw you getting your hopes up over her. And if you had gotten the rug pulled out from under you, I wouldn't have been able to forgive myself for not doing something."

"You made her think I'm a monster," I say, scratching at my beard.

Jesse sighs. "Yeah, I'm sorry."

"So, what's changed?" I ask. "You hate her, and you hated me with her, so—"

"I never *hated* her."

I snort. "Yeah, right."

"I didn't! Not the way you think I did. I just wanted . . . to keep things the same. I thought I was protecting you. But I was just protecting me and being a jerk."

As I stare into my brother's eyes, I see the little boy he once was. How much he needed me before he got bigger, taller than me. Before he hardened to the world. "I'm still your brother, Jesse. You're not going to lose that. But if you'd just given her a chance, a *real* one, then—"

"I know that. Now." Jesse diverts his attention to the tips of his shoes. "Gwen made me talk to someone."

I frown. "Talk to someone?"

"A therapist," Gwen says from her place outside the conversation.

Jesse's cheeks go red. "Yeah, one of those online things. She thinks I have anger management issues."

"Gwen or the therapist?"

"Both," Gwen answers for Jesse.

Jesse glares at her. "Hey!"

She merely smiles. Sister knows best.

"Why *are* you so angry, man?" I ask.

Jesse looks down. He seems tired. Tired of himself. I know that feeling. "I don't know. I think it's genetic. Apple doesn't fall far from the tree, right?"

I narrow my eyes.

"But, um, that's an excuse. Or, so I've been told by my therapist," Jesse says, then scratches the back of his head. "I think it started when we lost mom. You and Gwen always seemed to be able to handle it. But I just . . . I've never known how to talk about it. Thought if I was quiet about it, it might go away."

"But it didn't."

Jesse shakes his head. "No."

Part of me wants to give my brother a hug, but I'm not ready to be so close to him. I put my hand on his shoulder. "Don't be bitter like dad, okay?"

"I'm trying."

I rub his arm. "I know you are."

For a moment, I think he might burst into tears. However, he swallows the swell of emotion down. "Anyway, I don't suppose you might be able to forgive me."

"Someday."

"Yeah, someday," he says, clearly disappointed.

I hold out my hand to him. A truce. Jesse takes it, and we shake. There's a lot we have to recover from, but we're brothers. A lifetime of distance isn't in the cards.

Jesse shakes my hand and smiles.

"Okay, I've got to head out," I say. "I want to be in the air before it gets dark, and—"

Jesse holds onto my hand, keeping me from leaving. "Okay, but you're going to fly to LA and do what? Search for her high and low until you find her like a creep? Go to her office or something?"

I have tried to avoid thinking about the logistics, but he's right. I might scare her if I just . . . show up. "You have a better idea?"

"I do. But you have to give me your phone."

I look at Gwen. She shrugs. *What have I got to lose?* I've already lost Lillian. I thought I lost Jesse too. Maybe I can give him a chance to repent. I pull my phone out of the inside pocket of my jacket. "You're not going to make things worse, are you? Because if you do something stupid, I swear to God—"

Jesse pulls out his phone too. "Yeah, yeah, yeah. I'll let you have a clear shot to the face, how about it?"

I smile despite myself. "That's a fair trade."

Jesse smiles back and sits down at one of the tables. He taps on my phone for a few moments before typing something out on his.

Chapter 34

Is That the Opposite of Over It?

LILLIAN

I stare at my phone. At first, I thought the unidentified number was a spam message or some political campaign.

Imagine my surprise when I read the first line.

This is Jesse.

My stomach bottoms out.

I was the one who trashed your cabin. Matt had nothing to do with it. I owe you an apology.

I look away from the screen and scan my empty office. The room is blurry, thanks to the tears flooding my eyes. I didn't anticipate this. I mean . . . how could I have?

I take a deep breath. I need to see what else he has to say if only to sate my curiosity.

This isn't about me, though. Matt was going to fly down to

LA to find you, but I convinced him not to be a creep and let me do the talking. I know women get weird about the grand gesture thing these days.

I laugh before a tear slides down my cheek.

I promise, he had nothing to do with anything we did. He would never have hurt you, and it's not an excuse, but that's what scared me. I thought you were too different from each other. It wasn't my place to meddle, especially the way that I did.

My heart throbs in my chest.

So, do with that information what you will. I just don't think it's fair to my brother for you to go on thinking he's a bad guy. He's not. And he really cares for you. So maybe . . . give him a call.

Once I read the last sentence, I navigate to Matt's contact. I don't know what to say, or how the conversation will go, but I can't let another second go by now that I know the truth. I knew he couldn't have done something like that to me. I just knew it.

I press unblock trying to figure out what to say.

"Dr. Harvey."

I jump in my seat, nearly dropping my phone. "Dr. Harrison!"

"Did I scare you?" he asks in his dour voice.

Isn't that obvious? "Sorry, I was just—" I throw my phone into my desk drawer. "Um, did we have a meeting?"

"No, but I wanted to talk to you. Is this a bad time?" he asks, brow hardening.

Shit. I was crying. I rub the wetness away from my

cheeks. Hopefully, he's soulless enough not to notice or care. "No, it's a great time."

Dr. Harrison closes the door behind him and steps inside. Of course he won't take a seat. "I heard you're looking for approval to go on the coral reef project."

"Yes. Now that my report is done for Alaska, I thought I could lay the groundwork for next steps, and pass off the project to someone more capable," I say.

"More capable? You did all the research. Who could be more capable than you?"

I narrow my eyes at Dr. Harrison. This feels like a trap. "I thought I was supposed to find a project after my report was done to—"

"May I sit?"

"Please."

Dr. Harrison sits across from me and glances around my office. "I haven't gotten to commend you on your report in person."

"Oh. Thank you."

"It was extremely well-researched and thought out. I have to admit, given how the trip was unceremoniously cut short, I wasn't sure you'd be able to pull it off, but—"

"My safety was at risk, Dr. Harrison. I'm sorry if that isn't important to you, but—"

"It is," he says, clear as day.

I blink. "Forgive me, but that hasn't seemed like a priority since I've returned."

Dr. Harrison says nothing and looks out the window for a moment. "Yes, well, I lack a bedside manner with humans. I'm much better suited to marine life."

I stifle a laugh. I didn't know he could be funny.

"The reason I wanted to speak with you, is that . . . given how things ended for you, I wasn't sure if the report would reflect the severity of the situation. That is to say, I didn't think it would be so thoughtful."

"Well, I'm a professional."

He smiles. "That you are, Dr. Harvey."

What is going on here?

"It was more than professionalism, though. I've read your reports before. They're always good. Comprehensive, thoughtful, and empathetic in a way that is sometimes elusive in scientific literature. This report, though, felt like it came from a place much deeper."

I wait for him to say more.

"Not to mention you've been very eager and proactive when it comes to finding grants. More so than any other project."

I say nothing.

"Naknek very much impacted you. Am I wrong?"

"All my projects impact me."

"Of course." Dr. Harrison shifts in his chair, crossing his ankle over his knee. "But I'd go as far as to say you wouldn't have had such a strong reaction to needing to leave if there wasn't something deeper going on."

"I'm not sure what you want me to say."

Dr. Harrison purses his lips and looks away. "I had a similar project when I was younger. Ecological redlines in China. Working on coastal restoration." He clears his throat. "There was a man I worked with; he was native to

Naked in Naknek

the area. A fellow scientist. We became friends. Good friends."

Is Dr. Harrison opening up to me? I'm so confused, but my attention is rapt.

"And because we got close, I became closer to the area. Learned more about what it meant to the locals. It's easy for us to see the big picture as scientists. See all the problems. But it's not always easy to see it up close. There's no better way, though, to understand the subject of our research than with someone who is native to the area, right?" Dr. Harrison smiles.

Smiles. Who is this man?

"Anyway, when it came time to finish the project, and I was supposed to head back to the States—" He clears his throat. "It was clear the project had become much more to me than the work."

I wait for him to say more, but he doesn't. He fiddles with the ring on his left hand. I never thought much about his wedding band before. Maybe in passing, wondering who would put up with someone as cold as Dr. Harrison, but that's about it. "You wanted to stay?"

"I did stay. The work was important, but it had never been *more* important to me. So, I left behind my job in the States, and I moved onto the project in China permanently. I like to think I made a big impact because my heart was really in it." Dr. Harrison is quiet for a moment. "The only reason we moved back here is because we got tired of hiding. We wanted to be married and out."

I had no idea Dr. Harrison had a husband. Let alone one he met while he was working. "Do you miss it?"

"All the time. But we make sacrifices, don't we?" He looks me in the eye. "My point is, through our work sometimes we find a connection to a place that seems unearned or unrealistic. Makes it painful to leave."

I'm split open by his story. It feels so familiar and raw. The fact it's coming from *him*—this man I thought was entirely cold and emotionless—makes it more meaningful.

"Perhaps Naknek was a soul place for you?" he asks. "If I'm off the mark, please tell me and I'll move on, but—"

"No, you're right. It was. I really loved it there. I loved the people, too, for the most part, but—"

"You were an outsider. I get it."

I can only imagine his experience in a place that didn't even speak the same language with cultural differences even more severe than California and Alaska. "I would have stayed if it hadn't gotten so out of hand."

And if I'd known Matt had nothing to do with it, maybe I would have stayed. Given Naknek a chance. Given *us* a chance.

"Forgive me if I've been callous to you. I forget what it can be like out in the field."

"Thank you."

Dr. Harrison folds his hands in his lap. "I've got a lead on a grant that might be interesting to you. It's a tandem plan that provides jobs for fishermen during habitat restoration. I sent them your report, and they're quite impressed with your work. I'm sure they'd love to talk to you." He gestures to me. "To *you*. Do you understand what I mean?"

I do. They want me and my work. Not someone else.

"I'll send you the information should you want to look over it."

"I'd like that."

"You have my approval for Australia if you want, but something tells me you'd like to finish what you started." Dr. Harrison gives me a small smile before placing his hand on the front of my desk and standing. "You know where to find me."

"Thank you, Dr. Harrison."

He nods and then leaves me in my office, leaving me alone again.

I remember my phone in my drawer. I reopen the text message chain with Matt. Except I don't know what to say. I don't know if I can throw my heart back into Naknek after being so broken by it.

But I don't like leaving things unfinished. I'll regret it the rest of my life if I don't try once more to show Naknek how everything I've ever done for that little town is out of love and respect.

I'll regret it if I don't do it for Matt.

With shaking hands, I go to type out a message.

I'm sorry. For everything.

∞

THE SECOND I walk into Sarah's apartment; she knows I'm off.

"What's that face? What happened? Did Dr. Harrison do something to you? Should I go punch him? I will," she calls out from over a boiling pot of pasta on the stove.

Although my energy is sapped, I explain everything to her as best as I can. I have no idea how to go on or what to do. What more to say.

"So, to recap," Sarah says, turning down the heat on the stove. "Jesse was the vandal."

"Yes."

"Which means Matt had nothing to do with it."

"Yes."

"And your boss thinks you should finish the project because, shocker, he has feelings and fell in love with a guy in China."

"I'm filling in some blanks there, but—"

"And you texted Matt before you left work and immediately turned off your phone because you're a crazy person?" Sarah finishes.

This is true. The phone is face up on the counter. Off. I have no idea if Matt replied to my text.

"Lil—"

"I don't know what to do," I groan, dropping my head in my hands. "This is all so messed up and confusing. I thought I'd just move on and forget all about it, and you know, hook up with a hot Aussie."

Sarah scoffs. "You said you weren't going to mix business and pleasure anymore."

"That's not the point! The point is I was moving on! I was getting over it, and now—" I rub the heels of my hands into my eye sockets, stars popping in the darkness.

Sarah's hand lands on my shoulder. "Hey, I'm gonna say something you won't like."

"What else is new?"

There's a pause long enough to make me pull my hands off my eyes and look up at my sister.

She smiles. "You're not over it. You're not even *getting* over it. You're very much *under* it."

"Is that the opposite of over it?"

"Yup."

"I hate that."

Sarah laughs. "Okay, but you're not saying I'm wrong. So, I think that means you know I'm very, *very* right."

I do. And I hate it.

"Why don't we see what Matt said, huh?" Sarah reaches for my phone.

I tuck my hands under my armpits, or else I might reach out and snatch it from her.

She turns it on and types my passcode. "You want me to read it, or do you want to?"

"He replied?"

"Of course he replied! He's obsessed with you."

I tuck my chin against my chest and groan. "You do it."

"My pleasure."

I close my eyes and wait.

"No, you should read this."

"Sarah—"

"It's for you, Lillian. After all this time, just hear him out, okay?"

I glance up at the screen. *Deep breath, Lillian.* I wrap my hands around the phone and pull it close to read.

I'm the one who should be sorry for not going after you the second you left. It's my biggest regret.

"Oh . . ." My eyes fill with tears again. "That's nice."

"More than nice. He's clearly in love with you."

The tears from earlier return. Tears that I've scolded myself for shedding again and again since I left Naknek. Now, I let them fall. Without guilt. I thought I had lost him for the rest of time. And I had no idea just how much I *want* him.

Sarah comes over to me and wraps her arms around me. And I cry and cry until my face hurts.

"It's a good thing, Lillian," she says sweetly.

"I know, but I can't—I don't know how I'll go back there. I want to go back, but I don't know—"

"I'll go with you, obviously. I have vacation days that I need to use anyway," Sarah says as if it's the easiest decision in the world.

"Really?"

She kisses my temple. "Really. Besides, I can't wait to give Jesse a piece of my mind."

I wind my hand around her arm, leaning into my sister. "I don't know what I would do without you."

"Good thing you don't have to think about that," she says. "Now, tomorrow, we're going shopping. I have to figure out what to pack."

The rest of the night glows with hope and anticipation. I have a lot of work to do. Packing and planning. Looking into this grant and making sure it all makes sense. But I'll have Sarah at my side. And even more, Matt and I might get a chance again.

Chapter 35

Buy a Friend a Drink

LILLIAN

November in Naknek is frigid compared to the relative warmth of August. Sarah and I are bundled in many layers, bracing ourselves against the twenty-degree chill.

It feels more like early morning than noon, thanks to the lingering polar night. I already miss the endless summer days of the midnight sun.

And yet, after stepping off the plane and breathing in the Alaskan air, Naknek brings me a peace I haven't known since I left. It's confusing, considering how I was basically run out of town, but at the same time, it makes sense. Not only was I left broken-hearted by Matt, but I was torn away from a part of myself I had just discovered. A part of myself that found a place like a soulmate.

We drop our stuff off at the cabin—a different one. While I'd be happy to give Ian the money, my nerves can't handle being back at his cabin. We rent one a little closer to town. And though Sarah is tired of traveling, I drag her out to the Half-Hitch with the promise of coffee.

When we drive up, I'm unsettled by how full the parking lot is. I hesitate, getting out of the car long enough for Sarah to ask, "Are you good?"

"Yeah. Yeah, I'll be okay," I say, then shut off the truck. Yep, a truck again. A necessity for the often-slick roads and worsening weather.

"Let's do this," Sarah says, her lips pouted with determination.

I'm sure she'll throw down if anyone so much as breathes in my direction.

We get out of the car and head inside. There are groups peppered through the shop, almost the same as the first time I came here, except now with heavy boots and coats.

A few people look up. Faces I recognize. Lots of surprised looks. Some are more welcoming than others. I lock eyes with Marina, who smiles and gives me a flat-palmed wave. I wave back and smile brightly.

I belong here. Even if they don't agree I do.

"Were they expecting you?" Sarah asks, pointing up at the "Give a Coffee" board.

I look up, and sure enough, my name is up there. A chai tea, courtesy of Marina. "You got chai?" I exclaim, loud enough to get Gwen's attention from behind the espresso machine.

She beams. "You're *here!*"

Abandoning her drink, she comes out from behind the counter and embraces me. It's the kind of hug you give someone you've known for years, not only a few months. At least I know one member of the family likes me. "It's good to see you, Gwen."

"You, too! Did you see what we have on the menu?" She points up at the board.

"I did!"

"It was my idea, but Marina flew out to Dillingham to make sure we had it in stock in time for your arrival. Isn't that sweet of her?"

After deciding to return to Alaska, Gwen and Matt were the only ones I told I was coming back. But given how small Naknek is, I'm sure the knowledge of my return was disseminated quickly.

Gwen turns to Sarah. "Is this your sister?"

I introduce Gwen and Sarah, and Gwen turns to make two chais. "Marina will cover it," Gwen says, waving her hand.

"Who is this Marina person?" Sarah smirks. "And where can I get one of them?"

Gwen laughs it off, but Sarah's question makes me wonder if there's more going on.

I don't have long to wonder before she changes the subject. "Matt is so excited to see you."

"Me, too. I mean, I'm excited to see him," I say, knowing my cheeks are turning red. I haven't told him I arrived. He knows I'm coming today, but I lied about the timing so I could surprise him all on my own. Gwen was the only one who knew the true timing of my travels.

"Lillian?" Sarah and I turn to find Jesse behind us. His skin is paler than usual, and his eyes are wide.

"Hi, Jesse."

"Oh, *you're* Jesse," Sarah says, putting her hands on her hips.

"Not sure if I want to be anymore, but yeah," Jesse replies, clearly unnerved by my sister.

"Jesse, this is my sister, Sarah."

Jesse swallows. "I see the ... resemblance."

"Yeah, well, the resemblance ends with the physical, because unlike Lillian, I'm not so nice. In fact—" She points and pokes her finger into Jesse's sternum. "I'm a lawyer, so don't get any more funny ideas, or else—"

"*Sarah*," I hiss.

Sarah gives me a puppy-eyed look. "Why won't you let me threaten him?"

Jesse's cheeks turn red. "Trust me, uh, I feel ... threatened? I guess."

I bite my lower lip. I'm sure Jesse didn't expect I'd bring along my gorgeous bulldog of a sister.

"Good." Sarah gestures with a 'carry on' motion.

Jesse's eyes somehow widen even more. "Okay, um, well, I obviously owe you an apology in person."

"That's an understate—" Sarah begins.

"Sarah, you can give him a piece of your mind when we're done talking, okay? I'm good," I say, patting her arm.

Sarah inhales. "Fine. I'll be right over here." She makes the 'I'm watching you' gesture at Jesse before shifting her attention to Gwen.

"She ... "

I raise an eyebrow.

"Seems lovely," Jesse says. "Anyway, I wanted to apologize in person. I know it's not much, but it was wrong of me to—more than wrong. I'm guilty. If we were to go to court— please, don't take me to court for—"

"Jesse, I'm not taking you to court," I say, somehow managing a smile.

He lets out a genuine sigh of relief. "Good. Um, well, if there's anything I can do to make it up to you?"

"Make it up to Matt for breaking his trust. That's all that matters to me."

Jesse nods. "Heard."

"All I care about is making things easier on him. So, if that means going door to door, convincing people he's not a bad person for trying to make this community better, then that's what you should do."

"Trust me, I'm already stumping."

I'm surprised to hear that, but pleasantly so. I smile. "Good." I swipe my chai off the counter.

Gwen watches me expectantly. "Take a sip. Is it good?"

I do so, but I barely taste it, my anticipation building. "Perfect, Gwen. Just perfect."

She grins. "We'll put it on the menu and name it after you. The Chai-entist. Clever, right? Winnie came up with that."

"Don't get ahead of yourself," I say with a playful grimace, then elbow my sister's arm. "Sarah, he's all yours. I'm off to see Matt."

"He's home, getting ready for you," Gwen tells me with

a big grin. "He's going to be so surprised. Record his reaction, will you?"

"Only if you want an R-rated movie," Sarah says.

I ignore her. "Good luck, Jesse," I say as I pass him.

"I believe I'll need it," he mumbles.

As I leave the Half-Hitch, I laugh as I hear the beginning of Sarah laying into him.

∽

MATT'S TRUCK is parked out front. Everything is frosted from the chill in the air. Snow has already touched Alaska this season.

I climb out of the rental and head to the front door. *You can do this.* I knock, shoving my bare hand into my pocket as soon as I can since the cold is biting.

A minute passes. I know he's home, but maybe he didn't hear me. I raise my hand to knock again.

The door flies open before I can knock.

And there he is. In the flesh.

I hold my breath, taking Matt in for the first time since I left a month ago.

He's breathless, having clearly run from whatever part of the house he was in. His hair is wet, water dripping down his neck. And he's wearing a tight, long-sleeved shirt and jeans. No shoes. I've succeeded in surprising him.

"What are you doing here?" he asks, in shock.

"I'm here to see you."

"I know, but you weren't supposed to be here until—"

Naked in Naknek

He runs a hand through his wet hair. "I was showering. I haven't even shaved. I—"

I'm not sure if I'm shaking because of the nerves or the cold. "Can I come in? I'm freezing."

Matt's surprise melts into a warm smile. He grabs the front of my coat, pulls me into his house, into his arms, and hugs me tight to his chest.

Warmth floods through me. Not just physical, but emotional too. I hadn't realized just how frigid my heart had become.

I hold onto him, burying my face into his neck.

"I'm sorry," he murmurs.

"Why? Why are you—"

"For not—"

"Stop it."

"No, I should have—"

I cup his cheeks in my hands. "Stop. We're here now. We're here."

Matt furrows his brow, concentrating on my face.

I twirl a lock of his wet hair between my fingers, pushing it out of his face.

"I should have told you I loved you," Matt whispers.

I lean closer. "You can tell me now."

Our lips connect before he can. A long, grounding kiss. And when our mouths part, he says it. "I love you."

"I love you, too."

Absence makes the heart grow fonder. It's a cliché because it's true. Something about returning to the one you love is indescribable.

What happens next is both entirely unexpected and

absolutely right. My lips find Matt's again, and my hands move to the hem of his thermal shirt. I push the fabric up, feeling the warmth of his skin, his hardened abs. I want to be close to him again.

"Did I surprise you?" I ask between kisses.

"Was that not obvious?" he replies.

I laugh as he grabs the zipper on my jacket and shucks it off me in record time.

This is like the first time all over again. Except there isn't the anxiety of getting it right. It's the necessity of making it count, which is why Matt hauls me into his arms without a moment's hesitation.

I wrap my legs around him, allowing him to carry me upstairs to the bedroom and lay me down on the bed, his body over mine. He then presses me onto the bed, kissing me as he holds me tight.

"I've missed you," I whisper.

"I've needed you," he replies. "I just didn't know—"

I touch my fingers to his lips. "It's okay. It's okay. We didn't know what to do."

Matt's eyes flutter shut. He kisses each of my fingertips.

I want him to have me. I don't just mean my body. I mean everything I am, all my time, my adoration, my life. I want him to have all of it. There's so much yet to discover about one another, so much to process and apologize for.

Then, a sound trembles out of him, a sound like he's been waiting for a place to moor himself again all this time.

I am his place.

We cling to each other, basking in the glow of each

other. To have Matt in my arms again is heaven. A heaven I thought I had lost.

∽

"So, how was your trip?" Matt asks, cupping my cheek.

I burst into laughter, giving him a flurry of kisses all over his face. Cuteness fucking overload. How can a man be so sexy and adorable at the same time? Maybe because he's mine. Mine. "Good. Better now. It would be even better if I had remembered to bring my chai in from the car."

Matt sighs and rolls out of bed, pushing himself to his feet. "It would be my honor to retrieve your chai."

How did I get so lucky?

After Matt returns from the car, I eye him over the lid of my drink as I sip.

"So . . . you love me," I say.

We're sitting on the couch now, on opposite ends so as not to get handsy and distracted.

"That seems to be the case," he says. "And you love me, unless you were just trying to get in my pants."

I giggle. "I could have gotten in your pants for less, I think."

Matt blushes. "Yeah, you could have told me you had a mild tolerance for me, and I would have been at attention."

I smile. Correction, I haven't stopped smiling. "So, what happens next?"

Matt swallows. "Well, I don't want to lose you again. Obviously."

"Obviously," I repeat. For myself, because I can't even believe my luck.

"And I know asking you to stay here, with your work and everything, would be too much, so I'll go with you."

I blink. "What?"

"Yeah, I mean, there's fishing in California. I can find a job there, I think. I mean, maybe," Matt says.

"But your family, Matt."

He sighs and glances away. "Yeah, I'd hate to be away from Gwen and Winnie. Jesse and I are still patching things up. And my dad . . . well, I'm treating him as a lost cause at this point. The drinking and—" He stops and clears his throat. "I've done what I can."

"I'm not going to ask you to come to California to be with me," I say.

Matt shakes his head. "It's fine. I've thought about it. With everything going on here, I think it's time for me to . . . move on."

There's a solemnity in his voice that doesn't quite sound like acceptance.

"To tell the truth, I'm sure if I stayed here all year round, I might lose my mind," I say with a half-laugh. "But I love Naknek. I wouldn't ask you to leave it behind because I don't want to leave it behind either."

Matt screws his brows together. "You *love* Naknek?"

"Yes, I really do. Even if the people aren't thrilled about me, I saw it through your eyes. And *you* love Naknek. It's a piece of you. I love that piece."

His lips curl up in the sweetest smile.

"Maybe we can split our time. Spend summers here so

you can be here for the fishing season. Then, we can go somewhere else for the winter because twenty-four hours of darkness might kill me."

"Half the year here, half the year in LA."

I shrug. "Maybe LA . . . maybe Anchorage."

"Anchorage?"

"Yeah, well, depending how the town hall goes. Maybe it will open up some more opportunities with the Fishers First organization. Then, I can keep working on projects like this one."

"You want to help fishermen after everything they've put you through?" Matt asks.

I scootch over to him on the couch, placing my hand on his thigh. "There are some good ones, I think."

He's quiet for a moment, then moves some hair away from my face. "I'll go wherever you want. Say the word, I'm there."

"Let's get through the town hall first, and then . . ."

And then . . .

There are lots of questions and not many answers.

Matt wraps his arm around me, and then kisses my temple. If I only know one thing, it's that we love each other. And that's going to be enough.

No matter what happens.

Chapter 36

You Haven't Gone Pro, Have You?

MATTHEW

I've never seen a town hall meeting so full. Granted, I haven't been to many in my day. But still, I don't think there's an empty chair in the place.

The room is buzzing with nervous energy, wooden chairs squeaking as people sit, shift, and stand. Even the walls seem to pulse with the whispered hopes and fears of everyone crammed into the small space.

I stand in the back, taking everything in, sort of like a security guard. If someone does something stupid, I'll take care of them right away.

However, so far, it seems like everyone is on their best behavior.

At the front of the gray room, Lillian stands with a couple of city officials and representatives from Fishers

First, the foundation through which Lillian received the proposed grant.

The weight of the moment presses down on my shoulders. If the grant is received poorly, I'm not sure what more Lillian can do. What any of us can do. For selfish reasons, I want this to go well. I don't want her to feel she's a villain here anymore. I want to be able to hold up a big middle finger to Naknek and say, "I told you so."

But the bigger picture is this grant could save us. There's little hope these days when the climate is changing so fast. I know everybody here doesn't believe that. Some think it's some sort of conspiracy.

But that doesn't change the fact that the coho yield has been decreasing every year. And facts are fucking facts.

If Lillian can show them this can change, then we might all stand a chance.

"Now that you've seen the data," Lillian says, gesturing toward the PowerPoint presentation on the projector. "I know you're eager to hear what we *do* with this data."

Some folks mutter to each other in the crowd. I swallow, leaning my head back against the wall.

"She's good. Don't worry," Sarah whispers beside me.

I smile at Lillian's sister. She gives me a hearty wink. Over the past week, I've gotten to know her quite well. She's a sassy spitfire. A Lillian in a different font.

Tuma sits on my other side in solidarity.

Lillian continues. "We have a plan to protect the coho salmon populations and help sustain the lives of fishers here in Naknek as well as the greater Bristol Bay community," Lillian says. "This will all be done in tandem with

Fishers First, an Anchorage-based foundation, which has taken an interest in the issues here, thanks to the research I've done."

I withhold a chuckle. Lillian might love Naknek, but she's getting a kick out of flaunting what she's accomplished.

I am, too. That's my girl. She's smart, gorgeous, and takes no shit. I've never seen her in such clean-cut office wear before, and it's a crying shame because it's a side of her I want to see more of. Tailored slacks, a cream-colored blouse, and her auburn hair clipped back in an elegant, effortless bun finish off the look.

"Here to help me explain the plan is the head of grant allocation from Fishers First, Steve Yonnitz. Steve is a Native Alaskan with Aleut roots and has been advocating for fishermen during the climate crisis since the early 2000s," she says with a gesture toward her counterpart, an older man with olive skin and a worn face indicative of a life lived in Alaska.

Steve nods. "Thank you for that introduction, Dr. Harvey. I'd be happy to."

I smile every time someone calls her doctor. *I'm dating a doctor.* As Steve begins to wax poetic on the plan, Lillian looks away, her eyes searching the crowd. She sees me, and for a second, her hardened exterior breaks.

I give her a big smile and a nod. *It's going great.*

It's not a lie. I'm terrified the tides could turn at any given moment since Naknek has a groupthink mentality. But for the most part, she has them in her grip.

I scan the crowd. Marina and Rio are here, toward the

front. Jesse, too, with some of the younger fishermen. Whether or not he believes in Lillian's cause, he has made it clear he owes it to both of us to help. And help he has. Hell, he even managed to get Lefty to come.

"The two-point plan will hopefully cover all the concerns many of you have. Obviously, in order to preserve a population, we have to proceed conscientiously. Which means turning an eye toward overfishing coho. There is no way to do this without habitat rehabilitation and a more rigorous permit process."

There are audible groans and curses from the audience. I hold my breath, gripping the arms of my chair. "This won't impact the way you can fish sockeye or other populations at *this* time," the man goes on, unfazed. "However, Dr. Harvey has made it clear that is not an option on its own. This is why we think Naknek would be a prime candidate to institute a coho-stocking program. This is point two of our plan. We would provide money to repurpose one of the defunct canneries into a hatchery, where we can build up the population of salmon in the area. This would mean the creation of many jobs. Construction, management, operations, maintenance..."

There's something for everyone on that list.

"What we foresee is being able to employ fishers in the area for half of the season while the other half can be out on the water." Steve takes in the crowd as if anticipating the questions he might need to answer.

This grant would change more than just the future of Naknek. It would define what our lives can become. What our *town* can become. We don't have to be Egegik. We can *grow*.

"Seasonal job opportunities would increase, along with the potential of tourism and more money to the community." Steve goes on. "And with the spawn from the hatchery, we can stock the rivers with more fish as we better their habitat." Steve glances at Lillian. "Did I miss anything there, Lillian?"

She smiles. "I think you got it all. I think we should open the floor to questions."

I hold my breath.

And so does the rest of the room. No one moves for a long moment. I hope this is a good sign.

"You can make a line here at the center aisle," Lillian says. "We're happy to answer any questions you might have about the proposal."

Someone stands from the crowd.

It's Jesse.

I move to the edge of my seat.

"Let him go," Tuma whispers.

Jesse makes it to the center aisle as Lillian sits up. She doesn't betray any surprise on her face, just a pleasant, eager smile. "Good to see you, Mr. Benton," she says.

"What's he *doing*?" Sarah whispers, the disdain clear in her voice.

"I don't know." I gulp.

Sarah pulls up the sleeves of her sweater. "He better play nice or else I won't."

Yeah, she'd be good for Jesse.

"You, too, uh, Dr. Harvey. Um . . ." Jesse shoves his

hands in his pockets. "I'm just curious if the kind of work we'd be doing, if we were hired, would it come with benefits?"

Lillian's eyebrows lift as if she's remembering something. "Yes, there will be benefits for both part-time and full-time employees. Health insurance . . . retirement programs. There is even potential for the hatchery to have an ESOP, an employee stock ownership program."

More buzz in the room. Excited buzz. A buzz of potential.

Jesse nods. "Okay, just checking. Thank you."

"Thank you, Mr. Benton, that was a fantastic question," Lillian says.

He turns on his heel and goes back to his seat, catching my eye on the way. He gives me a lopsided smile.

I smile back.

"Did he just try to *help*?" Sarah whispers in disbelief.

"I think he did," I reply.

Sarah settles back into her seat, crossing her arms over her chest. "Hm."

I hold in a laugh. I know that "hm." It's an interested sort of "hm."

Lillian leans on the table in front of her. Now, she can't be stopped. She's beaming ear to ear. "Any more questions?"

Several people get up and move to the aisle. Although with an apparent endorsement from hard-ass Jesse Benton, I'm sure they're questions of curiosity rather than attack.

Sarah presses a knuckle into my arm. "I think she's got 'em."

I inhale, chest puffing, with both pride and relief. "Yeah. Me, too."

∽

AFTER ALL THE questions have been answered, the town council makes a motion in support of the grant. It's done and dusted. And sure, there's a long road ahead, but there's a road. It's no longer a foggy plain.

The hall clears out. I get a couple of apologetic looks and handshakes from the men I used to call friends. Perhaps, there will be a reckoning. Real apologies. But for now, I'll settle with knowing I'm right.

And, that I got the girl.

Once Lillian is settled with Steve and the Naknek council, she rushes over to me. I open my arms and hug her tight. "You did it."

"I can't believe it," she says. "I feel like I'm in a dream." She palms my biceps. "You can't be real."

"A big, sexy fisherman is in love with you, Lillian. Believe it," Sarah says.

Lillian turns to Jesse. "Thanks for setting me up with the benefits! It had totally slipped my mind."

Jesse shrugs. "I know health insurance gets people around here listening, so—"

"You were right!" Lillian exclaims. "I owe you a drink."

Warmth spreads through my chest at the sight of Lillian and my brother getting along.

Sarah intercedes, scooping Lillian away by the arm. "You don't owe *him* anything."

Jesse flushes and opens his mouth to speak as Sarah drags Lillian away, talking a mile a minute.

"It's like another language," Jesse says as he steps up beside me.

I give him a wry smile. "You just don't understand women."

He scratches the back of his head. "True."

"What happened to my cocky little brother? I thought you were good with the ladies."

I follow his gaze to Sarah. Yup. Totally infatuated.

Sarah looks over Lillian's shoulder, her smile turning into a thin line. "What are you looking at?"

Jesse holds up his hands. "Nothing."

Ignoring him, Sarah announces, "Let's go get drinks! On me! I've got *law* money." She grabs Lillian's hand and pulls her ahead of us.

Jesse, Tuma, and I stand there a moment before following.

Tuma grins at me. "He likes it when they're mean to him."

"Shut up, dude," Jesse retorts.

I laugh, shaking my brother's shoulder. "Come on, let's get you a drink."

We end up at Fat Fred's. And so does the rest of Naknek. It's a celebration for all. There's a palpable relief that something might be done for our community and our livelihood. I'm not sure everyone believes this is our reality. But at least, for tonight, we do.

"There she is!" Marina exclaims as soon as we walk in. "The woman of the hour!"

Lillian is pulled away from us to the bar, where she is peppered with compliments from Marina and Ian . . .and Lefty, of all people. He looks like a different man as he talks to Lillian. I'm sure he's trying to rub elbows and get her to put in a good word for him for management. He'd be a terrible manager. A total tyrant.

A problem for another day.

We grab one of the few available high-tops. It's rare for things to be *this* busy in Naknek. It's like the whole town is here.

"How are you liking Naknek, Sarah?" Tuma asks in a sweet, innocent tone.

"Well, it's not Los Angeles, that's for sure," she says. "But I can see what my sister likes about it." Her eyes stray around the room. "Hot fishermen everywhere."

Jesse shifts in his seat. Poor guy trying to hold in his jealousy.

We get drinks and let the warmth of intoxication take over. All the weight that's been on my shoulders is now gone. There's an unfamiliar straightness to my spine, an alignment I haven't experienced in a long time. Hell, maybe not ever.

But I have my girl. I have my home. And things feel *good*. I'm excited for what's to come next, rather than being scared.

"I bet you twenty bucks," Sarah says to Jesse.

I recenter myself in the conversation. Sarah's on her

second gin and tonic, probably more g than t, and is leaning closer to Jesse than someone does with their enemy.

"There's no way you can beat me at darts," he says. "I play almost every night."

"So? You haven't gone pro, have you?" she sasses.

A smile tweaks Jesse's lips. "Fine. Twenty bucks."

"You're on," Sarah says, jumping down from her stool and heading to the back of the bar where the pool tables and dartboards are.

Tuma and I watch them go.

"He's down bad," Tuma says.

"It's hilarious," I respond before finishing off my beer. It might do him some good to have a crush.

Tuma checks his watch. "I should head home to the kids."

"You're right, you should," I say with a nod. I would normally give him shit for leaving early. But I get it. Now, I really do.

Tuma gives me a salute, then disappears into the crowd.

I look at my empty glass, tipping it and watching the liquid drip around the glass.

This has been one of the hardest years of my life. Between the terrible fishing season and the way my town turned against me, it would be easy to say one of the worst too. Not to mention things with Dad going sour. But I got Lillian out of it. We rose above together.

I have no regrets.

With perfect timing, Lillian wraps her arms around my neck and presses her cheek to mine. "Having fun all alone here?"

I latch onto her arms. I'm not letting her get away again tonight. "A lot more now that you're here."

We kiss softly. I'd like to steal her away and kiss her until our lips are bruised. *Don't rush it. There's plenty of time.*

"Where is everybody?" she asks.

"Tuma went home, and Sarah and Jesse have a bet on who can win at darts," I say, pointing over to the corner where Sarah is lining up her shot, and Jesse is not so subtly staring at her ass.

"Oh, my god. They're going to kill each other," Lillian murmurs.

"We'll see. I think Jesse might have met his match." I pat her hand.

Steve Yonnitz interrupts us with a soft wave of his hand. "I just wanted to say congratulations before I head out."

"Oh, Steve. Thank you. I couldn't have done any of this without you." Lillian hugs the older man.

He chuckles. "Ah, it was all you and your work."

I place my hand on Lillian's lower back and smile at her fondly.

"I actually wanted to ask if you'd be interested in a lead role at the hatchery as we start putting the team together."

Lillian's jaw drops. "Me?"

"Of course. You understand the ecosystem, the town. I

think it would be a great bridge as we continue developing the project."

It's hard to believe how it's falling into place.

Lillian leans into me, pressing a hand to my chest. "I think you ought to talk to this guy. He taught me everything I know."

"Oh, I don't know about—"

Steve holds out his hand to me. "I don't believe we've met officially. Lillian's told me a lot about you. Matt, right?"

We shake hands.

"Matt's a local fisherman, but he's also the smartest guy in town. He'd be great on the management team."

Steve reaches into his pocket and hands me a business card. "Then, we'll talk, hm? Send me an email at your convenience."

"Thanks," I say, my mouth dry, still in shock.

Steve says his goodbyes, leaving Lillian and me alone again.

"I don't understand," I say with a frown.

Lillian's hand caresses my chest tenderly. "What? You don't think I'd want to try and help provide options?"

"Well, if I take on a management position, that's probably a year-round thing, right? What happened to half the year in Naknek, and—"

Lillian cuts me off with a kiss, and I don't have the strength to draw away. Her mouth is divine.

"I don't care where we are. I just want to be with you. We'll figure it out."

My eyes fall to her lips. "Can I take you home, or is it too early?"

"Why didn't you ask an hour ago?"

We leave the bar, the hubbub of the celebration, Jesse and Sarah, *all of it*.

I take her home. To *our* home. To our bed. And I fall asleep to the whisper of, "I love you," in my ear.

Chapter 37

I'm Not Getting Naked

LILLIAN

"I can't believe I'm doing this."
The Thanksgiving Day Polar Plunge is a yearly tradition in Naknek. The town gathers on one of the pebble beaches and strips down to their skivvies for a dip in the frigid November waters. Some people even go naked.

To my right, Matt pulls off his sweater, bare-chested to the winter air.

"You're insane!" I gasp.

He grins. "And you love me for it."

"I do," I grumble.

To my left, Jesse and Sarah are squabbling.

"I'll watch," Sarah says, casting a hand toward Jesse.

"Don't be a wuss."

I wince. Those are fighting words to Sarah.

"I'm not a wuss!" Sarah shouts back.

Jesse pulls off his shirt, and then pushes down his pants. I turn away just in time not to see my boyfriend's brother's birthday suit. "Prove it!"

As expected, Sarah responds, "You're on!" and a second later, her shirt lands beside me on the pebble beach.

"She's naked, isn't she?" I ask Matt.

Matt laughs. "You think I'm looking at your sister naked? No way."

I grin up at him.

I hear their feet trampling through the rocks, and then their screams as they leap into the cold water.

"Okay, Lil. You ready?" Matt asks.

"I'm not getting naked."

"Neither am I. I only do that when we're alone," Matt says with a cheeky smile.

I shiver. Not from the cold, but the memory of us skinny dipping in the Egegik months ago before anything really happened between us. Oh, how things change. "Can we go slow?"

Matt grabs my hand. "Of course."

We approach the water's edge. The riverbank is filled with people running in and out, shrieking at how cold it is. Jesse has Sarah wrapped up in his arms, keeping her from escaping the cold grips of the water. I'd be worried if she wasn't grinning ear to ear.

I probably wouldn't do this if I wasn't trying to be a good local. I've earned the trust of many, but I have to keep that trust.

And evidently, that means taking a dip in the nearly-frozen Naknek River.

I shrug off my robe, wearing only a bathing suit. "This is crazy."

"This is Alaska," Matt says, then taps the tip of my nose. "You ready?"

"Ready."

Hand in hand, we run into the water, so cold it's like knives. But I understand why Sarah is smiling. It's exciting to feel the shock and know the thrill of it all.

Matt dives under, and I follow suit because if you're going to do a polar plunge, you have to actually plunge. I come up for air with a brain freeze.

"Alright, let's get you warmed up, California!" Matt scoops me up in his arms and takes me back to shore.

"My hero." I wrap my arms around his neck and kiss him.

∽

"Who wants pie?" Gwen exclaims as she enters the room with a pie in each hand.

"Everyone wants pie, Gwen," Sarah says from her spot across from me at the dinner table.

Matt bought this table especially for Thanksgiving. It was the only room in the house still unfurnished. "It just feels sad to be a single guy in such a big house with a dinner table no one ever sits at," he told me one night under the covers.

Cue an immediate trip to Anchorage to pick out a table

all of our family could fit around for the very first Thanksgiving we are hosting together as a couple.

It's hard to believe that only a month ago I was in Los Angeles, and now, here we are, figuring out a life together in Alaska.

"These look amazing, Gwen," I say as she places the pumpkin pie in front of me and a pecan pie at the foot of the table.

"You have Marina to thank for the pecan. The supermarket ran out before I could get to them, so she—"

"Let me guess," Sarah says, eyeing Marina at the other end of the table. "She flew to Dillingham."

Marina goes red in the face. "It was King Salmon, actually."

"Yeah, it was King Thalmon, actually," Winnie parrots in defense.

The whole table laughs. Marina and Gwen are taking things slow. Slower than slow. Jesse and Matt were shocked when they found out the two of them were dancing around the idea of a relationship, but I wasn't. Not at all.

Marina returned to Anchorage for the season, but you wouldn't know it since she's back in Naknek almost every weekend. Yes, to spend time with Gwen, but also with Winnie. Marina's babysat on a few occasions so Gwen and I can have a girl's night.

The shy, dinosaur-loving kid comes alive around Marina now. The two are best buddies. I know that eases Gwen's burden of being with someone new. Not to mention being with a woman, something that sticks out around here like a sore thumb.

"Oh, my apologies," Sarah says, clutching her chest.

"You're such an asshole," Jesse teases my sister.

She shoulders him, and then he pokes her in the side. The two of them are a match made in younger-sibling heaven.

Matt and I exchange a smile. He sits at the head of the table with me on his right. It's so comfortable and fills a part of my soul I never realized was there. He grabs my hand and squeezes.

"Gwennie, give me a piece, will you?"

At the other end of the table sits Matt's father. I'm still getting my footing with Wayne. We didn't even know if he'd come tonight. I encouraged Matt to extend the invitation. Wayne is his dad after all. He showed up an hour late with a bottle of whiskey as a host gift that he immediately opened to pour himself a drink.

I guess it's a win that he's not abusing me anymore for my work. The way Naknek has responded to my grant proposal certainly hasn't been lost on him. Despite the ever-shortening days, Naknek has been infiltrated with hope and optimism.

In fact, when I greeted Wayne, he grunted at me in a way that felt... *friendly?*

It's the little things.

Gwen attends to her father's pie while the rest of us dig in.

"Oh! I forgot the vanilla ice cream!" Gwen says.

"I'll get it," I say, and find that I'm in chorus with Marina, who is halfway out of her chair. I cackle. "You're a guest, Marina. Please, sit."

Winnie grabs onto Marina's pullover and gives it a tug, which is enough to convince her to stay.

"Just trying to be helpful," she says with a sheepish smile.

"Yeah, we know. You want to be all kinds of helpful," Matt says.

More laughter. I playfully slap him on the shoulder as I go. "Dude."

The kitchen is a wreck of pots and pans, and the smell of our Thanksgiving dinner fills the air. It brings a smile to my face.

I go to the freezer to pull it open but find my attention grabbed by a movement outside the window. It gets so dark out here that sometimes you can't see into the night. But tonight, the sky is filled with shifting ribbons of green and blue—cosmic, unreal.

"Oh, my god." I abandon the ice cream and go to the window.

The Northern Lights.

I've never seen them before. They're mesmerizing. I grab a jacket and wrap it around myself as I step outside, looking up at the sky. It's so quiet out here. So still. Like the world has stopped everything except for the vivid, dancing rivers of light.

Tears prick my eyes. I'm surrounded by so much beauty every day. It's hard to describe just how lucky I feel.

"Lil?" Matt calls out.

I turn back to the house where Matt's peeking out from the kitchen door. "Aurora Borealis," I say, pointing up to the sky.

Matt comes outside and looks up. "Would you look at that?" He comes up behind me, wrapping his long arms around my waist and resting his chin on top of my head.

I lean into him, giving him all my weight. "It's beautiful."

"You know, I've seen them more times than I can count, and they've never been more beautiful than right now. Seeing them here with you."

I smile at him. He's the most handsome man in the world, even more beautiful because of his big heart and the unwavering confidence he's had in me from the start.

Matt nudges his cold nose against mine.

I melt further into his body, arms entwined, both of us looking at the heavens.

When love finds you, it can light up the entire sky.

Also by Lolu Sinclair

Lost Love on 6th Street

A Sanctuary for Fire & Fate

I Don't Date Hockey Players